YOU BELONG HERE

YOU BELONG HERE

A Novel

MEGAN MIRANDA

MARYSUE
RUCCI
BOOKS

New York Amsterdam/Antwerp London
Toronto Sydney/Melbourne New Delhi

An Imprint of Simon & Schuster, LLC
1230 Avenue of the Americas
New York, NY 10020

Manufactured in the United States of America

ISBN 978-1-6680-8097-9

For Alexa

YOU BELONG HERE

PROLOGUE

I knew how easily a story could shift. How quickly the public could turn. I'd seen it happen, twenty years earlier. A game sliding into a crime. A tradition twisting into a nightmare.

I watched as an arc slowly emerged from the series of headlines and police bulletins, until the story had a shape, the truth a sharp end point.

Structure Fire at Perimeter of Wyatt College Burns Through Night

Two Local Men Deceased in Steam Tunnels Under Campus

Police Seek Public's Assistance in Locating Missing Student, Adalyn Vale

Person of Interest Named in Fire Deaths of Two Men

Wanted for questioning: Adalyn Vale

Wanted for murder: Adalyn Vale

In the days that followed, I'd felt a shift happening inside of me, too.

Confusion. She'd been my roommate for nearly four years—had been my closest friend in those earliest years of adulthood.

Denial. Thinking that the witnesses were mistaken. That she hadn't meant to do it. It *must've* been an accident—flames in the wind, catching and spreading.

Anger. Because she had fled without a word. And in her absence, I was the only one left to answer for her.

And finally: *Fear*.

Fear that she'd done exactly what they claimed and I hadn't known her at all.

Fear because the police thought I was protecting her. And now they kept coming back to me.

PROLOGUE

PART 1

THE STILLNESS

CHAPTER 1

Wednesday, August 13
5:00 p.m.

For the moment, nothing outside moved. Not the tall grass lining the highway, encroaching on the edges of the asphalt; not the haze in the sky, hovering over the mountains; and not the sinuous curve of brake lights disappearing into the landscape in front of us.

Only Delilah fidgeting in the seat beside me, checking the time on her phone yet again.

"We're going to be late," she said, her leg bouncing from either nerves or excitement. With her, sometimes, it was hard to tell. She was a theater kid, functioning at all extremes, with conviction. But the nuances were harder to discern.

"It's just dinner," I said. Which was only partially true. Tonight it was dinner at my parents' house in town. But tomorrow it was dorm move-in. It was the start of my daughter's first semester. It was time to say goodbye.

I didn't understand how we had gotten here so quickly. The previous eighteen years had stretched into a lifetime, and suddenly time was catapulting, leapfrogging.

Over the past year, I'd often been caught off guard by the race of time, missing deadlines, receiving follow-up emails from the high school's commencement coordinator: *Did you order the graduation regalia? Reserve your tickets*? It seemed I wasn't quite ready to face it, so some primitive part of my brain was blocking out key facts.

You'll be ready when it's time, my friends who had crossed this milestone before me would say. *Trust me,* they'd say with a secret look, a knowing grin. *Wait until you see what an eighteen-year-old brings into your home.*

But she'd turned eighteen in the spring, and I still wasn't ready.

I was never ready.

Not for the first high fever or the first broken bone—my first failure to keep her safe. I wasn't ready for the first time I lost her in a store, calling her name frantically down the aisles. The first time she slammed her bedroom door (I'd never felt an echo in my heart like that before). The first secret.

I'd been trying to prepare myself for the feeling of an empty house. A new rhythm, a new routine—but I couldn't slip it into focus. I felt stranded somewhere in time, with no anchor.

It's not that Delilah never left. On the contrary, she was fiercely independent—a particular point of pride for both of us. She spent a month with her father each summer. A long weekend here and there with my parents. She went on trips with the school and had sleepovers with friends, got home late (she was always late), made plans and forgot to share them, intentional or not.

But these things were all so temporary, bookended by her presence.

Now she rested her forehead against the window and groaned—as if I could do anything about the standstill traffic on the single route through the Virginia mountains.

I wanted to say: *We can turn around. It's not too late.*

I wanted to say: *We shouldn't even be here.*

Up until the spring, I'd thought we had a different plan: Two acceptances to in-state schools. A partial scholarship tilting the balance toward one. Easy driving distances.

But somehow we were here instead, on this winding mountain road, driving the four—now six—hours back to the one place I'd tried so hard to leave behind.

I could still feel that jolt of surprise and betrayal when the decision letter arrived—the familiar *W* of the emblem, sharp as a knife. The realization that she'd applied without telling me.

There were other people I'd tried to blame first: my parents, for still living in Wyatt Valley, just beyond the edge of campus, even after retiring from the faculty. I imagined the stories they must've told my daughter, poisoning her with promise. Not to mention the view I knew Delilah had out my old bedroom window on her visits, of the gray stone buildings climbing up the hillside in the distance, like a secret idyll.

The admissions committee, for accepting her in the first place and then making it impossible to say no by offering her a fully covered Presidential Scholarship. If they cared—if they *really* cared—they would've rejected her, in a disguised act of kindness.

I found myself blaming Delilah, even, who had probably marked on the application that she was a legacy, even though that wasn't technically true. I'd left midway through my senior year, transferred my credits, and finished abroad at a sister school, so my diploma carried the name of a different college.

But I knew the fault was mostly mine. I'd wanted to keep the past from her, pretend it never existed. And in doing so, I had only managed to push her closer, like a magnet. Shouldn't I have known better by now? It was the singular truth of the teenage years, binding us all across time—a yearning for the forbidden.

Even as she'd sent back her acceptance, I'd imagined all the things I could've done to prevent this moment, tracing my missteps all the way back to the start.

I shouldn't have been so determined to give her my last name instead of her father's—which would have provided her a layer of removal, making her surname unrecognizable to the town. *Delilah Bowery . . . daughter of Beckett? Granddaughter of the professors Bowery?*

I should've invited my parents to visit us in Charlotte more often so they wouldn't insist on having Delilah in Wyatt Valley, so close to campus. I should've paid more attention during her senior year, asked the obvious question: *Are you planning to apply anywhere else?* So I could say: *Don't you know what happened there? Don't you know why I left? Why I* had *to?*

Two men had died. My roommate, the prime suspect, had fled without a trace. And in her absence, I had briefly become a *person of interest*. Someone the police thought might have more answers than I gave them. Someone the town thought might have been complicit, might have helped the guilty party disappear.

But that was twenty years ago now. Delilah had no fears, and that was purely my fault.

Because I should have told her the truth. Or at least the parts that mattered. The reasons I'd spent so many years avoiding this place.

The town has a long memory.

Not everyone has forgiven.

I should have begged: *Please, I can't go back.*

The distance had turned me dangerously complacent. Foolishly confident.

I'd thought I knew my daughter better. I'd thought I knew how best to keep her safe.

But by the time she opened the acceptance letter, it was already too late.

There was no one left to blame but me.

And now here we were, with a trunk full of luggage, backseat piled high with crates and bedding and decor—though I couldn't imagine it all fitting in her dorm room. My own move-in day: a cinder-block double with narrow beds and a single closet. The memory was crisp and shimmery, even after all these years.

Time had been working like that recently, with moments from the past coming into sharp clarity from nowhere. But the present skewing out of focus, slipping behind me too fast, like the way the fog swept out of the valley with a sharp gust of wind in the fall.

"Mom," Delilah said, gesturing to the open space of road in front of us, just as the car behind us laid on the horn.

"Finally," I said, tightening my grip on the wheel.

I knew we were getting closer by the feeling in my chest: that familiar sense of claustrophobia and the way the mountains seemed visible no matter which way we turned—always in the distance, a blue haze hanging in the summer sky.

If I closed my eyes, I could still picture the campus so clearly: The worn gray steps emerging from the hillside, our footsteps racing the hourly chime of the bell. The curved stone walls of the main building and their cool, gritty texture as I dragged my fingertips across them.

In the silence, I could hear the echo of my name in the long hall, laughter in the dark.

On a deep breath in, I could still smell the smoke.

Now Delilah wore a T-shirt with the school's insignia, a walking advertisement of all I'd hoped to leave in the past. Her dark wavy hair held back with oversize sunglasses, a sparkling phone case in her hand—her name written in loopy cursive with a neon gel pen—and suddenly I was desperate to hold on to it all. Terrified that this place would strip her of the things that made her.

"Doc says the blue is an illusion . . ." Delilah said, as if she could feel me watching her from the corner of my vision.

"Is that what she says," I responded, sounding like my mother now, too. My mother, a professor of psychology, never answered questions directly, just led you to the answer she wanted you to find for yourself.

"I'm sure she's right," I added. She'd probably read studies about the importance of being honest with children of all ages, as a way to establish trust.

Delilah turned sideways. Her mouth had stretched wide into that beguiling smile that could throw anyone off kilter—even me.

"You know what else Doc told me?" she asked.

"I have no idea." The motivations of my mother remained one of life's great mysteries to me. I pressed my lips together.

"She said that you were a total wild child."

A bark of laughter escaped. My mother was not a fan of idioms, found them lazy or, worse, more revealing of the person who used them than what they were describing. "I just didn't turn out like she expected, I think."

"Apparently, by comparison, I'm a *breath of fresh air,*" she continued, grinning. "I don't think this is appreciated enough in our household."

"She did *not* use that term," I said, laughing.

"That might've been Hal."

"Somehow I find that equally unlikely."

Delilah had taken to calling my parents Doc and Hal. I wasn't sure if it was their idea, but knowing my mother, she would've found this charming, delightful. Precocious. *A breath of fresh air.* Maybe she missed being known as Doc by all her students now that she was retired. When I was growing up, there had been a rotating group of upperclassmen who'd come over for family-style dinners on Friday nights, with a new topic of conversation each week. Even when I was young, I was encouraged to participate. If nothing else, my parents had taught me to develop strong opinions and prepare to defend them. I had learned to hold my own, regardless of my age. I had also honed a stubbornness early; seen conversations as something to win.

"There it is," Delilah said, just as the sign for Wyatt Valley came into view.

I tried to focus on the things I loved about this place—because once upon a time, I did. I loved this place fiercely. The town was set in the foothills, tucked against the Blue Ridge, where the haze drifted down into the valley and hovered over the trees. It was hard not to appreciate the clarity of the view, the distinct ridgeline in the distance. Something I could trace like my own heartbeat.

I could feel Delilah's gaze on me instead of the road. I wondered if she had ever clocked the view herself, noticed the way it matched the tattoo on my wrist, hidden under the wide strap of my watch—the number of peaks like a barcode transporting you to this one place, from this one view.

But she was just looking at my grip on the steering wheel, white knuckles and blanched fingertips.

Her fingers drummed against her knee, as if my nerves were transferring to her. As if she could feel it, too—a sense of dread with no apparent cause.

Maybe it was the unnatural stillness of the place. The silence. The way the flags hung down from the front porches and the leaves on the trees seemed eerily static, like you were moving through a movie set.

I lowered the windows, just for a sense of movement, felt the hot rush of humidity pushing in, sensed a wavering of air over the tar-black pavement—an illusion in the stillness.

There are two states of being in Wyatt Valley: the stillness, when the fog settles like a cocoon, and the tree branches hang slack, and nothing stirs; and the howling, when the wind funnels down from the mountain like a cry in the night, first the leaves spiraling, then the snow swirling in eddies up and down the terrain.

In town, we used to await the first howling, welcome it like a ritual. For us, it marked the unofficial turn of the season, ushering in the fall. The stillness always made me antsy, like I was slowly being suffocated. Even the arrival of a new batch of students each year couldn't shake things up on its own.

There were just over a thousand undergrads on campus, and they stayed largely behind the iron gates up on the hill. When they spilled out, they generally kept to the first perimeter, with the places that had been built and dedicated to them. But the town sprawled downward through the valley.

We drove past the fixtures that hadn't changed in all the time I'd been gone: the town square, with its maze of streets and restaurants in a grid; and the old sign for Cryer's Quarry, now with a chain hung across an unpaved access road, though I knew there was a shortcut by foot—a hiking path branching off from the parking lot behind the deli.

Instead of pointing these out to Delilah, I felt the sharpness of twenty years prior.

On the hill in the distance, I saw the campus where I'd spent so much of my youth, and thought: *The spot where the smoke rose over the trees, ash falling over fresh snow.*

I pulled onto my parents' street, two blocks from campus, and thought: *The corner where Adalyn Vale was last tracked before disappearing, never to be seen again.*

I was lost in my own memories, so I hadn't noticed at first how Delilah had leaned forward until her hands were on the dashboard.

I followed her gaze to the end of the block, where my parents' street intersected with College Lane—which had once been Fraternity Row, before a series of incidents in the nineties led to their systematic shutdown. The properties had since been annexed back to the town, where they typically housed a rotating assortment of employees and their families.

Now there was a noticeable gap in the row of homes, an empty plot at the T intersection—so that we could see straight through to the edge of campus.

"What happened?" Delilah asked.

"I have no idea," I said, feeling the unease that came whenever my memory did not line up with reality. "Renovation?" There was always construction happening around campus, and I could see a dumpster beside a heap of wood. But there were people lingering on the other side of the gap, staring.

I pulled up to the curb in front of my parents' home, half a block from the empty plot. The sun was setting behind the mountains, the sky turning a golden hue, dusk falling.

I heard the distant chime of the bell tower marking the hour, and thought, like I had long ago: *Run.*

CHAPTER 2

Wednesday, August 13
8:00 p.m.

"Look who's here!" The door to the house swung open under the porch light, screen door balanced on my father's hip. He dressed like he always did, no matter the season: khaki pants, checkered button-down tucked in, loose gold watch. My mother hovered just behind him, her close-cropped, stylish brown hair making her look younger than her seventy-plus years, while my father's receding hairline and hunched posture had the opposite effect.

Delilah raced up the porch steps of the old Victorian, a quick pitter-patter on the wood floorboards. Sometimes she seemed like an ethereal figment I had created from air, from nothing, gliding effortlessly through a space.

"Hello, dear," my mother said as she reached up to hug Delilah. And then to me: "We already ate. I didn't know how late you would be."

"I sent you a text," Delilah said. "We were stuck in traffic."

"You need to *call,*" my mother said, looking at me instead of her. I could never imagine her reprimanding my daughter. And then she frowned at my father. "Someone probably needs to reset the Wi-Fi." Which was apparently as close as I'd get to an apology. Here in the valley, text messages didn't always come through if you weren't connected to a local wireless network.

"Well, come in, come in," my father said. "We'll warm up the food in a minute." I could already smell the lasagna, his specialty, the heat from the kitchen permeating the downstairs.

"Let me bring in Delilah's things," I said, gesturing back to the car at the curb. "She's got half her life in there."

"Oh, please," my mother said. "Like anyone's going to break into your car here." She shook her head once. "You've lived in a city for too long."

As if the isolation here somehow inoculated them from crime.

I ignored her and grabbed our backpacks, electronics, and overnight bag, handing Delilah her purple fluff pillow that she carried in front of her like a stuffed animal.

I often felt like Delilah had grown up more slowly than I had, a member of the post-Covid generation, where the rules seemed more important, the consequences more direct. There was no carefree game about their adolescence, as there had been in ours.

"What happened to the house down the street?" Delilah asked, pulling the pillow to her chest, with her oversize khaki backpack hitched on one shoulder. She tipped her head toward the darkening lane.

"Oh," my father said, following our gaze. "It burned down." He scratched at the side of his white beard like he'd forgotten. Ancient history.

But I felt my shoulders tense, the evening splinter. A gateway opening up between the present and the past. *The crunch of fresh snow. Flames rising over the treetops. The scent of smoke carrying on the wind—*

"When?" I asked. The dumpster was still on site, and I was sure the school wasn't thrilled with the optics during move-in.

"Oh," he said, shifting slowly on his feet. "Maybe a week ago?"

"Two," my mother corrected.

This was a hallmark of my father's perception. All past was the past. Whether a week or a decade. The moment it was behind us, it became something to study.

I felt my mother's steady gaze on me before her eyes drifted to the side. "Happened in the middle of the night, when no one was home," she added, as if she could read the tension in my demeanor and needed to clarify. "It was between renters. Old wiring, they said."

An accident. An old home.

No deaths. No locked doors. No accusations. No mystery.

"Okay, come in, come in," she said, beckoning. "Don't stare."

I trailed Delilah inside, trying, as my mother had requested, not to stare.

The homes on this block had all been built in a much more distant past, and ours was no exception. It was full of quirks and secrets, from the hexagonal front porch to the kitchen dumbwaiter and the attic door that opened beside my bathroom sink upstairs. It was the type of place a child would love exploring—and Delilah always had.

But there was a fine line between run-down and charming, old and historic, and we were currently walking that line. The trinkets from my father's trips had taken over the space, dust settling in the remaining gaps on the mantel. The floorboards popped on the narrow staircase, and the thin windows shook in the howling wind. The old radiators near the baseboards had to work double time to keep up and suddenly seemed like a fire hazard.

Unlike most of their original neighbors, they'd held on to the property since my childhood. There had been no renovations, no fast sell in a market high. They owned it outright, which they claimed allowed them to spend their retirement however they pleased.

But now my parents' luggage was cluttering the foyer, adding to the sense of claustrophobia. They were leaving soon for my father's new assignment, a guest professor role for a semester abroad in Peru. Neither of my parents was truly suited for retirement. They guest-lectured, and wrote papers, and accompanied student groups on excursions. My mother said they had to seize the opportunities while they still could—as if they could hear a clock ticking down.

They had postponed the start of their trip to see Delilah into college. Though I'd told them they didn't need to be here for move-in, my mother had scoffed. *My only granddaughter?* Of course she would be here. But now I felt the luggage was a stark reminder of the imposition. As if she wanted me to see their sacrifice.

Beside their bags were several brown boxes marked *Fragile*.

"I don't think the bottom of an airplane is the safest place for these," I said, frowning.

"I know that," my mother said, crossing her arms. "They'll be our carry-ons."

I raised an eyebrow at Delilah. "And here I thought *you* had overpacked."

Delilah and I ate dinner at the circular kitchen table with both of them hovering over us, watching like we were a foreign specimen. They cleaned the kitchen around us, wiping down the counters, refilling Delilah's cup whenever it got half empty. When I was a teenager, I often felt that I was in the center of a snow globe, visible from all angles.

My dad was a professor of anthropology, my mother of psychology, and their attention managed to feel somehow too close and too aloof at the same time. My father, seeing things from a remove—he'd said once that college itself was nothing but a huge social experiment—while my mother always seemed to be peering deeply into my psyche. I grew to believe that she could sense a lie as easily as the truth. It had taught me to be both clever and closed. Careful, always, to mask my thoughts, if I wanted to keep them for myself.

"Oh, we ran into Maggie," my father said, dipping into the past again. "She says hi." Which I doubted. My father never seemed to notice that we'd drifted apart after high school. "And she says good luck to *you,*" my father said, patting Delilah on the head as he passed behind her.

Delilah's gaze trailed after him. "I have no idea who you're talking about," she said.

"Your mom's old friend. You've met her once or twice," he said, squinting out the window over the sink.

"We dropped off a baby gift," my mother added, like she was the keeper of his memories. "It was a while ago, but you were here visiting us."

This was the first I had heard about Delilah meeting Maggie. I knew she'd had twins—my parents kept their annual holiday card on the fridge just below ours—but that must've been five or six years ago now.

"How's your work going?" my mother asked with a tilt of her head. My mother always seemed confused that I'd managed to make a career as a ghostwriter. But it played to my strengths—I could copy any voice, any style, slip into someone else's story and make it my own. I took on both fiction and nonfiction projects for all ages and audiences. And when I was done, I could leave them behind. Nothing to either own or answer for.

"Good," I said, scraping the last of my lasagna from the plate. "Busy. I'm almost finished with a big project." I'd taken on the last few books in a middle-grade series over the past year, writing under a shared pen name, racing against a string of very tight deadlines. But the project was coming to an end; my agent was starting to put out feelers for what would come next.

"Marcia Greene was asking when we saw her last," she said, like my old literature professor was the main reason for the question.

Delilah leaned back in her chair, scrolling through her phone. "Can someone check the Wi-Fi?" she asked. "I can't log into my school email for tomorrow's schedule."

My father sighed, heading for the hall. "I'll reboot it again."

"We were shutting things down for the semester," my mother explained, eyes wide like she was sharing a secret. "I'm not sure if he got the dates right." She gave Delilah a tight smile. "Sorry about that. As soon as you're close to campus tomorrow, you'll be able to log onto their network."

Delilah's eyes cut to mine in a moment of pure panic. No Wi-Fi, no texting. No entertainment here but my parents' outdated over-the-airwaves television.

"Early to bed, I guess," I teased as she scrunched her nose at me in disgust.

"We made up the futon in your father's office," my mother said, either not catching or ignoring the joke. "It's up to you who sleeps where."

The side of Delilah's mouth quirked up. She held out her fist, preparing for a round of rock-paper-scissors.

"Go ahead," I said. "You might as well have a real room to yourself for the last time in a while."

She quickly disappeared up the narrow steps behind the kitchen. I had no desire to sleep up there anyway. My parents had left my room exactly as I'd abandoned it, the walls covered in quotes I'd accumulated over time. They circled the room on pieces of glued-down paper, or hung in frames, or written in paint or Sharpie taken directly to the wall. Once upon a time, they'd brought me comfort, made the world feel smaller—connecting strangers across time. But I found them disorienting now, like the past was whispering from the walls.

It was just like my parents to want to preserve it—a living history. Another version of me, in a different lifetime. Maybe the one they believed I would become.

But Delilah loved it up there. She loved the history that you could see all around us.

My mother was still staring at the narrow steps behind the kitchen where Delilah had disappeared.

"I'm surprised she wanted to come here," she said, lowering her voice. She turned to look at me slowly, waiting for me to fill in the blanks. My mother never wore makeup, but there was a flush to her cheeks now. Some emotion simmering under her words.

"I thought it might've been your idea." Planting the seed, drawing her home—like she was righting a wrong, making up for the fact that I'd left.

She shook her head. "No, but then kids always like to keep you on your toes, don't they, Beck?" She smiled tightly, then left the room, her final words trailing behind her.

Maybe she was right; maybe I deserved this. Hadn't I done the same to her? I hadn't told my parents I was pregnant with Delilah until I came back from my year abroad, visibly showing—something already tangible instead of hypothetical. They were confused, disoriented, by the sudden existence of what was to come. I remembered the heat of my mother's gaze, the cool shock of her words.

She wanted me to stay home with them, claiming I'd need help—that I'd need *their* help. That I had no idea what to expect; that I wasn't ready.

But I couldn't stay. I felt only the claustrophobia of the mountains. The accusations of the people who lived here fresh in my memory, even after a full year away. A nausea that seemed to creep in from the mere proximity. I couldn't stand to look out my bedroom window and see the rise of campus, the place the smoke once billowed above the trees. I couldn't raise a child here—not with the presence of the past like it existed beside us.

I didn't want their help. I didn't want anyone's. I knew by then that I was better on my own. Had gotten through that last year by trusting only myself and my own decisions.

I'd graduated after an extra semester that winter, and then I'd moved to Charlotte by myself—had already lined up a job in marketing and graphic design. A few years later, when the logistics of preschool and childcare became tougher to juggle, I'd leveraged my experience in copywriting for an audition with a ghostwriting agency. I'd had a steady stream of work ever since.

I'd met friends who had become like family. Gone on dates here and there. But for the last eighteen years, I had devoted myself fully to my daughter—and my career. It was a simple life but a meaningful one—and, more importantly, it was the right one for me.

I had created an entire second life for myself by leaving, and it had begun with Delilah.

The futon in my father's office was set against the wall under the window, across from his large cherry desk. But the gauzy curtains did nothing to prevent the glare of the full moon, long shadows falling across the assortment of artifacts that doubled as decor: tiny figurines across the edge of his desk; chipped pottery on the bookshelves; and the masks, of course. They lined the walls in a zigzag pattern—hollow faces and empty eyes. Things that seemed better suited for a museum.

Some were gifts from colleagues and former students, or items he'd picked up at markets around the world. He'd once loaned a good portion of his collection to an exhibit for the school. I imagined he was bringing some of the pieces to show his students in Peru, carefully cocooned within the boxes in the foyer.

I opened the window, hoping for a breeze, but felt only the thick humidity. I needed to move, to walk off the day's adrenaline, so I slipped on my sneakers and stepped through the window gap directly onto the front porch, careful not to wake anyone.

There were no streetlights, but the front porch lights of a few of the houses remained on. I could see the dark gap of night where the house should have been at the far end of the street. I felt myself drawn there, just like others must've been earlier—passing by on their way to campus, taking note. Something out of place. Something *wrong.*

I stood in the middle of the empty street. Shadowed cars lined the curbs, from resident parking. In the distance, behind the gaping plot of land, dim lights trailed up the hillside, Wyatt College coming back to life from its summer hibernation. I saw a lonely glow of blue in the darkness from a campus security system. One of the safety additions in the last twenty years.

I walked down the street and stopped just before the wreckage.

The dumpster sat at the edge of where the lawn once was, before a pile of blackened wood and debris, rotted from both the flames and the water. Yellow tape that I hadn't noticed at first traced the perimeter but had fallen to the ground, twisted and half covered with dirt.

I took a step back just as a noise jarred me from the dumpster. I turned on the light from my phone and shone it around but saw no one.

I climbed onto a stack of cinder blocks beside the dumpster, then carefully peered over the edge, wondering if an animal had gotten trapped inside.

At the bottom, the waterlogged wood appeared dark and splintered. There were also seared photographs, blackened at the edges, soot-covered silverware and broken dishes, and for a moment, I wondered if my mother had lied after all about the house being empty.

A glow in the bottom corner caught my eye.

A scent rose from below—a lingering smoke. An ember left burning.

No, I thought. *Not after two weeks.* This was something fresh. New.

The glowing edge of a match, yellow-red. I watched as it faded to nothing, finally extinguished. A wisp of smoke the only thing left behind.

A warning that I wasn't alone out here.

BEFORE:
THE RULES

It was a tradition up there, on the campus. The first howling of the year—a call to move after the long stillness. A chase through the woods. A game for bragging rights. A chance to prove you belonged.

It started with a whistle. Something sharp and piercing.

Heads rising, eyes locking from across the classroom. A small smile.

A warning that it would be coming.

Throughout the day, the sound would gradually deepen as the strong winds funneled into the valley—blowing in the colder weather from the north, pushing out the stagnant humidity.

It was the promise of change, ushering in the windy season.

By night, the whistle would turn to a howl. And it would be time.

The students all knew the rules, passed down in whispers: Don't get caught by the seniors in masks. Don't be last. Don't be scared. Don't cry for help. Don't, don't, don't.

If caught, you had to give your name and make your way back to the dorms in the dark—alone.

The seniors kept their own tallies, for after. And each year, the winner's name would be etched into the bottom of a growing list. A secret piece of history.

From the woods, we could hear the first of the freshmen scrambling from their dorms, shadows in the night.

We knew where they were heading. It was the same every year.

They gripped one another as they raced blindly through the woods toward home base: the ruins of the old president's house on the far edge of the campus property, where a fire would be burning in the half-standing chimney just inside the stone perimeter, to guide the way. The supply barn beside it, no longer in use by the school, would be stocked full of warm beer and the type of liquor designed only to burn your throat going down.

A celebration, for those who made it.

In town growing up, we had learned those same rules—they were whispered up and down the halls of our high school.

It was a tradition, a game, for us, too.

We knew how to access the power panels of the campus buildings, turn them off, blame it on the wind. We knew how to move through these woods in the dark. We knew this place much, much better than they did.

Ours were the footsteps that made them walk faster, that turned them around, that separated them from a group and got them disoriented.

We didn't touch them. We never did.

But we got them lost, kept them on edge—followed them and declared our own wins.

Every year, for one evening, these woods were full of college students racing through the night, heading for the far edge of campus.

They never seemed to notice that they weren't the only ones out there.

CHAPTER 3

Thursday, August 14
9:30 a.m.

Delilah and I stood at the edge of campus, staring up at the landscape. The gates to the college stood open, as they tended to be only twice each year, by tradition: once at orientation and again at graduation—though there were open walkways on either side. The college property extended back from the gates, stone buildings and grass quads connected by brick paths and flights of steps disappearing into the trees.

Delilah walked like she knew where she was going, pausing only briefly to read each academic building name as she passed. I wondered if my parents had taken her here on her visits, letting her explore the empty campus when she was young, like I had done.

The dorms were set farther up the hill, deeper in the woods—designated as upper campus. My father was set to meet us there with my car for move-in.

Delilah stopped abruptly in front of the stone building with arched wooden doors that had always reminded me of a church from the Middle Ages. Her smile stretched wide. "This is it, right? Beckett Hall?"

I nodded, grinning back. Only the people I'd grown up with knew I was named after the building where both of my parents once taught—my mother on the second floor, my father on the third. It was the original structure of the campus from back when it was an all-boys school, with classes and dorm rooms in a single building. Now it was the center of social sciences. Sometimes I feared it was the place of my conception.

"Take my picture," she instructed. She posed beside the sign, arms outstretched, tilting her head back and smiling at the sky.

I stood across the path and took several shots as she changed positions. She didn't care that people were watching, and I loved that about her. I envied the way she didn't feel compelled to choose words carefully, as if she had to present a curated version of herself. She was all rough edges, moving through the world like an unstoppable force that had not yet been tested.

There was a poster taped to the wooden doors that seemed student-made: *Orientation Tours!* written in purple marker and outlined in silver Sharpie.

I followed her inside, where I saw a group congregated in the second atrium, presumably ready for the start of tour.

"Hold on," I said as Delilah started walking that way. I needed a moment to take it all in, recalibrate. I ran my fingers against the lobby wall, where the paint must've smoothed over the once-gritty stone. I tapped at a low door that was now painted the same color as the walls, so it almost disappeared to the eye. There was no knob, but a keyhole was faintly visible next to the seam.

"What *is* that?" Delilah asked, eyes tracing the border of the doorframe.

"This used to be the entrance to the old steam tunnels," I told her, voice low. "They connected all the buildings of lower campus. They're mostly sealed off now."

Sealed off, I knew, after two people had succumbed to the smoke, trapped inside the tunnel system at the far edge of campus, underneath the old storage barn.

Delilah ran her hands across the hidden doorway, grinning. "Have you been down there?" she asked, like it was all fun and games. There was a time when I saw it the same way. *A dancing beam of light. The hiss of steam. Laughter in the dark.*

A door slammed shut from down the hall, jolting me back to the present. Now all I could imagine was the claustrophobia. The dark and the disorientation, hands desperately groping for an exit—

I felt a rush of panic but tried to play it off. "You're forgetting I practically grew up in this building."

I'd been raised in these halls. My father had been the first person to take me down to the tunnels, as a way to avoid the winter weather. By high school, I could lead the other town kids through every secret shortcut, winding through the narrow, arched tunnels, using the pipes as a road map.

Most of us from town knew the ins and outs of campus. We thought of it as our own—the students only temporary inhabitants.

For fun, Cliff Simmons once sneaked onto campus during orientation, pretending to be a new student, seeing how much he could get away with. I'd been helping my parents, so I'd seen him asking questions on a campus tour; sitting with a group of students in the cafeteria; playing Ultimate Frisbee on the quad. Sometimes he'd catch my eye as I passed, give me a secret grin.

I was a year behind Cliff in high school, dated him on and off during my junior year, and then something a little more casual after he graduated. He worked construction, I knew; he hadn't been able to afford college full-time and took classes at night. But by the time I'd graduated and enrolled at Wyatt, we had moved further down diverging paths, until I stopped seeing him around—like he was avoiding me. As if I could no longer be trusted now that I was on the other side of the divide between the town and the college.

"What else?" Delilah asked, eyes flashing. Maybe this was the way to bridge the time, grasp the past and fully acknowledge it—letting it go in the process.

I grinned and lowered my voice even more. "Everything echoes in here. If it were just the two of us, I could go to the back atrium and hear you perfectly."

The acoustical quirk was an architectural feature but generally impractical, considering this building was usually bustling with activity.

"Here," I said, hands on her shoulders, positioning her at the center of the atrium. "Be quiet."

I stood beside her, listening to the sudden proximity of the conversation down the hall, in the opposite atrium. Their words were indecipherable, blurring together, but it sounded like we were almost in the same room.

Delilah took a step closer, head tilted to the side, like she was trying to make something out. I knew, of course, that Delilah would love things like this. A history full of secrets, passed on just to her.

"Shhh," Delilah said abruptly, though I hadn't spoken. "They're coming." She pulled me back from the center of the atrium, like we were about to be caught eavesdropping.

A young woman in a red polo was walking backward toward us, giving an overview of the school's history. She paused when she noticed us lingering at the edge of the lobby. "Are you two here for the tour? We're just getting started."

Delilah glanced over at me before nodding. "We are," she said, slipping into the group.

I kept at a distance as we moved through lower campus, though Delilah stayed near the front, listening to the guide's practiced speech, highlighting the health center hours, the logistics of the meal plan—all the things they might've skipped over on a general admissions tour.

The guide tried to hurry us along as we passed the location of the old student center, which was now surrounded by cones and razed to the ground; she claimed that the construction for the new center was a sign of strong financial health, of progress. But in the in-between, all that remained was a gaping, empty pit where a few yellow construction vehicles sat idle behind the hole.

It was a huge eyesore, and presumably loud. I guessed *progress* was a better pitch. A reframing, which we were always good at here.

"This is a very safe campus," the tour guide continued, stopping at one of the blue-light emergency phone towers I'd seen glowing in the night. "But if you press the button on any of these"—she tapped the metal pole—"the campus police will be here within minutes." Then she smirked. "Don't try it for kicks, though. There are cameras."

We'd stopped at the bell tower just before a set of steps leading to upper campus when I felt a hand on my shoulder.

"Oh my God," a voice said from just behind me. "Beck?"

I spun around, stomach plummeting. Like I'd been waiting for this moment. Or as if something had been waiting, all this time, for me. A petite woman with wide-set hazel eyes stared back. I didn't recognize her at first. Her straight blond hair was cut to her shoulders, and she wore a tight white tank over her tanned, athletic build. I thought she might've been wearing a tennis skort. "Violet Wharton," she said, one manicured hand to her chest. "Violet Harvey, once upon a time."

"Oh my God," I said, repeating her sentiment—buying myself some time. I hadn't seen Violet in *years,* and it took me a moment to reconcile the woman in front of me with the one I'd known growing up, in ripped jeans and heavy eyeliner. It was possible I'd last seen her at a party in the quarry, stumbling close to the edge with a drink in one hand, cigarette in the other.

Violet had been four years ahead of me in school, so I knew *of* her more than anything. Our high school was about the same size as the college, pulling from a handful of surrounding towns. From what I remembered, she was sharp and funny and magnetic. With our age difference, she'd mostly ignored me back then. But now she was talking to me like we'd been old friends, finally reconnecting.

She grabbed my wrist as if to share a confidence, then nodded to Delilah, who had sidled up next to me, drawn by the conversation. "She looks just like you did at that age. I thought I was seeing a *ghost*," she said. Then she smiled. "It's a compliment," she continued, getting a grin from Delilah in response. "I promise."

My shoulders tensed. Wasn't that a big part of my fear here? Anyone could see that Delilah belonged to me. Instead of my traits dulling, blending with Trevor's fairer features, it was like each of mine had only grown stronger in her. Hair, a richer shade of brown. Eyes, a deeper blue. Her smile wider, cheekbones sharper, limbs longer. I could even see myself in her expressions, slightly exaggerated but there all the same.

"This is Bryce," Violet said, gesturing to the lanky teenager towering over her, dark hair falling haphazardly in his eyes, shoulders hunched forward like he was trying to go unnoticed at well over six feet tall.

Bryce, I assumed, took after his father.

"Delilah," my daughter answered, shaking hands with both Violet and her son.

"I can't believe it," Violet said. "Both of our kids in the same school. Like old times!"

Which wasn't entirely true. Violet had graduated before I'd started high school, and she'd never been a student at Wyatt College that I knew of.

"I didn't know you had a son," I said. I tried to remember anything I'd heard about Violet in the years since high school, but I came up blank.

"I'd heard *you* had a kid," she continued in a way that sent a chill down my spine as I thought of how my name had continued to circle through town even after I'd left. "I just didn't know she was starting college already. And coming here! What a surprise."

I could say the same about her. Violet Harvey had grown up in Wyatt Valley, but it was unusual for locals to also attend college here. There was a divide in the town; it was hard to truly exist as a member of both. Most people didn't want to try.

Besides, not many families chose to fork over the price tag for private tuition to live exactly where they'd always lived. I, with my two professor parents, named after the building at the heart of the campus, had the privilege of a free ride.

"Well, you know how this place can be," Violet said, and I nodded. Though we probably had opposing views on that now.

Our tour guide had moved on from the bell tower, and we all rushed to catch up. We joined late as she was speaking of the famed traditions of the college. She pointed in the direction of the fountain at center campus where students tossed offerings for luck before finals. She paused in front of the marble *steps to nowhere* that reminded me of the ruins of the Athens Acropolis, and relayed their history as the bones left behind from the original footprint of campus.

I felt Violet lean over. "I guess they don't highlight how many people end up in the infirmary each year from these steps."

"Any of the steps, really," I added. How many kids had broken a bone each year running down from upper campus, inebriated?

"Or the heart attack on parents' weekend last year," she said, and I widened my eyes in surprise. "Had to be airlifted," she whispered.

The tour guide took a step up the marble so she was visible to the semicircle around her. "Our favorite tradition is to decorate these steps in the spring . . ."

I felt Violet lean even closer. "*That's* their favorite tradition now?" she said under her breath with a laugh.

I cut my eyes to the side, but she was staring straight ahead.

But I knew exactly what she meant. Our favorite tradition had officially died twenty years ago—abruptly halted and banned by the school after the town's biggest tragedy.

"You know what they say now at the first howling?" Violet said as we headed toward Beckett Hall, ending the tour.

I didn't answer, heard only the sound of air rushing in and out of my ears.

Violet grinned, leaned closer, so I could feel the words against the side of my cheek. "They say it's Adalyn."

She pulled back and smiled at me—like she was telling ghost stories around a campfire, waiting to gauge my reaction.

For all the change to her outer appearance, the old Violet I remembered was still there. Sharp and funny, just as long as it wasn't at your expense. Violet Harvey had always suffered no fools.

"So nice catching up, Violet," I said, one hand on Delilah's elbow, guiding her away. "I think it's our turn to check in."

This was what I had wanted to explain to Delilah about the town. The way no one had forgotten. The way a simple comment could carry layers of history underneath.

The way I could never be sure whether the implication was meant for me.

Before that final, fateful howling, the scandals on campus rarely spilled over to the town itself. There was the series of hazing incidents that led to the Wyatt fraternities and sororities shutting down. Faculty campaigned to get a president booted. There had been embezzling of athletic funds, traced back to that same president, who was sacked but somehow not charged, which thankfully prevented it from becoming national news.

That was the trick, really, to a place like this. Keep the dirt to the bubble. Control the narrative.

But my senior year, that became impossible. Two young men from town were dead, on campus property. Their names were Charlie Rivers and Micah White. They were twenty-four years old. And a Wyatt College student had allegedly set the fire that killed them.

Adalyn Vale had a soft, rounded face, cheeks that pressed upward when she smiled, red in the cold. Hair she'd tie into a pair of blond braids under a winter hat, so that from a distance she could pass for a child. Maybe that's why it was so hard to believe the witness reports at first. Maybe that's why people were so intrigued by her crime.

Eventually the police tracked her movements across campus, out the gates, to the intersection of College Lane. And that was the last concrete trace of Adalyn's existence.

All that remained were two sets of footprints in the snow: hers and a men's size-ten winter boots. And the wind ultimately erased even that evidence.

The college settled in a civil suit brought by the victims' families—though they tried at first to fight it. The men were not their students. They'd been trespassing; the tunnels were off limits; they must've sneaked inside.

I'd been long gone by the time it was all settled, but I'd kept up with it all online. And I'd been there for the worst of it: the smoke in the sky, flames rising over the trees; fire engine sirens in the night and the coroner's van by dawn.

Their deaths had exacerbated every tension, every slight, between the town and the school. Every fight over a property line expansion; every noise ordinance complaint and trespassing citation. Every allocation of funds and diversion of resources.

It didn't matter that the main suspect had vanished.

Someone had to pay.

CHAPTER 4

Thursday, August 14
11:00 a.m.

There was someone already inside Delilah's third-floor dorm room when we arrived at her move-in time. I could hear the catch of their rubber soles on the linoleum floor through the heavy door as Delilah fumbled for her key, already lost somewhere in the recesses of her backpack.

The building layout was the same as I remembered from my own freshman dorm, when I'd hauled my essentials over by myself. My parents had been busy with their own orientation responsibilities—there was no ceremony to my start here, no need for the formality of a long goodbye.

Now, when Delilah slipped the key into the lock, the movement on the other side stopped. But instead of her roommate, a man in a gray uniform stood beside the single window in the center of her dorm room, with a set of keys dangling from his belt loop.

Delilah froze in the open doorway just in front of me.

The man blinked twice, like we'd been the ones to surprise him.

"Hi! Welcome," he said, squinting as his expression shifted to a smile. He was in his fifties, maybe, rounded face, ruddy cheeks, hair buzzed military-short, receding at the corners. He gestured to the toolbox open on the desk beside him. "I was trying to beat you here. Stuck window. Should be all set now."

"Oh, thanks," Delilah said, carrying her bags to the nearest bed. Both were currently stripped bare.

The man clamped his toolbox shut, preparing to leave. "Would you be Delilah or Hana, then?" he asked, as if he had the room assignments already memorized.

"Delilah," she answered, tucking a loose wave of hair behind her ear. "This is my mom."

He nodded. "I'm Lenny. This here's my building." Up close, a line of sweat was visible along his forehead, despite the cool blast of air-conditioning coming from above. He cleared his throat. "I've got an office in the basement, but I'm on call day and night if there are any maintenance issues. The number's posted on the hall bulletin."

"Nice to meet you," I said, trying to prod him along. We had limited time to set up, and the room felt too claustrophobic for the three of us.

"One last tip," he continued, lingering in the doorway. "The doors lock automatically. Don't go anywhere without your keys. Otherwise the only person who can let you in is your roommate, or me." He pointed to the alarm system overhead. "Can't tell you how many kids get locked out after a fire alarm in the middle of the night and have to wait for security to show up."

That seemed to get Delilah's attention, at least. I watched as she slipped the dorm key onto the carabiner clip hanging from her bag.

"Don't worry," Lenny added, with a wink in my direction. "We take good care of them here."

Three trips to the car and nearly an hour later, we were finally putting the finishing touches on her side of the room. I was helping Delilah string the lights of her name over her bed when I felt the presence of another person in the entrance.

I turned to welcome a roommate named Hana, but the woman in the doorway introduced herself as the RA. Her shoulder-length hair was an unnatural shade of maroon that perfectly matched her lipstick.

"You must be Delilah." She greeted Delilah with open arms, sharp chin resting on her shoulder, winged eyeliner accentuating amber eyes. "I'm Raven," she said. "I'll just be in the lounge when you're ready." She gave me a quick, tight smile but didn't address me at all. As if I had already overstayed my welcome.

I stepped back, taking in the room. It felt like Delilah's, even though it was half bare and mostly beige. But she'd managed to make it her own, from the electric blue bedspread to the glowing lights, an assortment of hardy plants in small pots, and a photo montage of her friends over her desk.

"Smile," I said, taking a picture of her in front of the decor.

And then, because I was feeling nostalgic, I sent the photo to Trevor. It was a generosity he'd always afforded me during her visits: Delilah on his shoulders at the Washington Mall, her toddler hands gripped into his light brown hair; Delilah in front of a fossilized dinosaur, copying its pose; Delilah and him eating hot dogs at the ballpark last summer, in matching caps flipped backward. She still used that one as his contact photo in her phone.

Here we go, I wrote.

His response came immediately, like he'd been watching the clock himself.

God. Give her a hug from me please.

Though I knew that Delilah was geographically closer to him now, halfway between me in Charlotte and him in D.C., it felt like she was somehow farther from us both, stranded in between. There was a difference from shuttling her on a ninety-minute plane ride between our cities than in driving through the mountains. The closest major airport was over two hours away.

I slipped the phone away; could feel our time running out.

"Can I help with anything else?" I asked Delilah, not ready to leave her alone just yet.

But Delilah shook her head. "I have a lunch soon," she said, checking the schedule on her phone, happily back on Wi-Fi. "And then a group orientation. I think Raven is waiting for me to meet them in the lounge."

I nodded. "Right."

She shifted on her feet, like she didn't want to have to tell me to go.

I knew it was time.

Though I made my living with language, sometimes, when the moment felt too big, I struggled to find any words at all. I'd short-circuit, say something that barely grazed the surface, forgettable and meaningless at the same time.

I wanted to tell her how proud I was. I wanted to tell her that the world was so large. So much larger than this.

I wanted to tell her to be careful.

"Don't forget to call me," I said instead, pulling her in for a hug—and then one more, from her father.

There was a moment of hesitation, a break in her demeanor—something that seized my heart. A pause of uncertainty. A chance where I could've done something different. Said something else: *You don't have to do this. We can go. Right now.*

But then it was gone, and she wrapped her arms around my back tight and quick in that familiar teenage way.

"See you soon," she said.

I tried to freeze the moment. Remember her exactly this way, at this singular fulcrum in time, right on the cusp of the rest of her life—where I could suddenly see both Delilah the child and the Delilah she might soon become.

BEFORE:
THE ROOMMATE

I arrived on campus for freshman move-in with nothing but the large hiking bag strapped to my back, the key in my hand, and a healthy dose of confidence. There were no first-day jitters. No fears of what to expect.

I'd been in these halls many times before. First when I was young, playing a game of hide-and-seek across campus with the other faculty kids. And then when I was in high school, helping clean out the dorms after spring semester, when I volunteered to lug the items left behind to the donation center downtown.

As I walked through the open doors, I thought: This is my home.

I thought: No one belongs here more than I do.

But something happened in the lobby. Boxes were stacked along the walls, making the dimensions feel off. Families chatted in line for the elevator, giving the names of their prep schools instead of their towns. Like there was another thread that connected people here—something I hadn't considered.

The door to my room was already propped open, a pair of black Chelsea boots haphazardly kicked off at the entrance.

A girl with long blond hair was standing on one of the beds, hanging a set of dream catchers against the cinder-block wall behind her. She hummed along to the Killers, music blaring from the speaker on her desk.

I felt the sudden urge to knock, but she was already turning around.

I didn't know how she heard me over the noise. Maybe she just sensed me there, a disturbance to her world.

"Hello," she said, eyes trailing over me quickly—the rugged sneakers, the single bag, the high ponytail cinched tight—like she was tallying off things about me, deciding whether I had anything to offer her.

"Hi." I waved, then took a step inside.

She pursed her lips, like she was still thinking things over. "I'm Adalyn. From Maryland." She pointed toward the ceiling, which could've meant either up north *or* someplace better than here.

She'd layered a strand of pearls with a graphic T-shirt and baggy jeans. The room already smelled like hair product and vanilla, as if there was a candle burning just out of sight.

"Beckett," I answered. The window was open, but I felt only the humidity of the August stillness, a wave of sudden self-consciousness, and the realization that, for me, nothing at all had changed. "I'm from right here."

Adalyn climbed down from the bed and smiled then, waiting for me to look at her. A precursor to a question. Something that seemed both practiced and disarming.

"Tell me, Beckett-from-right-here, what does one do around this place for fun?"

I soon learned that Adalyn was a legacy. That she was here not for the experience, or the ambiance, or even the education, but in a deal with her parents: a promise of their continued financial support as long as she made it through. And she intended to make the most of it.

We discovered the likeness in each other first, before the differences.

Neither of us had been truly given the choice to be here, and it bonded us together, swift and furious. She was a legacy, and I was a faculty kid, and we both arrived on campus with one leg up, knowing the secrets of the place.

How quickly I felt at ease after those first jarring moments.

How lucky we were, I thought, coming from two very different worlds, to meet.

CHAPTER 5

Thursday, August 14
1:00 p.m.

Outside of the dorm, a new set of students was arriving, pulling their cars up the road in the distance, so I kept to the side steps, tracing the far perimeter through the trees, heading back down on foot.

The bell tower of lower campus began to chime just as I emerged from the woods, drawing my attention up. I thought I saw a figure up there, looking down. Watching. But the sun was making my eyes water, and I couldn't be sure.

My mind was playing tricks on me here, seeing the danger in everything. *So what* if there was someone up there, for some innocent reason? *So what* if there was someone out at the plot of the burned-down house last night, drawn by the same curiosity I was? Maybe they'd seen me out there first. Maybe my arrival in the night had spooked them instead.

The back door of the bell tower pushed open slightly, making me pause. It was the way the door hovered, half closed, like whoever was inside was peering out, making sure they weren't spotted.

I stepped back into the tree line and waited until a slender man slipped out, locking the door behind him. He looked quickly over his shoulder before heading toward the main quad. He was dressed like a professor, in a khaki blazer and navy blue pants, and his sandy blond hair was overlong, brushing his shoulders, pushed back from his face. There was something familiar in the lope of his stride, the quick bounce of his step.

I found myself trailing after him, through the main quad, my mind trying to place the details. A woman in a skirt suit was heading our way, and they both paused briefly, exchanged a few pleasant words. He turned to the side, and I took in the hooked ridge of his nose, the sharp angle of his chin—and then it clicked.

Cliff Simmons. My ex from high school. The same man who once pretended to be a student during orientation, for entertainment. Was he still doing it? Only now he seemed to be pretending to be a professor.

He had always been a chameleon, at ease with any group. It had lured me in when I was younger, but looking back, I could never be sure which parts of him were real.

I kept pace as he continued through campus, curious where he would head next. To the cafeteria, where he'd grab lunch at the discount faculty rate? To the cluster of new students gathered on the lawn, to pretend to give them directions or advice?

But he moved at a quick, determined pace, straight down the brick path.

Eventually he turned for Beckett Hall and entered through the back lobby, the same place the tours had begun.

I was maybe ten seconds behind him when I pulled open the heavy wood door. I was not afraid to call him out, report him to campus security. It wasn't a cute prank anymore, at the age of forty-two. It was unnerving, disturbing.

But when I stepped inside, the back atrium was empty. I started walking down the long hall, where the walls were interspersed with glass windows, displaying the lobbies for the administrative offices beyond.

I spotted him in the second window, at the Office of Student Life. His back was to the glass, and he was shaking hands with another man in the waiting area—as if he'd scheduled a meeting.

I checked the listing on the door to see who he was visiting.

My eyes trailed down the names for the offices within. And then I felt every muscle in my body tense: *Cliff Simmons, Associate Dean.*

The past was creeping out with the ivy here. I shouldn't have been surprised to see people I once knew. Just because my parents barely mentioned them didn't mean they were gone. They were from a different phase of my life—a time *before.* Before I crossed the divide from local resident to college student. They were the people I left behind, before I fully left.

This was why I'd always avoided lingering in the area when I brought Delilah for a visit. Because I knew it was only a matter of time before a familiar face appeared. Maggie running into my parents in the grocery store. Violet on a tour. Cliff Simmons in Beckett Hall.

Would he recognize my daughter's name? See the ghost of me in her appearance, walking across campus? What would he say to her under the guise of kindness?

I knew your mother. We grew up together. The stories I could tell you . . .

Or maybe he had also become someone new over the course of two decades. He would've had to, to become a dean there. The Cliff I knew had coasted through high school with no particular direction, getting by on wry humor and natural charm. He'd stayed in town after graduation, juggling night classes and odd construction jobs, hopping between local crews and pitching himself as a jack-of-all-trades handyman, though I wasn't sure he had the qualifications for either.

He must've changed since then, found a new path, crafted his own second life.

I sat on a bench at the edge of campus and pulled out my phone, searching *Cliff Simmons, Wyatt College.* His administrative listing popped up immediately—a smiling headshot, along with his office contact.

This was the problem with avoiding a place for so long. You didn't even realize what you might be missing.

His presence here wasn't a secret, if only I'd been looking.

My parents were cleaning the house when I returned—the drone of a vacuum in the living room and the scent of lemon cleaner coming from the kitchen. Final preparations for the semester away.

In the office, the sheets from the futon had been stripped, and I imagined the washing machine in the basement was already running.

My mother appeared in the entrance of the office; I hadn't heard her approaching over the sound of the vacuum. She crossed her arms, frowning at my things scattered across the fading patterned throw rug.

"Do you want lunch before you go? I was about to see what I could scrape together with the leftovers before we clean out the refrigerator."

"Sure," I said, because I was in no rush to leave yet.

"Sorry, I didn't know how long you'd be staying today or I'd have been more prepared."

I felt a pang as I followed her into the kitchen, passing an old family photo on the wall—the three of us posing in front of Beckett Hall, me as a toddler in my father's arms. How long had it been since it was just the three of us in the house? A jarring before and after, bookending the last eighteen years.

"Did you know Cliff Simmons works at the school now?" I asked as my father joined us in the kitchen.

My mother paused, peering into the refrigerator. "Now, that's a name I haven't heard in a while." A nonanswer, her specialty.

"I think he started a couple years ago. After we left," my father said, taking off his glasses and cleaning the lenses with the hem of his shirt.

My mother pulled out a few packets of sliced meat and cheese from the fridge drawer. "I don't know why you're so surprised," she said. "The college is the second largest employer in town. Who else do you think works on the staff there?"

I felt myself gritting my teeth. "I'm *surprised* that no one told me," I said.

She spun around, taking me in. "I barely remember him, Beckett," she said, clearly exasperated. "You dated for, what, a year in high school, on and off? Not like you brought him around much back then. I doubt I'd even recognize him if I saw him now."

My father opened the pantry and pulled out a stack of paper plates and a mostly empty bag of sliced bread. "Think this is enough?" he asked, dangling the bread between us. "I can run over to the deli if not."

I frowned. The pantry behind him was practically bare. "When do you fly out?" I asked.

"Early tomorrow," my mother said. "So we're getting a car to Richmond tonight."

I froze, imagining this empty house. I had thought they would be here for a few more days, in case of emergency.

"I'm thinking of staying an extra night," I said suddenly, though I hadn't packed for it. "In case Delilah decides she needs anything before the start of school."

My mother laughed, turning to my father. "*Now* she wants to stay." And then, with a shake of her head, "You'll be back for parents' weekend in no time. And Amazon delivers here, you know."

"We need to close up the house, Beckett," my father added, in a gentler type of nudge. *It's time to go.*

"I know how to lock a door," I said, sharper than anticipated.

He blinked twice, light blue eyes unnaturally large behind his bifocals. And then he smiled slightly. "Look at you. Same as every other parent who's come before you after all," he said.

This was my father's main argument about humanity. I'd heard it at their dinner parties more times than I could count. He always said human behavior doesn't change, it just finds a new frame of reference. *Forced gladiators become paid players, but we all still fill the stadiums and cheer for blood, don't we?*

My mother leaned against the counter and smiled like she could see right through me. "Everyone has to let go, Beck."

I gestured in the direction of campus. "I literally went to college across the street. And you worked there. I don't think it's really the same, Mom."

I felt her gaze sharpen. "And yet you never came back home after, did you?"

My father sighed, hands out, as if trying to defuse a situation before it began. "She's going to be fine, Beck." Then he gestured to the leftovers on the counter. "Eat something and go, before you have to drive through the mountains in the dark. You know I don't like when you do that."

I didn't like the way they were talking down to me. I understood, of course, that my parents were probably right.

But I also knew that driving in the night wasn't the only dangerous thing here.

CHAPTER 6

Thursday, August 14
4:00 p.m.

I left my parents' house without eating. The true pulse of the town was in the outer veins. On this street were two hallmarks of town: the deli on the corner, with a line stretching uncharacteristically out the door, and the Low Bar.

The Low Bar had existed for as long as I could remember. By the evening, this place would be packed. But it was still pretty early for the dinner crowd. It was situated at the lowest point of the valley, or so they claimed, and was frequented mostly by locals—though it also had been the one spot that would serve the underage college kids back in my day.

This was a place that once was dimly lit and hazy, with windows that seemed to be fogged up from the smoke, or dust, or both. The slogan had been hand-painted in script on the back wooden wall: *Everything's up from here.* There used to be pool tables in the back room, high-top tables with too many stools, a dartboard on the far wall, and a jukebox that I knew was just for show.

When I stepped inside now, most of the tables were currently occupied—definitely by out-of-town families, but also by locals who had gathered to watch the baseball game on the televisions around the room.

I opted for an open stool at the bar and was quickly handed a laminated menu by a man who looked barely old enough to serve liquor.

I texted Delilah while I waited: *I'm heading home soon. All good?*

Her thumbs-up reply came as I ordered Coke and a burger, my comfort food of choice.

My phone chimed again, but with a message from Trevor: *How'd it go? Let me know when it's a good time to visit her.*

Trevor always defaulted to me instead of Delilah. I was used to receiving daily questions from him throughout each summer visit: *Is she allowed to watch* The Shining*? She says yes . . .*

Over the years, he and I had become civil, friendly. Dare I say *friends,* even.

I remembered the time he had called out of the blue, voice shaking: *I thought you should hear it from me first. I lost her today. She ended up with a security guard at the museum, my name over the loudspeaker.*

She's okay, was all I could say. A question but also an answer. A grace I had learned to give him over time. I never told him about the times I'd lost her, too.

She was upset, he told me. *But she knew what to do.*

In the end, Delilah never told me about it. I thought that was telling, too. She was keeping his secret, protecting him.

Now I sent him a screenshot of the flyer for parents' weekend in mid-October, along with a note: *Book early. My parents don't even want me staying in their empty house. Don't take it personally.*

Tell them I say hi, he replied. And then: *Or maybe don't. Your call.*

I smiled, just as my burger was delivered.

The last time we'd all been together was for Delilah's graduation party, in the fenced backyard of my townhome. Trevor had made the trip but stayed at a nearby hotel. He and my father had made surface-level small talk—their fields of expertise overlapped at the edges, and Trevor told him about the newest exhibit at his museum. But my mother didn't engage with him, pretending he hadn't spoken or acting like he wasn't standing in a room with us.

For a psychology professor, I thought she had some pretty giant blind spots. But then I wondered if instead this was a master move designed to keep him on his toes, make him sweat, question his choices—even all these years later.

My mother was horrified from the start that we didn't share custody and that I wouldn't accept his support. But I didn't want it—refused it, even—and that was something she couldn't understand.

But by then there was so much about me she didn't understand. He was a good person, I was sure—but he wasn't for me.

Trevor and I had met abroad while he was in the midst of an art history master's program and I was finishing up my disastrous final year. It was a reprieve from our normal lives. We never meant for it to be anything serious or permanent.

He'd been working in a coffee shop on campus the first time we met, in the early London spring, cold and gray and wet. *Beckett,* he'd said in a distinctly American accent, handing me my drink, one side of his mouth quirked up. *Like Samuel Beckett?*

My parents are both professors, I answered, warming my hands on the cup, and a slow grin spread across his face. I knew, from that first crooked smile, that I was in trouble.

One morning later that week, he ran his thumb across the tattoo on my wrist and asked if it was a heartbeat. The idea sounded so beautiful, and I said yes. He asked whose it was, and I told him it was mine.

And in that moment I became Beckett Bowery, named for a great Irish writer, who tattooed her own heartbeat on her wrist, as a proof of life, of living. I liked his vision of me better than the truth. He was studying the classics. What chance did either of us have?

I'd been in the middle of a disappearing act. And suddenly I was seen.

At the end of that summer, while trying to catch up on my degree requirements, I realized I was pregnant. I was twenty-two. I kept it to myself for a week, then two, then three, letting the idea take root and grow. I'd close my eyes and try to imagine a different life stretching out in front of me, starting over in a town I'd never been—a place with no history.

When I finally told Trevor, sitting across from him at that same coffee shop, his face went pale, mouth half open, mug hovering in the space between us, frozen in midair. And when he spoke, it was knee-jerk and all wrong. *I don't think I'm ready for that, Beckett—*

It knocked the wind from my lungs, turned my limbs numb. But I had already run through all the scenarios. I had already decided that I didn't need his help. That I could do it on my own.

Delilah had always belonged fully to me.

I asked for the check just as a man slid onto the barstool two down from me, hands laced together on the countertop.

"What's the word, Wes?" he asked as I handed over my credit card. A local, I assumed as he fished the phone from his pocket, placing it on the bar.

"Nonstop busy," the bartender—Wes—said, eyes widening at the growing crowd behind us. "The usual, sir?" he asked.

"Please," the man said, repositioning on the stool, pivoting to watch the game.

Wes brought him a Sprite, then leaned forward, resting his arms on the bar between them. "Getting lots of questions today about the house on College Lane," he said. "Parents, I guess."

"I'm not surprised," the other man said, dragging his glass closer.

"I can't believe they didn't get it cleaned up before move-in," Wes added. He must've understood the optics, even at his age.

The man sighed. "Insurance is still investigating."

"Was it not an accident?" I asked, looking directly at the man beside me for the first time.

He was about my age, broadly built, with jet black hair, slicked back and just starting to gray along the sideburns.

"Have we met?" he asked, grinning slightly. A line, or maybe not.

Wes handed me my credit card and a receipt to sign. "Thanks, Ms. Bowery."

There was a twitch at the corner of the other man's mouth. "Ms. Bowery," he repeated.

Wes tapped the bar top between us. "The sandwich will be out in just a minute, Detective."

My heart sank as the recognition clicked. It had taken a moment for me to see the other version of the man before me from twenty years earlier. Time had softened his physique—and his demeanor.

"Fred Mayhew," he said, extending his hand. "Been a long time, Beckett." His eyes, a rich brown, held my gaze.

I took his hand, warm and large, then pulled away to sign the check.

He'd been a young patrol cop when Adalyn disappeared, pulled into the biggest investigation this town had ever seen. A couple years older than I was, with something to prove. The same age as the victims. He and Charlie and Micah had all gone to school together.

It seemed that Officer Mayhew was now a plainclothes detective.

"You back in town to see your folks?" he asked.

"On my way out," I said, slipping off the stool.

"Drive safe," he said with a smile, in a way that made me wonder if he knew I'd been here all along.

I sat in the car, engine idling, unable to shake the feeling of dread.

There was so much to sift through, and I had a hard time deciphering the true threats from the hypothetical.

It was the fact that my parents were leaving, while it seemed like everyone knew I was back. It was the four hours of distance between my home and here, which had always seemed like a buffer and now felt an improbable distance.

Or maybe it wasn't this place at all. Maybe it was the fact that I was leaving Delilah. Maybe I'd feel this way no matter where I was leaving her.

Were the dangers here really any different from elsewhere?

My parents had lived in town for the last twenty years without incident. They'd continued teaching there even after I'd been asked to leave. Time moved on.

I was the only one who let the past creep in every time I stepped foot in town.

I pulled away from the curb, heading up the sloping road—heading home.

I passed the spot I'd once stood with Maggie during high school, at a clearing beside the road, tracing out the ridgeline that would one day become the tattoo on my wrist.

And then, on a whim, I veered off at the next unlabeled drive. The gravel road wove back through the wooded landscape, then widened as the trees gave way to green farmland and Maggie's family home, like the set of a postcard.

My parents had always loved Maggie, who had been a friend since elementary school. She was trustworthy, where I was not. Loyal, where I had failed. A good daughter, with a sense of responsibility, returning home after college to continue the family business.

Maggie's farm had always instilled a sense of calm. Maybe that's what I was seeking now as I walked up their horseshoe-shaped drive. It was the sound of the crickets, the tall grass brushing soft against my ankles. The curtains pulled wide open on the large white house and the long, welcoming front porch.

I'd just stepped onto the porch when a voice came from behind me.

"Beckett?"

Maggie stood at the corner of the house, muck boots pulled over jeans, like she'd been working around back. She was tall and skinny, with a strong jaw and auburn hair that was currently tied into a messy ponytail, frizz escaping from the sides.

“Hi,” I said. “I didn’t know if you’d be home.”

She didn’t seem too surprised to see me, considering I hadn’t been on this property in decades. But then my parents had run into her recently.

“I heard you’d be in town,” she said, stepping onto the far side of the porch. “Is everything okay?”

I nodded. “I just dropped off my daughter.” I gestured in the direction of campus, toward the mountains.

“I can’t believe it,” she said. Which could’ve meant: *I can’t believe your daughter is eighteen*. Or, more likely, *I can’t believe your daughter is coming here, of all places.*

She waited then. Waited for me to say something. Do something. Apologize, maybe, for drifting apart when she’d left for college. And then after: For not answering her calls. For pushing her away, just like everyone else.

“My parents are going to Peru,” I said, shifting on my feet. “They’re leaving tonight. And I just . . . I’d feel better if there was someone in town who Delilah could call in an emergency.”

Maggie stared back like she was waiting for me to continue—before realizing I meant *her*. That the only person I trusted enough here was someone I hadn’t spoken to in decades.

She blinked twice, then nodded rapidly. “Of course. Here.” She held out her hand for my phone, then entered her contact.

Two boys suddenly rounded the corner from the backyard, one right after the other, water guns in hand, yelling after each other.

“Careful!” Maggie called. She cleared her throat. “Did you want to stay a bit?” she began, but I couldn’t tell whether she meant it.

“I should really get on the road,” I said, gesturing into the distance.

“Next time,” she said, hopping off the porch, striding after her boys.

By the time I made it back to Charlotte, it was after ten p.m., and I had a message from Delilah. *Roommate finally arrived. Hana likes the color black. A lot of black. So much black.*

I smiled, then responded: *I'm going to need pictures.*

I waited for her to reply, but my phone remained silent. I wondered whether she was out, but the day she'd turned eighteen, she'd removed my ability to track her phone without telling me. I discovered it that same day, when she was late for curfew and I was checking to make sure she was on the way.

I never said anything, pretended I didn't notice. I didn't want her to realize how often I'd checked in the past.

As I was waiting, a new message popped up on my screen, from a number not in my contacts:

Welcome home

A chill rose up my spine.

I was alone in the house, curtains pulled shut. The only noise was the periodic drip of the kitchen faucet.

Slowly, I opened the text.

A photo had been included below the message. A picture of the campus from an aerial view, *Wyatt College* printed in deep red script over the top.

It must've been sent from the school, part of the automated system for parents that I'd just signed up for.

I laughed to myself, poured a drink, trying to shake it off.

It reminded me of the months after I'd first left home, when I could so easily be overcome by a sense of panic, for any reason. A knock on the door I wasn't expecting. An unknown incoming number. News of a fire in a local restaurant or an abandoned building. Or anywhere at all.

It was a spiral that I'd learned to escape only by acknowledging it at the start: *Oh, there it is.* Where now I could look it in the eye for a brief, fleeting moment and keep going.

BEFORE: THE INTERVIEW

It was routine, the message claimed. An invitation *to come back in. A chance to clear up a few lingering questions that had come up in the witness statements.*

The initial statements had also been routine, requested of each Wyatt College student who had been out in the woods that night. Campus security had taken down the statements, one by one, in their building:

Where did you last see Adalyn Vale? *When we left our dorm room that evening.*

Did you see the victims at all that night? *No.*

Do you know what she was planning? *Not at all.*

Now I sat in an interview room at the Wyatt Valley Police Department, alone. I'd walked to the station from home, where I'd been staying ever since Adalyn had been named the prime suspect and our dorm room suddenly teemed with potential evidence or clues.

A young officer named Fred Mayhew entered the small room. He had nothing in his hands; no list of questions or pen to take notes. Just a camera set up on the corner of the table, with a red blinking light.

"Thanks for coming back in," he said, pulling out the metal chair across from me. He glanced toward the door, then leaned forward. "Everyone talks about you as a pair, you know. BeckettAndAdalyn." He slurred our names together until they sounded like a single word. A single entity. "So I was surprised to see your statement that you weren't with her. That you"—he raised his hands to form air quotes—"went your separate ways that night."

I waited for the question. He grinned.

"I grew up here, too, you know," he continued. "I know what happens during the first howling of the year." He ran his hand through his jet black hair. "And you're a senior now, right? Strange to imagine you wouldn't be together out there."

"It's a competition," I said, shaking my head. If he'd ever been part of it, he would know this.

He drummed his fingers on the table. I could feel his energy crackling. "How many?" he asked.

The question hung in the air. "Excuse me?"

He rested his arms on the table, leaning forward. "How many people did you catch? That's the game, right?"

I swallowed, felt unexpectedly parched. "None," I whispered.

He leaned back, crossed his arms. "And here, from someone who knows these woods so well."

"I saw the fire," I said, gritting my teeth. "I knew something was wrong. I ran straight there."

He nodded. "Now, that I heard. Heard that you were the one yelling for people to call 911."

"The building was on fire, and everyone was just staring *at it." My hands started to shake from the memory. Just like they'd done when I saw the wooden barn fully ablaze. The lick of orange flames, the sound of wood splintering, and everyone dazzled by it, like they were standing around nothing more than a bonfire—*

"The other students said you were screaming for Adalyn," he said.

"Because there was a fire *and I didn't know where she was," I snapped. I took a slow breath before continuing. "I didn't know she was the one who started the fire until later. I was just trying to find her."*

"So you were looking for her," he said. "Where?"

"Anywhere I could think. In the woods. At the school." I glanced at the camera. "Back at our dorm."

He raised an eyebrow. "And did you find her?"

I knew this was already clear in my statement. "No," I reiterated for the official record.

Officer Mayhew took a deep breath, opened his hands, palms up, on the table. "So here's the thing. It was snowing and she had no car. She's not from the area. How did she get out of town with no witnesses, Beckett?"

I shook my head. "I don't know."

"Or," he began, drawing out the word, "maybe she didn't."

My eyes locked on his. This *was something I hadn't heard. Hadn't even considered.*

"I think maybe someone's protecting her." He stared at me hard, unblinking. I felt my eyes burning. "Maybe she's still here."

I blinked twice, just as the door to the room swung open. Another officer started to enter the room, then froze, frowning.

"Be right out," Mayhew said, quickly turning off the camera. It occurred to me then that it was possible no one else knew we were in here.

He stood abruptly, metal chair legs scratching against the concrete floor. Then he leaned down, hands pressed into the table, so I could see his fingertips blanch white.

"Someone saw you, Beckett," he said, voice low.

"Saw me where?" I asked. It wasn't possible.

But I understood then: He was running out of time, and he was desperate.

"They saw you together," he added.

The room felt charged. I'd made a mistake, coming here. I shouldn't have trusted his request. Or him.

But I knew that he shouldn't be in here with me, either. Fred Mayhew was too close to the case. Too close to the victims. He shouldn't have been the one interviewing me, all alone.

"No," I said. "They didn't."

Later that night, after my parents had gotten ready for bed, I was sure I heard something out front. An engine idling in the silence. I turned off the lights and stared out the living room window, searching the darkness.

A hand dropped onto my shoulder, and I jumped. But it was just my father. "What are you doing standing here in the dark?" he asked.

"I thought I heard something," I said, eyes wide, voice low.

He frowned, eyes drifting from me to the night. "The press are like vultures around campus right now." Then he stepped back from the window. "Okay, come on. You need to sleep, Beckett."

I hadn't been sleeping much at all since the fire. He must've been able to read it in the hollows under my eyes.

My father thought the media was the biggest concern, but I couldn't shake the thought that the police were out there now, watching for Adalyn to emerge in the night. As if they believed I was keeping her hidden.

The interview with Fred Mayhew had messed with my head. For a brief moment, I wondered if it was Adalyn herself out there, keeping an eye on things. Keeping track of those she left behind.

Deep down I knew that couldn't be true. She'd never come back; never risk being caught. She was too smart for that. She knew you couldn't return to the scene of a crime.

CHAPTER 7

Friday, October 3
6:00 p.m.

It had been seven weeks. Seven weeks of new routines for the both of us. A *Good morning!* text from Delilah each day, sometime between eight and ten—and as late as noon on the weekends. A FaceTime in the evening, if she was alone on her walk back from dinner, where I'd accumulate snippets of her life: *Intro theater class surprisingly hard; math surprisingly easy; cafeteria enchiladas surprisingly good.*

She hadn't been cast in the fall play, but—she continued in the same breath, before I could respond—she'd joined the stagecraft crew. An upperclassman, Gen with a *G*, was showing her the ropes. It sounded like Delilah spent weekends exploring the town with a girl named Sierra. She was adjusting. Keeping busy.

I was trying to do the same. I'd even let my neighbor set me up on a blind date with her colleague, which she'd been asking to do for a year. But I'd also been counting down the time: Eight more nights until I'd be heading back for parents' weekend. Seven. Six.

Evenings unsettled me the most. I was so used to her presence in our townhouse, the way I could hear her get up every morning, the rush of steps when I called her name, knowing she'd overslept.

In the night, I restrained myself from checking in, worried when she called me—and equally worried when she didn't. I found myself marking time by my parents' weekly emails, with updates and photos of their trip.

I kept my phone close, turned off the *Do Not Disturb* feature, and was woken hourly by the motion-notification alerts from passing cars or the sway of branches in the wind.

Sometimes when my mind started reaching—imagining all the things outside of my control in the universe, all the things that could happen to her—I would focus down to a single point. Sink into a project, immerse myself completely in someone else's story.

I needed that now. I was being considered for a nonfiction series on famous serial killers and had submitted a formal writing sample a week ago. But I was currently in a holding pattern, waiting for their feedback.

I hadn't heard from my agent yet, which was unusual.

Just in case, I checked the junk folder while finishing my dinner. I didn't see a response for the proposal, but I did see several emails I'd missed, all from the same sender, with the subject line in all caps:

REFERRAL FOR MEMOIR

I didn't usually take on work from outside my agency, other than freelance edits from people I'd worked with before. I didn't post my contact information on a website or advertise on any social media. Whoever had sent this request must've gotten my details from a previous client.

I wasn't generally picky when it came to the type of projects I took on, but memoirs made me nervous. There was an added layer of expectation that the story was being told authentically. A voice I'd have to inhabit perfectly. Loads of interviews with the subject. The challenge of finding the arc, the shape.

And then there was the personality combination. The fact that a collaboration didn't always pan out after months of working together. The nontraditional schedules to accommodate. The fight over final payments if the client wasn't happy with the finished product.

I opened the message, from *FordGroup:*

Hello Beckett, checking to see if you've received my prior emails. You came highly recommended as a ghostwriter for a memoir. It's a tight turnaround but our client is offering considerable compensation—200K, half on agreement and half on completion. Please let us know if you're interested in discussing further.

So the client was anonymous and the project very light on details, which also made me nervous. I didn't recognize the name of the sender. The note was unsigned.

But it was so much money. Three or four solid projects' worth—and for a fraction of the time.

And time, I had been learning, was the gift.

I didn't want to loop in my agent just yet, in case it complicated the progress of the other deal. Not until I was sure.

I'd be happy to hear more, I wrote. I added my cell number and logged off for the weekend, thinking: *Six more nights.*

The call came in the middle of the night, just after two a.m.

I fumbled for my cell on the bedside table, heart racing from the surprise. It took my eyes a moment to focus and register Delilah's name on the display.

"Hello?" I answered, groggy and trying to orient myself. But all I heard was dead air.

A pocket dial, maybe. Out on a Friday night with friends. Except there was no background noise—no laughter or music or chatter.

I stared at the phone, saw it was still connected. "Delilah?" I said again, pressing the phone to my ear.

Static.

No, not static—a whistle. I recognized it immediately—the wind funneling through the valley. The noise deepening as it picked up speed, heralding the change of the season. I heard it clearly then, a deep and haunting rush of air, that familiar cry in the night.

Every nerve was on high alert.

The howling.

And then a quick gust—or a gasp—before the call dropped.

I immediately tried her again, but it went straight to voicemail.

I was fully awake then, panic seizing my lungs, hands shaking as I repeatedly called her number, over and over.

I tried tracking her location, even though I knew she'd turned the feature off. I sent her a text just to see if it would go through—but it went undelivered.

I tried to slow my heartbeat. Tried to acknowledge the dread and move on to rational thoughts. She was probably out of Wi-Fi range. Or the phone had lost charge. Maybe she hadn't meant to call me. Maybe she was just walking home, and the cell was in her pocket, and she'd accidentally called the last dialed number—me.

But I was out of bed now, limbs tingling with a surge of adrenaline.

I gave her ten minutes. Then twenty. Trying her again as the digits on the clock ticked forward—imagining her getting back to her dorm, plugging in the phone. But all of my calls kept going straight to voicemail.

I paced the downstairs, watching the clock keep moving. Thirty minutes. An hour. Getting closer and closer to something that felt dangerous.

I felt a crackle in the air. Kept hearing that noise in my head just before the call dropped. A breath of fear? The wind?

I imagined her running through the woods, lost, confused, with no idea what was happening. I imagined her hiding behind a tree, back pressed into the bark, calling me, scared to speak—to give herself away. I imagined the danger of that place, twenty years earlier, getting closer.

I knew I was overreacting. Seeing the danger in the hypotheticals instead of the reality. But I couldn't stop the spiral. Instead, I was seeing everything I couldn't stop. Everything I should've told her. Every secret of that place.

It was a four-hour drive through the mountains in the dead of night. I knew what would probably happen. I'd get a text an hour in that said: *Oops, sorry, didn't mean to wake you.*

Or: *Why are you calling me at 3 a.m., Mom?*

I knew these things were the most likely scenarios. But I was also calculating the hours of space between us.

My parents' house sat empty a few blocks from campus, and I knew exactly where the spare key was.

Delilah would never have to know that I'd panicked, driving through the night, if I was wrong.

BEFORE:
THE LETTER

The letter was waiting for me on the kitchen table, four days after my interview.

Four days of an engine idling in the dark. Four days of leaving the phone off the hook to prevent the calls from the media, who had somehow gotten my name. Four days of my parents warning: Don't answer the door; stay inside.

My mother had already pulled the letter from the envelope, but the creases still bent the paper into thirds.

"What is it?" I asked as my mother backed away from the table, leaving space for me to see.

"It's from the school," she said, frowning.

I unfolded the page, printed on the college's official letterhead. My eyes skimmed the page:

Due to the ongoing investigation—

In order to protect the learning environment—

We believe it would be in your best interest to take a leave of absence—

"They're kicking me out?" I asked, paper shaking in my hand.

"No," my father said. "It's just temporary. A semester away, until this all blows over. They're trying to keep this from becoming a national story."

Of course—the school valued their reputation above all. This was a narrative they couldn't control. A story that was spiraling outside of their reach. My presence was only making it worse.

I looked to my mother, but her eyes drifted away. "There's a sister school in London," she said, as if they'd already discussed it. "I'll talk to the deans tomorrow, see if we can get the process started. Really, if they're asking you to take a leave, they owe you."

I didn't put up a fight. Found myself overwhelmed, with no words to pull forth. It seemed fitting, somehow, to lose everything all at once: my best friend, my home, my future.

"Just for a little while," said my father. "By the time you come back, this will all be in the past."

But even then, I knew: This place would never forget.

It would never be safe to return.

PART 2

THE HOWLING

CHAPTER 8

Saturday, October 4
7:00 a.m.

I made it back to Wyatt Valley in record time, just after seven in the morning, as the sun crested the mountains, the town ablaze in orange, like the sky was on fire.

Five hours since the dropped phone call, and still no word from Delilah.

As I drove through the grid of downtown, I didn't notice anyone out on the streets or sidewalks—but the air felt alive.

The branches and the leaves were swaying overhead; an empty plastic bag, caught in the breeze, drifted along the edge of the pavement; an American flag fluttered from the front porch of the white corner house, colors vibrant.

The howling had swept through the valley in the night.

The windy season was here.

The downtown seemed like it always did after a windstorm. Leaves had blown from the trees into the yards and driveways. Pieces of debris and loose paper crept along the edges of the streets, caught at the lip of the curb.

I passed my parents' empty house, then the burned-out lot on College Lane, yellow caution tape rippling across the yard next door. I entered campus through the service road, weaving around the perimeter. The construction vehicles were more visible from this side, tucked away from the central footpaths. Muddy tire tracks veered on and off the pavement as I passed the location of the old student center, now a gaping hole.

I lowered the windows of the car as I approached upper campus, as if I might hear something in the wind. But the only noise was the churn of my engine, gears shifting on the incline.

The dorm parking area was mostly empty—students weren't permitted to keep cars on campus—but the bike rack was overflowing.

I parked in the back corner, just inside the edge of the lot, knowing Delilah's room was on the third floor, with a clear view down.

Behind the building, the wind funneled through in a soft whistle, and I felt the mountain chill of the early-morning hour.

Delilah had probably gotten back late and was sleeping soundly upstairs. She rarely called me before noon on a weekend.

I stood behind the dorm, staring up, counting the windows to where I believed hers would be.

What would she think if she saw me out here?

I called her cell one last time, but it went straight to voicemail again. My text from the night before still hadn't been delivered. My throat was tight with fear. I had convinced myself that by the time I arrived here, she would've checked in.

Now that I was here, the panic had taken hold fully.

I tried to talk myself down. To act rationally.

I circled the building until I was in the front quad connecting all the dorms, a span of green between a perimeter of gray stone buildings, the forest stretching outward beyond them.

I wasn't surprised to find the front door of the building locked. The doors to the dorms had an electronic entry system that worked with the physical ID cards the students received at orientation or the digital ones on their phones. Unlike the academic buildings, which were locked only at night, the dorms required the tap of a card or phone at all hours.

I turned around, taking in the quad. There were blue-light emergency phones positioned on the brick pathways between each building, a promise of safety. The closest one to her dorm was just before the spot where a trail branched off into the woods.

My eyes traced the route from the woods to the phone, and from the phone to the front door of the dorm, looking for signs that something had happened here—evidence of chaos, of a chase, of an accident—but everything felt typical for a sleepy college campus on a Saturday morning. It was probably too early even for the dining hall to be open.

I sat on the bench at the corner of the path. I'd have to find the number for Raven the RA, ask if she could let me in. But just as I pulled out my cell, ready to search the website for a directory, the front door swung open.

I jumped up as a man in a gray uniform emerged. In the morning chill, he wore a black windbreaker, zipped closed, straining against his gut. *Lenny,* I thought—the man who had fixed the window inside Delilah's room, who'd told us this was his building.

He stood in the entrance as I quickly approached, door resting against his shoulder, like I'd startled him yet again.

"Well, hey there," he said.

"Hi, Lenny," I said. "I'm Beckett Bowery, Delilah's mom." I gestured toward the rooms overhead.

He nodded. "I remember. Room 302." The keys jangled off his hip as he shifted, checking the time on his watch.

"She's not answering my calls," I said, feeling the lump tightening my throat. "She's late," I added, the lie slipping out so easily.

He looked over his shoulder into the lobby. "Probably the power surges," he said, frowning. "Bet her alarm never even went off. That's why I was out here this morning at the crack of dawn. Systems had to be reset." He narrowed his eyes at the rustling trees along the perimeter. "The wind last night, if you can believe it."

I nodded. But I wasn't sure if I did believe it. No, I knew what used to happen during the first howling—how local kids would flip off the power under the guise of the wind. I'd done it once myself, senior year of high school. Getting a boost from Cliff over the high locked gate, dropping into the utility space before climbing back over on my own.

"Well," Lenny said, stepping to the side, "you enjoy your visit."

In the end, for all the safety protocols on campus, nothing could beat human instinct: He held the door right open for me.

I veered from the lobby, heading up the steps to the third floor. About half the doors here had a sign with the roommates' names. Delilah and I had hung a blue-and-white-striped *D* on the left side of her door, leaving space for her roommate's.

But now the door to Room 302 was bare. I rechecked the room number, frowning, then felt a surge of anger displacing the fear. Wondering if this place had already started to change her.

There were signs of life all around: a pair of muddy sneakers left outside the door across the hall; a toilet flushing somewhere above, water rushing in the pipes. But nothing stirred from inside Delilah's room.

I imagined her inside—dead asleep, maybe even hungover. Out of my watch for the first time and taking full advantage. I thought of how I would explain my presence to her—*Surprise, I'm taking you to eat! I tried calling first*—hoping she didn't read the panic in the hollows under my eyes.

I knocked gently on the door, cringing at the way it echoed down the hall. I strained to hear motion inside, but the only thing that registered was a cough coming from another room nearby.

I used the side of my fist, knocked harder, the noise managing to sound both dull and violent—something that shook the door against the frame.

Movement then—a rustling of sheets. I pictured Delilah slipping out of bed, bare feet on the cool tile floor, wearing a matching pajama set, hair in that messy bun she slept in each night.

I stepped back in a wave of anticipation. The door cracked open, and one sleepy dark eye peered out.

Her roommate, Hana. I'd seen pictures of her during their first week. Tall and thin, Korean descent, and, like my daughter had noted, a fan of all black.

"Hi," I said, "Hana, right?" I craned my neck, trying to peer past her, deeper into the room. "I'm Delilah's mom."

Hana just frowned, not opening the door any farther. In the pictures Delilah had sent, I'd only seen Hana smiling. I couldn't reconcile it with the girl in front of me, who seemed unmoved by my presence.

Her silence stretched on, though it was probably because I'd woken her and she was confused. "Can I . . ." I gestured to the door, trying to push it open, but she stuck a foot in the way just as I got a better view of the room.

Delilah's bed: fully made, electric blue comforter pulled up. No shoes kicked off on the throw carpet or laptop open on the desk. Hana's decor, dark and moody, had encroached across the center line, so that it was her black backpack hanging from Delilah's desk chair, her dark clothes folded in a pile on Delilah's bed, like she was using it as a staging area. Delilah's name in lights over her bed had been removed as well.

"She's not here?" Hana said, but like a question—like I should know better.

My eyes slid back to Hana's, as if I had been wrong about the source of the danger after all. As if it were Hana, and not the school, who had managed to strip Delilah's personality from this place.

"She doesn't stay here anymore," she added, something sly in her tone. As if she were telling on my daughter. Looking to embarrass me. Something I surely would have known if I were a better parent.

The school chose the roommates based on surveys they turned in beforehand. Delilah had told me they weren't a great match, but I figured they just didn't have much in common. Not that there was any animosity. But standing here, I wasn't so sure. I wondered if she'd come to find it unmanageable. If she instead stayed with other friends whom she meshed with better.

"Where—" I began.

"Excuse me!" A voice carried sharply from down the hall. A woman in a terry-cloth robe with her hair wrapped in a towel stood just outside the bathrooms, shower caddy in hand. "How did you get in here?"

I frowned, trying to understand why this young woman was acting as an authority figure. A strand of dark red hair had fallen free of her hair towel, and the white fabric was stained slightly pink around the edges from the hair dye. She looked different, younger, without the maroon lipstick and winged eyeliner, but this was the RA, Raven.

Hana pushed the door fully shut then, the click of the lock resounding through the hall.

I turned to face Raven—I'd been trying to find her number after all.

"Hi, Raven, right?" I said. "Delilah wasn't answering her phone, and I assumed she was sleeping."

Raven frowned, moving the shower caddy from one hand to the other. "You aren't allowed in here without a resident."

"Delilah *is* a resident," I said. Not to mention, Lenny seemed to have no issue with it.

Raven widened her eyes, took a step forward, the squeak of her shower shoes almost comical given the situation. "But she's not here."

I wondered how much she knew about Delilah's rooming situation—or lack thereof. I swallowed dry air, a lump of panic stuck in my throat. "Have you seen her?" I asked, facade giving way to desperation.

Her expression softened for a moment, and she tugged at the edge of her towel. "Look," she said. "There are policies about this." Her eyes slid away. "She's an adult."

As if she, too, were embarrassed for me. As if I were not the first parent to arrive on campus, demanding answers about my child's whereabouts. As if there were a protocol for this—parents who couldn't let go—and she'd seen it before. Like my father had claimed: *Same as every other parent who's come before you . . .*

But the legality of adulthood seemed so arbitrary. A sudden and jarring before and after, when I was the one who still coordinated her doctors' appointments. I was the one who made sure she paid any bills for miscellaneous funds due to the school, even though she had a scholarship.

I had signed her up for the dining plan, purchased the books, filled out the paperwork.

But it was her name on the contract.

"It's a family emergency," I said, to spare Delilah the future embarrassment of my panic. Hoping for any sort of information to put my mind at ease.

I looked Raven over carefully, trying to see any signs of a long night on her. I assumed she was a senior. But Raven was up and showered early in the morning, and there was no evidence of anything unusual in the building. Nothing more than typical for a freshman dorm early on a Saturday morning.

"Then you'll have to call your daughter," she said, free hand up, absolving herself. "I'm sorry, I can't give you anything more."

My daughter was eighteen, and officially I had no right to her comings and goings. How many students got into fights with their parents and didn't answer their calls? But there had to be a policy to reach them in an emergency. Administrators who would know how to track them down. Cameras situated around campus. An electronic log of their movements.

It was a Saturday morning, so there was no class schedule I could follow.

It was so different from the last year of high school, when the school sent an automated call if your kid hadn't shown up for class. When I knew I'd always be able to track her down through the parents of friends or the friends themselves—a group of kids who'd spent the past decade in the back of my car singing along to the radio, or filled my kitchen, or were the topic of dinner conversations.

Her friends—mostly other theater kids—had been loud and dramatic. They didn't seem to believe in secrets, stage-whispering in a way that made sure those around them heard. Wearing their emotions on their sleeves. Always, it seemed, believing this life was their great performance and we were their audience. Watching, carefully, to gauge our reactions.

Now all I had were snippets that Delilah chose to share, and where did that get me? She liked enchilada day. Joined the stagecraft crew. Barely mentioned her roommate.

None of this led me any closer to her.

I mumbled a few words to Raven in understanding, drifted down the steps, back out the front door, and thought of Delilah walking home from dinner, calling before she got back to her room.

Maybe this was the reason she always called from outside the dorm. A roommate she didn't get along with. Or . . . someone she preferred to be with instead.

A boy she didn't want to tell me about just yet. A secret.

In my memory, the gasp before the phone went dead became a laugh. Someone sneaking up behind her—the phone slipping from her hand at the shock of it. Her expression, a welcome surprise. Someone she was happy to see. The phone had broken, but it was an issue to deal with later, in the daylight. *Tomorrow,* she'd say with a shrug.

I returned to the wooden bench, wondering where to go next. I thought about how I could track down her friends—Gen, Sierra—without embarrassing her. They had to be somewhere in this quad of dorms. On-campus housing was required.

But first I opened my phone, connected to the campus Wi-Fi, and sent her an email.

Hey, I've been trying to reach you. I'm in town (surprise!) and wanted to take you out. Can you call me please?

If she'd damaged her phone, she'd at least be able to call me from someone else's. She knew my number by heart. It was the first thing I had her memorize as a child, in case she was ever lost.

I also checked her Instagram account and saw she was last active eighteen hours earlier. But I decided to cover my bases, figuring she'd be more likely to scroll social media before checking email, and sent a message there, too: *My texts don't seem to be going through. Call me?*

I prepared to head back to my parents' place, settle down, regroup. Wait for a reasonable hour—sometime in the afternoon, when I knew she'd be up.

It would be best to come back to campus when it was more active, when Delilah would have to log onto her laptop or venture out for food. When her friends would be roaming around as well.

I had just stood from the bench when a runner darted out from the woods, emerging from a trail that had been obscured.

A young man, gangly limbs, dressed in all black. He paused for a moment, pushed his dark hair off his eyes. He was tall, slightly hunched, like he was trying to remain inconspicuous—I recognized him then as Violet's son Bryce.

He seemed out of breath, and I took a step forward, wondering if he could help me.

But there was something about the way he moved—with an awkward, sporadic gait—so that suddenly I questioned whether he'd been out for a run or was returning from his night out.

It was the way he had emerged from the woods, like he was being chased. As if he had successfully reached safety and was finally able to recover—bent over, hands on his thighs.

He took a quick glance behind him into the woods before continuing across the quad, toward another dorm.

I narrowed my eyes at the place he'd just been, felt a pull drawing me closer.

Nearly six hours after Delilah's dropped call and there were kids still out there.

Whatever was happening, it might still be going on.

As I approached the trees, another strong gust of wind funneled through the woods, stinging my eyes.

Please *let me be overreacting.*

But if I'd learned anything from twenty years earlier, it was that you had to act fast. Before the clues drifted, before the trail faded, before the possibilities branched out, endless and cold. Before she was well and truly gone.

There was always a chance, in hindsight, to alter the series of events to follow. But you had to make a decision. You had to *move.*

I ducked my head and pushed forward, straight into the trees.

BEFORE:

THE TUNNELS

"We're not supposed to be here," Maggie said. It was the same thing she'd said at fifteen, during the first party we attended together at Cryer's Quarry. And at sixteen, arriving at the tattoo parlor two towns away that was notoriously lax with the age requirement. And now, at seventeen, as I slipped a skeleton key into the door to the tunnels under Beckett Hall.

She said it like an involuntary impulse. But she still always came.

Cliff was with us, and I was showing off—campus was supposed to be shut for winter break.

I flicked my flashlight, shining the beam down the steps, guiding the way.

At the bottom of the stairs, Cliff reached his hand up to the pipes running above our heads. I could hear the hiss of steam moving through the system.

"Don't touch that," I said. I had no idea if they were dangerous; if they were flammable; if they could burn you.

"We're going to get lost," Maggie said, her footsteps quickening behind me.

"We're not," I said. There were no labels on the tunnel walls, but there was a map in the archive room. "This was how they used to transport goods from the president's house to the main campus in the winter and vice versa." I was repeating the story my father had told me.

We reached a T intersection, a locked door to either side—a dead end, it seemed. But my key worked on every door down here. We veered left.

I felt Maggie close on my heels, felt her nerves transferring to me. We were deep in the underbelly of campus. I knew how easy it would be to get disoriented down here.

"Cliff?" I called. I spun around, flashlight searching the long empty hall.

"Right here," he said, grabbing me from behind, laughing. The flashlight fell from my hand as I gasped, light spinning and then cutting out.

"Asshole," I said, but I was smiling, fingers lacing with his in the dark.

My heart was still racing as Maggie picked up the flashlight and turned it back on. "That's not funny," she said.

"It was a little bit," I said, grinning. "But we have to stay together. You need the key for every door down here."

We kept moving—left, then right, my memory growing a little hazy down here on my own, without my dad's insight—but we eventually reached the end of the path, where a stone staircase led to a door directly overhead.

I used the key and pushed the exit open, emerging from what seemed like a trapdoor in the floor.

We were inside a wooden structure, slants of light cutting through the gaps.

"Okay," Cliff said, stepping into the empty room. "We're definitely *not supposed to be here."*

Maggie hesitated for a moment before joining us. "Where are we?" she asked.

"The barn by the old president's house," I said. It was chilly, uninsulated. Outside, I knew, a perimeter of stone circled what used to be a home, fireplace still half standing.

I felt Cliff eyeing the skeleton key hanging from around my neck. "Can I borrow that? Get a copy made?" he asked. "We could use this as a shortcut during the howling next year."

"No," I said, tucking it away, under my shirt. "I have to get it back into the archive room before my dad notices I borrowed his access."

As I led them back down the steps, I wondered if I should've shared this with them. Next year, I would be a student here. On the other side.

Cliff pushed at the closed door in front of him in the tunnel. "It's locked," he said.

"I know. They lock behind you," I said. My dad said the inner doors had been installed as a safety feature, to keep the sections sealed off in the event of an issue with the steam pipes. "You need the key."

When what I really meant was: You need me.

I led them into the next section of the dark maze, heading back.

"Pull the door shut behind you," I said, waiting until I heard the latch.

CHAPTER 9

Saturday, October 4
8:00 a.m.

The kids were clever.

The path here had not existed when I was a student. The access point was barely visible until you were inside the tree line, hidden from view. It was narrow, unmarked, like offshoots of a main trail on a mountain hike that would lure you to a hidden overlook.

All it took was one step inside the trees, and I was back—racing through the woods, screaming her name into the night. *Adalyn, where are you?* The crunch of fresh snow and the cold wind stinging my cheeks, my exposed neck, my bare hands.

Twenty years later and the panic and adrenaline from the past were seeping into this moment, tinging it with something else—dark and dangerous and unspoken.

Inside the woods, there were no blue emergency lights guiding the way, promising safety. Here, there were no cameras to follow your trail. Here, you were on your own.

This was a place you'd go if you didn't want to be seen.

The trail was just wide enough for one person to walk comfortably, though I had to duck under the branches at times. I couldn't imagine this being used for running. No, I was sure—Bryce had been out here for something else.

I moved with the terrain, letting gravity guide me, drawing me down, down, down. Soon I was sure I was off campus, but the trail kept going, briefly disappearing in sections, only to pick up again on the other side of a tree. In the dark, it would be so easy to take a wrong step and head deeper into the woods, disoriented.

To panic. To lose a phone—or your way.

A rustling sound came from my left, and I stopped, standing perfectly still. But the wind quickly drowned out any signs of movement.

"Hello?" I called.

Nothing. My imagination, maybe. An animal. A dead branch knocked loose in the wind, falling to earth.

In the daylight, the wind was nothing to fear, just a hindrance, something to push against as you walked up the hill to your dorms. We used to call the slight dip between upper and lower campuses *the border,* where the wind caught in a gully behind the bell tower, pushing sideways—like it was some supernatural boundary trying to keep us from crossing.

In front of me, the trail abruptly stopped at a row of trees. This path had gone nowhere but down, and I'd have to retrace my steps up to make it back to my car. But before I turned around, there was a flash of movement through the trees. A blur of silver, moving quickly—here and gone.

A car. A road.

I wove between the trees, maneuvering over a hedge of low bushes, prickly burrs clinging to my joggers. The end of the path was hidden from the other side as well. When I finally emerged from the woods, I found myself at the edge of a familiar road—directly across from the Low Bar.

The front window was dark, but a subtle green glow came from within. The back room had always been for the late-night crowd, with people packed in the gaps between tables. As I approached, I spotted a collection of cigarette butts on the sidewalk, a *No Smoking* sign on the front door, and another below it that said *We Check IDs.*

They'd gotten stricter—or at least put on a show of it.

I pulled at the glass front door, but it was locked. Inside, I could see straight to the pool tables in the back room, and the outline of neon signs gone dark. There was one left glowing, probably by accident, in the outline of a green beer bottle—the cause of the eerie glow. The shadow of a jukebox fell just below.

It was probably the same one I used to lean against, dart in hand, shot glass in another. Aiming, and bracing myself backward for balance. A collection of dollar bills strewn on the high-top table beside me, from people who should've known better by now. Adalyn, catching my eye from across the room, already tracking down the next victim. Growing up, I'd spent years practicing on the dartboard in the old student center before asking my parents to buy me one for my birthday; I'd hung it against the house in our backyard.

This was our place that final year—just one of the many things in town I'd introduced her to. Something very different from her country club upbringing.

Adalyn loved making money off the local patrons, even though she didn't need it. She loved being the one in control. I think, above all, she loved a game. We'd spent so many Friday nights at the Low Bar that final fall, pushing past closing time, convincing the bartender to stay *just a little longer*.

She'd tip him from our winnings, order drinks she didn't consume, offer cash for things around the room she had no intention of wearing: a chunky bracelet; cheap rhinestone sunglasses; a hat for a sports team she didn't follow.

But I couldn't imagine that Bryce had been coming back from the bar at this hour. It was closed down, with no signs of activity. Maybe he'd been at his own house, somewhere nearby. I wasn't sure where Violet Harvey, now Wharton, lived anymore, though I could probably find out easily with a question or two.

The only storefront open—and just barely—was the deli, catty-corner across the intersection. The sign on the inside of the front door was turning from *Closed* to *Open* as I watched.

My heart thudded, then skipped. The deli.

I pictured Bryce not coming from the bar at all. But from behind the deli, where—anyone who lived here would know—you'd find the best shortcut to the quarry.

The back of the deli had no windows—just a metal access door used mostly for deliveries. A single black sedan was parked in the small makeshift lot, which was really an unpaved area of patchy grass that was never able to fully take root under the car traffic. The black sedan was parked directly in front of the trailhead, as if barricading the entrance, hiding it from view.

Unlike the path from the campus to the bar, the trail entrance here would be readily apparent without this car in the way. There once was a sign stuck in the dirt—a hand-painted arrow beside the words *Cryer's Quarry*—but it had long since been removed, probably to dull the allure of it.

There was also an unpaved access road that led to the quarry from the other side. But a chain hung across the dirt road, with *Private Property* signs nailed into the surrounding trees.

Years ago, it belonged to the mining company that had dug it out for granite or limestone—I was never sure which. I wondered if, like Fraternity Row, the property had been relinquished back to the town.

There had been signs all around warning us to keep out, but we did not. I doubted the kids who lived here now did, either.

When I was in high school, Cryer's Quarry was the place the locals met up on weekend nights. Where the dark yawn of the abyss and the darker water below beckoned. Where Cliff Simmons dared his friends to jump. Where I floated on my back in the dark and dared him to find me. Where the water rushing in and out of my ears sounded like a revving engine, a thrumming pulse—something threatening to consume me.

This place used to belong just to the locals. But maybe things had changed—another shifting boundary; another change of ownership.

I wove around the car and started down the path, which was wider than the one hidden across the street. This was more official: a hiking trail that continued to weave upward, even beyond the quarry. I could orient myself perfectly as the terrain rose and fell, even after all this time. Like something seared into the core of me.

Eventually the woods opened up to a dirt picnic area set just before the old mining site—the original reason for this town's existence. Now there were newer *Do Not Enter* signs, courtesy of JW Enterprises. I couldn't imagine what they intended to do with this place. There was just exposed sedimentary rock and a forbidden swimming pit below. The water was always shockingly cold, seeping in from the cool underground, no matter the summer heat.

It had been nearly seven hours since the dropped call—seven hours when Delilah could've been out here in the dark. And suddenly I felt the same fear as my father, who'd reprimanded me for driving through the mountains in the night. How easy it would be to someone unfamiliar with the landscape to slip and fall in.

The water had never been deep enough that we couldn't touch the bottom, but that somehow made it even more dangerous. There were so many ways to get hurt. To jump where you shouldn't, bones jarring against the shallow bottom; to trip, hit your head on the exposed rock, legs gently sliding out beneath you as your body disappeared under the surface.

I'd heard enough news stories, seen enough grainy video footage—the type that shook every parent to the core: a teen, seemingly disoriented, under the influence, last seen wandering into the dark. Wandering toward a river. Toward a dark alley. Toward a stranger.

I imagined Delilah running through these woods, lost. Hearing footsteps gaining on her from behind, difficult to distinguish under the sound of the howling. Turning to look over her shoulder, phone in hand, dark hair wild. Tripping and falling forward. Her phone slipping from her grip as she braced for anything to break her fall. The shock of cold water stealing her breath—

I was practically running now, racing to the crest of the quarry, thighs burning, heartbeat resounding in my skull. I needed to see. To disprove all the horrors of my imagination.

The last time I'd been out here was during the search for Adalyn. That night, I'd tried to imagine anyplace she might go. I'd thought she might be hiding out at a place where only I might find her. That was before I realized that while I'd been out desperately searching for her, she'd raced back to the dorm, preparing to flee.

It had been much colder then, the surface of the swimming hole frozen over, with a fresh layer of snow on top so that you couldn't even tell there was water underneath. Then, like now, there was no disturbance to the surrounding area.

Finally the edge: The water below was protected from the wind, eerily still, and eerily blue—so clear I could see straight to the rocky bottom. I found myself relaxing, hand to heart, like I was willing it to slow down.

In the daylight, the bright blue water appeared deeper than it did in my memory, the walls lighter, rimmed with chalky white, landscape greener, with trees taking root in the grooves, like some sort of Eden.

I took a moment to sit, muscles trembling. I was out of shape and out of breath, and I wondered if the water was safe to drink.

I felt like I had escaped something. Proved to myself that history had not repeated itself. That humanity wasn't stuck in the same vicious cycle with only a new frame of reference.

No, it was just me, panicking. *Unable to let go,* as my mother had so keenly implied. Unprepared to deal with all the uncertainty of my daughter out in the world on her own for the first time.

Whatever may have happened last night, it was over and done. Most likely, Delilah was being a college kid, staying out late, crashing with new friends—or a boyfriend she hadn't yet told me about—and would eventually see my messages when she logged onto her accounts.

I was standing, brushing the dirt from the back of my pants, when a flash of red at the corner of the quarry caught my eye.

Something new. Recent.

I leaned over the edge to get a better view but couldn't quite make it out. No, I'd have to go down.

The stratified levels of rock provided sloping steps; we'd used them to climb out of the quarry during high school. I had also used them to ease myself into the cool water, rather than jump.

The steps seemed more precarious now. My shoes had less traction; my age had made me more cautious. I lowered myself carefully, leaning into the landscape, one hand on the chalky rock as I descended.

When I reached the lowest level, I still had to lean out over the water to see clearly. The flash of red looked like a glove or a scarf.

I used a nearby stick to reach forward, pull it closer in the water.

When I lifted the stick, the red fabric hung limply, dripping water. A hat, I was guessing. Something lost nearby in another time of year, until the howling wind last night blew it over the edge.

I removed it from the stick, stuck my hand inside.

There were three round holes cut into the lower fabric.

A face, hollow-eyed, staring back.

A mask.

An old hat, holes cut with a pair of scissors.

My hand started shaking, the cold water trailing down my forearm.

I knew what this was from. What it was *for.*

Kids, out in the first howling of the year. A game of chase. A tally of names.

Like the tradition, banned or not, was still here.

CHAPTER 10

Saturday, October 4
9:30 a.m.

I took the mask with me, ice-cold and dripping with the quarry water, like some sort of proof.

Something had happened. Something was still happening. I felt the cold shock work its way through my bones. Felt something else coming alive in the process. The need to *move,* to act.

Seven and a half hours since the dropped call. One hour since Bryce had emerged from the woods, looking for someone behind him.

I was trying to put the pieces together.

By the time I made it back to the lot behind the deli, a second sedan, gray and rusted, was parked behind the other vehicle at the trailhead. I circled to the front of the building and stuffed the wet mask in my bag. It was instinct, a secret that belonged to the past—something I needed to keep for myself.

Bells chimed overhead as I pushed through the front door of the deli. The two girls behind the counter quickly looked up and pulled slightly away from each other, as if they'd been leaning close, whispering.

They were both striking, with angular features and bone-straight dark hair slicked back into tight ponytails. One was taller than the other, but I thought they could've been sisters. Or it could've just been the style of the current generation. They looked about Delilah's age—maybe still in high school; maybe not. The taller girl wore an apron with the name tag *Carly*.

They both looked to me expectantly. I'd been up since two in the morning, and I couldn't find my grounding in the present.

"Large coffee, please," I said. It seemed the smartest choice at the moment.

Carly turned for the coffee machine while the shorter girl rang me up at the cash register, her white nail polish just starting to chip.

The deli had clung to its roots—tip jar on the side of the counter, a request written in marker for *CASH ONLY PLEASE*. That was maybe the biggest surprise of the town: how little it had changed in comparison to the shifting generations and the new construction on campus. But that was also the charm of this place. They didn't bend their rules to accommodate the population from the outside. They held strong, waited for the outsiders to adapt.

There was an ATM strategically placed outside in the brick wall around the corner. I wondered if they got a kickback from the bank.

I rummaged in my wallet, thankful I had a worn ten-dollar bill, which had probably been there for months. I slid it across the thick wooden countertop that had been covered in graffiti over the years, notes and names and drawings. Another tradition, one that was encouraged.

If you were to strip back the layers, somewhere underneath the years of ink, you'd find my name in block letters, the ridge of the mountains in the distance engraved underneath. Something I was practicing, trying on for size, before I committed to my tattoo.

"Will that be all?" Carly asked as she handed me the cup.

I took a sip of the coffee, scalding against the roof of my mouth. "Do you know," I began, like the thought had just occurred to me, "where I can find the Harv—the Whartons? I think their son Bryce is about your age." I could've tried a Google search, checked the White Pages, but word of mouth was the most reliable resource here. I wanted to know if he lived close to downtown. I wanted to know if there was another reason he could've been cutting through the woods this morning.

The other girl paused as the cash drawer slid open, then cut her eyes to the side. A question.

"I went to school with his mother, Violet," I added. And then, with a grin, "A long time ago."

Carly stared back, straight-faced. I felt her looking me over. She was too young to know me but not too young to know *of* me.

This was another benefit of their cash operation—I didn't have to hand over my credit card, watch as my name registered on their faces.

"I think they live in the Estates," said the girl with the white nail polish as she pushed the drawer shut and handed me my change. "I graduated with Bryce last year." I caught a twitch at the corner of her mouth that did nothing to make me think they were friends.

"Thanks," I said, nodding like: *Of course that makes sense.*

I placed my change in the tip jar and turned to go, the heat of the coffee searing my grip.

"Hey," a voice called from behind. I turned around slowly, like I'd been caught doing something I shouldn't. But Carly was just holding out a receipt. "You forgot this." Her eyes were locked on mine as I took it from her outstretched hand.

There was no way Bryce had been returning from a night at home. The Estates was a solid drive up the winding mountain roads, large and showy on sprawling lots, with manicured hedges and wide front porches. And he hadn't been coming from the deli—it had been closed when I first arrived.

No, he was coming from Cryer's Quarry. He had to be. I knew there were technically other options—friends, a significant other. But the first howling of the year had presumably swept through the valley last night, and I'd just found a mask, eyeholes cut into the red fabric, floating in the quarry water.

He'd been there. I was sure of it. And, as much as I hoped against it, there was a good chance Delilah had been out there, too.

It took me a moment to find the entrance to the hidden path again, and it was much slower going on the way back, uphill with a coffee in my hand. But I felt the caffeine and the warmth hitting my bloodstream, waking me up. Students should be waking up soon, too.

I waited until I was at my car behind the dorm to check my emails.

It had been almost two hours since I'd emailed Delilah. Eight since her dropped call. And I worried my parents' house would have spotty coverage, with their Wi-Fi service turned off temporarily.

I did a quick scan for Delilah's name down my inbox, but came up empty. There were a handful of other messages that had come in since the evening before: an update from my parents, sent every Friday like clockwork, to a list of anonymous recipients including me; a reply to that request for a memoir—had that really been only yesterday?—and a reminder of an upcoming bill's due date. I didn't bother reading any of them. Instead I hit refresh, willing something to happen.

Her Instagram account was still idle, my note unread. My text message still showed as undelivered.

An electric golf cart pulled into the lot, driven by a man in an orange vest. Security, I was guessing, with nothing better to do at the moment than check for parking permits. I slipped inside my car and started the engine before I had to explain myself.

My father was a creature of habit, though he was prone to adventures. Even in Peru, I was sure, he'd be wearing a checkered button-down and khaki pants, waking at the same time each day, eating oatmeal and raisins for breakfast while he checked the same gold watch that once belonged to his father. The email updates were probably from him, though they came from a shared email address, so it was impossible to send a note to one of my parents without the other.

We do have separate cell phones, my father had said with a shrug when I pointed this out. *It's easier this way. Your mother keeps the calendar.* After they retired, practically in unison, they lost their school email accounts and defaulted to a single username that could double for either or both: *TheProfBowery*.

I found the idea of sharing an email address with *anyone* alarming, like giving access to my private thoughts. But maybe my mother had long since pried every secret from my father, so that he found the prospect a useless endeavor.

Other things I could count on my father doing: raising the flag on the mailbox, even though there were no outgoing letters, so that he would know when the mail had arrived; closing every door behind him when he exited a room, an old habit from trying to conserve heat in the bedrooms at home; and leaving the spare key around back, in the hollow of an antique weathervane.

Now I drove up their street until I found a spot along the curb. I walked up their narrow single-car driveway, which was occupied by their small gold sedan, then reached over the high picket fence for the latch.

The gate shuddered against the ground as I pushed it open, catching on patches of grass and dirt, the hinges starting to pull away from the wood, everything shifting off balance. I squeezed through the entrance and followed the paving stones to the back door.

The weathervane remained where it always had, on a slate stone beside the back steps. It was made of a dark, heavy metal, with a figurine of a coiled-up dragon just below the spinning arrow.

I tilted the weathervane to the side and reached into the hollow underneath, fingers grasping for the spare key. But I felt only the dirt and grit of the underside. I ran my hand over the slate, brushing the surrounding dirt and grass.

The key was missing.

I peered around the yard, looking for other options. The potted plants had been moved, only the rusted rings left behind on the steps. I groaned, irritated by my parents' preparations. One of them must've taken the key inside for safekeeping.

I returned to the front of the house and pulled the gate shut behind me until I could hear the click of the latch. So much for my plan to regroup here, think of my next step.

Looking up at the house, I had one more idea. One last place to check.

From the front porch, I stood before the window to my father's office, visible through the gauzy curtain. Inside, the row of masks along the back wall stared out at me, like a warning. I pushed the window from the base, and it gave, sliding upward. I almost laughed to myself. This, I knew, was my own oversight. My irresponsibility from a month earlier, when I'd neglected to lock up after slipping out into the night.

What was it they had said? I wasn't in a city anymore. Shouldn't worry about my full car left at the curb. They'd never had an alarm system or cameras pointed outside. And they'd left a spare key on the back porch, in the same place it had always been, for years.

I peered over my shoulder once just to make sure the neighbors weren't watching as I stepped inside my father's office, directly over the ledge, and onto the dark futon.

When I closed the window behind me, I was engulfed in silence. Without their presence, the house had a different scent to it. Something that existed deep in its bones, in the walls. A sweetness from old cooking, maybe. A remnant of those who had existed before.

I couldn't remember the last time I'd been in here all alone. Twenty years probably, give or take.

I removed the red mask from my bag, still cool and damp, and brought it to the kitchen. I draped it on top of the table, hollow face staring back up at me, then emptied the rest of my bag to give everything a chance to dry out.

I took a cup from the cabinet to fill in the sink, then paused. There was a single plate beside the sink, like something my mother had forgotten in their rush to leave, after a last-minute snack. And then, in the basin of the sink, a glass, pink lip print marking the rim.

Not my mother, then. I'd be shocked if she owned any makeup, and she definitely wouldn't be wearing it on her way to the airport.

I opened the trash cabinet under the sink, knowing it should be empty—something they surely would've handled before leaving for three months—to find the remnants of a bagel, and a Styrofoam cup, just like the one I'd received from the deli.

My heart raced. Of course. *Of course.* Who else would know the place my parents hid their spare key? If she hadn't been getting along with her roommate, *of course* she would come here. A safe place, a whole house, all for herself.

"Delilah?" I called as I headed straight for the steps, up to my old bedroom. "It's just me!"

When I reached the landing, I could see straight through the open doorway—empty. But there were signs that someone had been staying up here. In the bathroom, toothpaste residue was visible in the sink, and a dark green bath towel hung from the shower rod. Beside the sink, the attic door was unlatched. I pulled it shut as I passed, on instinct. Then, in my bedroom: a rumpled comforter, partially pulled up; a tissue in the trash can beside the desk.

I sat on the edge of my bed, feeling myself relax for the first time since that dropped call. I'd finally found a trace of Delilah, discovered why she hadn't been in her dorm. She wouldn't be able to check messages here with the Wi-Fi turned off. She wouldn't even know I was looking.

I lay back on the bed, feeling the imprint of my daughter in this same place.

I imagined what she thought when she looked around the room from this angle. All the words circling the room—the ghost of who I used to be.

Even when I was her age, I had already wanted to be a writer. I felt like I was reaching for some great truth, frustratingly out of reach. One that I believed I could wrestle into form, make concrete.

There was the string of lyrics in cursive painted sideways down the wall. A stanza from Poe behind an empty ornate frame that Maggie had found in a thrift shop. On the wall directly over my wooden headboard, a collection of the first and last lines from every novel I'd read during my senior year of high school, in my own secret project. A meaning I believed I could extract from the pattern.

At seventeen, I had watched Cliff's eyes widen in surprise when I sneaked him upstairs—a side of me he hadn't expected. And at eighteen, I'd listened to Adalyn reciting the lines back to me as she dragged her fingers across the walls, claiming it was *like looking straight into the heart of you*.

I wasn't so different from my parents, who wanted to pry into the human psyche or understand the predictable rhythms of humanity. We just had a different angle of approach.

After I left home, after Delilah, I switched my aim to marketing and graphic design, where I learned to refocus someone else's message most efficiently. And then I learned to inhabit other people's stories completely—my fingerprints on everything, my name on nothing.

Still, my parents kept my room intact, like proof of who I was supposed to be.

The ghostwriting had surprised them both. But the evidence was right here all along: I had always preferred to live inside other people's words.

The adrenaline from the morning was wearing off, fatigue settling into my limbs.

I scrolled to Maggie's new contact in my phone. It was after ten, and with young twins, I was sure she'd be up by now.

She answered on the fourth ring, sounding out of breath, like she'd been running after them through the yard again. "Beckett?" she said—just like she had when she found me on her porch.

"Hi, sorry to call you on a Saturday morning. I was wondering if you've seen Delilah around? Has she called you at all?"

"No. Is everything okay?"

"Yeah, I'm at my parents' house. I came up here on a whim, and I think she's been staying here. I'm just trying to track her down."

"Sorry, I haven't heard from her," Maggie said. "I'm not on campus much, so I haven't had the chance to run into her."

"Thanks. I'm gonna head over that way soon." I ended the call, then rolled onto my side, like I would when talking to Maggie during a sleepover, one ear pressed to the pillow, whispering until we fell asleep.

Another line caught my eye. Something near the top of the far wall in blocky black ink. Something I didn't remember.

I sat up, the words tilting into focus: *Hey there, Delilah*

The line jarred me at first—how long had it been since I'd sat in this spot, reading the quotes? I imagined my father dragging my desk chair over to the wall, marker in hand, adding another layer of history. It was the name of a song he would sing to her as a child. Maybe he still did.

I scanned the walls for evidence of any other new additions. And *there,* another, also near the ceiling, in that same deep black, thick lettering.

I can still see you

Goose bumps rose up the back of my neck. Was this another song title? Something Delilah listened to? Part of a game they played? I couldn't imagine my father writing that. It sounded so unsettling without context. Threatening, even. Not something to include on the wall where his granddaughter slept.

I stood from the bed, walking closer, searching now, scanning for anything out of place. One more, just over the open doorway—

I swallowed air, my throat tight.

Not a list of song titles at all.

Above me, instead, I read the final line of the message:

Did you think you could hide?

CHAPTER 11

Saturday, October 4
10:30 a.m.

Someone had been in my room. Someone who was *not Delilah*. And they had written on the walls—a threat, that they were watching.

Was it a message for me? A warning? Or was it something meant just for my daughter?

The message was spread across the three walls visible from the bed where she must've slept. It had been addressed directly to her:

Hey there, Delilah
I can still see you
Did you think you could hide?

A wave of nausea rolled through me, and a sound escaped my throat. I felt sick, fury rising to the surface. Someone had targeted her, taunted her, *haunted* her. Had they chased her out of her dorm room, followed her back to this place—determined to let her know she wasn't safe even here, in her family's home?

The people who grew up in Wyatt Valley would know that this was a likely place for her to go.

Please, I can't go back—

It was the mantra in my head when I learned she'd been accepted here.

I had always feared it wasn't safe for me to return. I had fallen under suspicion of knowing more than I did about Adalyn: what she'd planned, where she'd gone, and how she'd gotten away. The memory of the crime may have been lost for the students, but the fractures in the town ran deep. They thought I was protecting her, saw me as a traitor. Like I had picked a side and chosen wrong.

But it had never occurred to me that, in my absence, they would target my daughter instead. My parents had continued to live here for the last twenty years without any issues.

What could have driven her here? Where would she go next?

How scared she must've been, reading that message on the wall. Why hadn't she told me?

In all our calls, she'd never given me any indication that there was something seriously amiss—nothing that seemed beyond the normal issues of rooming with someone else for the first time, keeping her own schedule, trying to make new friends. Her Instagram feed had become annoyingly sparse over the last month. I'd thought it was just a sign of her busy schedule or shifting priorities. She used to post photos to her page from her theater shows, dressed up with friends. Over the summer, there'd been a photo dump from her graduation party; another from our summer backpacking trip. I could always pick up on small things she didn't say directly in what she chose to show. But nothing new had been posted since last month, when she'd shared a picture of the mountain ridge in the distance, peaks disappearing into the clouds. The caption read, succinctly: *Here.*

It was a view I knew she could've seen only off campus, standing at the entrance to town, on the crest of a familiar road, near Maggie's house. It was the view I'd once mapped out and tattooed onto my own wrist.

My breath had caught in my throat at first, seeing that same picture on her page. But then I'd thought: *Good. She's exploring. She's getting out there, discovering her world. Finding her place.*

It hadn't occurred to me that she had been escaping something instead.

I could feel the presence of her now—eating breakfast downstairs, sleeping in this bed, *hiding* from something—and wondered if the scent I'd noticed first was not the staleness from the bones of the house but a lingering fear.

For whatever reason, she hadn't told me. And she hadn't reached out to Maggie.

There was only one other adult I could think of whom she'd be in contact with.

I sent her father a text, hand trembling, trying not to panic him. *Trevor, when was the last time you talked to Delilah?*

I was trying to be vague, hoping for nonchalance. It was just after ten a.m. on a Saturday, and he might be sleeping. I was no longer privy to the details of his private life.

There was a time when Delilah used to tell me things after her visits in D.C. When she'd mentioned someone else hanging around with them, I'd asked him about it point-blank. I wanted to know whom my daughter was spending time with. He'd said, *Her name is Raya. She's a preschool teacher*. But by the next year, it was a new woman—this time Kelly, a kindergarten teacher.

I asked if it was on purpose, a trend. Aging up his girlfriends' careers to match Delilah's grade.

I'd meant it as a joke, but he'd said he needed to be sure whomever he brought home loved kids, and this seemed the safest bet.

I'd laughed, told him the safest bet was just to find someone who loved him, and the rest would follow—Delilah was an extension of him after all.

He'd gotten engaged to the second one—the kindergarten teacher, Kelly. He'd even asked me if Delilah could be the flower girl. But they'd broken it off before we bought a dress. Delilah was too young then to share any insights as to what had happened, and there were lines I wouldn't cross on my own.

I stared at my phone, waiting for an answer. But my message was still sending—stuck in limbo. Just like when I'd arrived in August and my mother had chastised us about our communication methods: *You have to call*.

I'd thought it was partly because my mother, from a different generation, just preferred phone conversations. She had a joint email account, for the love of God. But it was also a matter of practicality here in the valley, especially with their Internet service currently disconnected.

My finger hovered over his contact. *Trevor Dayton.* I placed the call, pacing the tiny square of my old bedroom. The phone rang three times—I imagined him sleeping, in bed with someone else, disoriented by my name on the display.

"Hello?" he answered, sounding out of breath—but also unusually close.

"Hi, sorry, am I interrupting something?" I asked.

"No, I'm just running. I was, anyway." I heard a car in the distance, imagined him at the edge of a sidewalk, standing on a city corner, pacing. And then: "Is everything okay?"

"Yes," I said. "I was just wondering if you'd talked to Delilah recently."

He didn't speak at first. I heard the cars moving in the background in a steady rhythm, the honk of a horn. And then he sighed. "She texted me last week," he said. "Asking if I could Venmo her some cash. I guess she was having problems with her bank account?"

He left the question hanging. Waiting for me to answer—to provide some insight.

"I didn't know that," I said, my stomach dropping. "How much?"

"I sent five hundred. Should I not have?" he asked. "I'm sorry, she just so rarely asks me for anything . . ."

But I was trying to understand what he was saying. Delilah had needed money, and she hadn't told me. She had saved a lot over the last few years of working at our local community theater during the summers. There were ATMs around town if she needed cash. If she was short on funds, she could've asked.

But she'd gone to her father instead.

"Beckett?" Trevor said, and I realized I hadn't responded. "What's going on?"

Like he could read it in my silence. Feel something simmering through the open line of the phone. Something coming for him, too.

"I got a dropped call from her last night," I said. "I couldn't reach her after, and I panicked. Drove straight up here." I tried to laugh it off, waited for him to tell me I was being ridiculous. Or imply something like my mother would, that *I just couldn't let go.*

"Okay," he said, voice rising slightly, waiting for the punch line.

I stared at the thick black lettering on the wall. The implicit threat of the words. The danger I could feel, pulsing through the room.

"Something's off here," I began. "I don't know, I might be panicking for nothing . . ."

"Beckett, tell me." His voice was so close, like the phone was pressed to his face in a white-knuckle grip.

I sucked in a breath. "I can't reach her. I can't find her, Trevor." My throat was tight, and then I spoke the four words I swore I'd never say to him. "I need your help."

I knew as the words left my mouth that I'd made it real. Taken an abstract idea and turned it solid, brought it to life with my words alone, like I'd once thought possible. All it took was a singular fear, a desperate plea.

Delilah was missing. Someone had been inside this house. And now Trevor was coming.

Maybe she was spooked and hiding. Maybe she'd asked Trevor for cash so she could disappear for a bit. Without a credit card trail. Without a phone.

Maybe she had been calling to tell me, had meant to leave a message but gotten caught up in the night.

It used to be easier to disappear, to go completely off the grid. Adalyn Vale had done it twenty years earlier. Back then Facebook was in its infancy; we didn't even know the word for social media. It wasn't prevalent on every campus yet—and definitely not on this one, with a crowd who preferred to shun popular culture.

Back then only a few of us carried phones, and when we did, they were flip-screen, with limited data plans and crappy coverage. It was easy to overlook a missing person as a series of missed connections: notes left on a whiteboard; a dorm landline ringing in an empty room.

Even now I didn't have Facebook. Used Instagram only as a practical way to keep up with Delilah, with an alias that wouldn't come up if someone were to search my name. Had an unlisted address, a decision made mostly for safety. Chose not to have my own website to advertise. But I was bound by my relationships. To truly disappear, you had to leave everything.

Adalyn had left behind her entire life. Her bank account; her family. Me.

And the police were convinced she had help.

There had to have been a car—we all knew that. Someone had picked her up and smuggled her out of town after her trail in the snow ended. There must've been a call she made from the dorm, or from a phone somewhere else in town. There had to be someone who'd agreed to come and get her out, shuttle her away, help her start over—while the rest of us were still out searching.

Even I knew there were some things you couldn't do alone.

I kept pacing the room, wondering where to go next—find Violet, get ahold of Bryce? I couldn't think straight, shaken by the knowledge that someone else had been in this room.

The attic door had been slightly ajar when I'd come upstairs. And suddenly I wondered if someone else had been in here, waiting—watching.

The access point to the unfinished space up here was one of the quirks of this house, with a narrow door cut into the wall beside the bathroom sink. When I was young, I'd keep an eye on it from my spot behind the shower curtain, its presence unnerving. There was no lock, and I used to imagine someone on the other side, waiting to emerge.

Once, a bat had gotten trapped in the attic space on the other side of my bedroom, desperate to escape. Scratching at the walls, flapping against the ceiling. The sound had haunted me long after the bat had been captured and freed.

When I was a teenager, I used the attic space to store anything I didn't want my parents to see: the bag with my fake ID, a collection of empty bottles after a party until I could sneak them out on recycling day.

From inside, I could hear everything below: my mother emptying the dishwasher in the kitchen; my father on the phone in his office; the noise of the television carrying from the living room.

Now I pushed open the narrow door to the attic and felt a warm gust of air from inside. I stepped into the darkness and got a whiff of staleness—a stronger scent than downstairs now that I was closer to the bones of the house.

I used the light on my phone to illuminate the space, looking for any evidence that someone else had been inside. It was obvious my parents had used it for storage since I'd moved out. File boxes now lined the near wall, lids closed, labeled by time. The first said: *'80s–'90s*. I tipped the lid and saw a collection of baby books, report cards in manila envelopes, school artwork.

The next box was labeled *2000s*. My college years. When I opened it, a pile of old photos were scattered on top from my parents' various trips and house gatherings. Things that hadn't made it into an album. I shifted aside the top layer of photos, and there

I was, in the backyard during their annual Labor Day barbecue. There was a mixture of faculty and friends milling about and, in the lawn chair beside mine, Adalyn. She sat with her feet up on a folding table, knees bent, head tilted toward me, peace sign thrown up at the camera. Even in jean shorts at a backyard barbecue, she wore pearls layered over a ribbed tank. A reminder of who she was, lest anyone forget.

Since my freshman year, my parents had grown accustomed to her presence at our home. My mother tolerated her but didn't quite take to her—as if she were holding space for Maggie's return. My father was ambivalent, like he was with most of my friends—as if he knew everything from that period of my life was just a precursor; that none of this was permanent.

But Adalyn took strongly to them.

Adalyn even took my mother's class, told me it was her favorite, that my mother was a *genius,* though wondered aloud whether she had just managed to hypnotize the class. She fawned over my mother at the dinner table, asked her about her research, her papers, like she was trying to crack the surface of her in a way my mother wasn't accustomed to—most students never dared to get so familiar. It made me smile. Made me feel I had an ally—a second line of defense.

But after the fire, my mother would tell people: *That girl was always a problem. Grew up being handed everything she ever wanted. And still always looking for something more . . .*

In her professional and personal opinion, as both Adalyn's professor and the mother of her best friend, she was *a dangerous narcissist.*

I didn't know if I agreed. I thought Adalyn was provocative, yes, but for a different reason: She didn't want to be in this small mountain town. She had no interest in college, or dorms, or a degree. She wanted to travel the world, maybe document her trips, write a guide. But I was drawn to the very thing that made my mother wary—Adalyn was *exciting.* Someone who raised the stakes in any room. In another generation, I thought later, she would've made a great travel influencer, posting aspirational photos, seeing what she could convince people to give her for free.

She was at Wyatt College only in a financial agreement with her parents. Perhaps I should have asked more questions about this contingency and what had inspired it. But she'd told me that the very first day we met. Everything I knew of her grew from this place.

And when she circled my bedroom, dragged her fingers along the wall and whispered, *Like looking straight into the heart of you*—it felt like that was something she'd been searching for all along.

I dropped the photos back in the box, closed the lid. Left the past to the past, where it belonged.

I shone the light around the rest of the attic space. There was a pile of old blankets in the far corner, in need of disposal. My parents were lucky another animal hadn't taken up residence.

And beside the discarded linens, another set of boxes, unlabeled, stacked into a careful pyramid. One of the upper boxes was missing a lid, so I could see delicate objects cushioned with newspaper and bubble wrap.

These must've been the valuables my parents had decided needed to be hidden away for safekeeping. There was no sign someone else had disturbed the space.

I stepped backward, toward the entrance. And then I froze.

A sound from somewhere below.

A creaking door. The thud of it latching shut. I tried to orient myself: the back of the house.

Someone coming in the back door? Someone who had a key. Delilah—

I stepped once, then paused, not wanting to spook her any more than she already might be. I imagined her perspective: *Someone upstairs, in an empty house, where there was writing on the wall—*

I listened, waiting for her to move deeper into the house.

There were a lot of things that I knew by heart: The way she could float through a room, light on her toes, like she was in the middle of a performance. Or the quick flutter of her steps upstairs when I called her name, late for school.

Which was why a chill washed over me, standing in the warm and stagnant attic space.

The footsteps below kept moving through the house, but they were slow, deliberate. Heavier than I thought hers should be.

Or maybe it was the acoustics up here, distorting everything.

A cabinet door fell shut—the kitchen, then. More footsteps, crossing the room.

I'd left my bag out on the kitchen table. Delilah would recognize it. She'd know it was mine. She'd know I was *here*.

The footsteps paused. Whoever was down there did not call out to me. *Not Delilah.*

Someone else was downstairs. Someone who had a key, who'd let themselves into my parents' house. Who'd written threatening messages along the perimeter of my bedroom wall.

And I'd cornered myself inside the attic.

I held my breath, terrified to make a sound. Waiting for the inevitable moment when the footsteps started upstairs, looking for me.

But they didn't. They slowly retreated, moving with the same deliberate speed, until they were at the back of the house again. Another creaking door. A thud as the door latched shut.

It took me a handful of seconds to rush out of the attic, back to my room, where I strained at the window to see down into the backyard. But all I could see was the gate hanging slightly ajar, and the mountains rising up in the distance beyond.

I hurried down the steps, threw open the front door, racing into the middle of the street, looking up and down the stretch of pavement, searching for any sign of movement. Someone slipping into one of the cars parked along the curb, maybe. Or someone cutting through another yard.

Nothing.

And then, at the very end of the street, I saw a figure. Someone standing at the intersection of College Lane, facing the empty, gaping plot.

Half a block away, and I knew him by the hair blowing over his shoulders. By the way he tilted his head and then turned slowly, as if he could sense me.

Cliff Simmons stared back, waiting for me.

BEFORE:
THE FIRST HOWLING

Freshman year, the sound of the howling was different from inside the dorm. We were closer to the woods, higher up the slope. You could feel it in the shudder of the windows, see it in the shadows of the arcing trees, hear it in the nervous laughter of the other students. Everyone on edge, waiting for dark.

Just after nightfall, one of the seniors came running down our hall, banging on each door, like a warning.

Adalyn stared at me from the other side of the room, blue eyes wide. For the first time, I thought she was nervous.

But I wasn't afraid. I knew these woods so well.

I had a plan: While most of the underclassmen would frantically head toward the president's house in the most direct line, we would circle around the long way, far off the typical paths.

I grabbed her hand as we rushed into the woods, so I wouldn't lose her. I used a small penlight sparingly, turning it on briefly to make sure we were on the right course.

But it was different in the dark, from the other side. I'd never been the one being chased.

We weren't far in when I heard someone in the woods. I paused, dragging Adalyn to a stop. In the moonlight, I could just make out a person in shadow, steadily moving through the trees. They flicked a flashlight in our direction, barely missing us.

I held my finger to my lips until they passed.

I'd thought most of the seniors would be on the direct path. They'd catch the most people that way. The ones out this way, I thought, must've been here to prove a point.

"Which way?" Adalyn whispered after the footsteps had faded away. I shone the penlight around in a circle. But suddenly I couldn't orient myself. I had to do it by the feel of the terrain.

"Up," I said, taking her hand again. And then I started to run, trying to make up for the longer route.

"Did you see that?" she asked, stopping abruptly.

And I had. A flash of light in the trees, to the side. But whoever was out there didn't come any closer. If it was a senior, I thought, they would've caught us by now.

No, this was someone else.

"Run," I said, pushing her forward. I could smell the smoke from the chimney fire. "We're almost there."

Her grip loosened, fingers slipping from mine just as an arm came around my waist, pulling me back, tight.

A hand over my mouth. A breath close to my ear.

"Boo."

I knew him by the feel of his hand. By his slender frame. By the laughter that followed, so I could imagine the charm of his smile.

Of course Cliff Simmons had come out for the howling. He'd followed me. Found me. Caught me.

It was the first time I'd seen him since he'd cut off contact that summer.

I felt a surge of anger. Threw an elbow into his gut so that he grunted, dropped his hand, cursed to himself. To me.

I shone the light on him, so all I could see was his overexposed grimace. Then I scanned the woods around him, looking for Adalyn.

"I think your friend ditched you," he said with a grin.

I didn't answer. I turned off the light and spun. I didn't hear him follow.

Adalyn was already there when I emerged in the clearing of the old president's house—home base. She stood in the middle of the stone ruins, warming her hands near the fire, shadows dancing across her face. She'd made it by herself after all.

I joined her at the fire, the wind pushing at the flames, sending the smoke into the trees. A signal, a homing device, drawing people closer.

"I thought you got caught," she said with a slight smile.

"No," I said. But even then I didn't want to tell her. Didn't want to say: There are other people out there. Another tradition. A different game.

"Don't worry," she said, "I won't tell." As if she were the holder of my secrets, decider of my fate.

But she was new here. She only knew half the rules.

"He didn't count," I told her, rubbing my palms together. "That was just someone I used to know."

CHAPTER 12

Saturday, October 4
11:30 a.m.

Cliff didn't seem surprised to see me. Other than a twitch of his left hand hanging at his side, where a cigarette was dangling from his fingers, his body gave nothing away.

Even after all these years, this was the trait I remembered most about him—the way he always seemed to be observing, or pretending, so that it was hard to differentiate the real Cliff from the performance. When I was young, it had intrigued me, as if I could be the one to crack the act, bend his reality. A dare I'd given myself.

But that was before I realized Cliff was a chameleon, inclined to change his persona to suit whatever group he was with. I'd watched him cycle through plenty of identities, from preppy student to blue-collar worker. How quickly I'd watched him change on me, too. By the end of my time in Wyatt Valley, I had no idea what part of him was real at his core.

And now he had reemerged as a school administrator in the place he'd once only pretended to belong. I wanted to reach out and shake him, see what finally came to the surface.

"What the hell are you doing?" I asked as I strode up the road with single-minded purpose. Anger had displaced the fear—I *knew* this man. He could've been watching Delilah from the day we arrived.

His expression gave nothing away. Cliff had always been on the slender side, but last I'd seen him, he'd been working in construction, had grown tanned and sinewy and had dressed to show it. Now his olive skin seemed paler, crow's-feet branching out from the corners of his hooded eyes. His sandy brown hair wasn't tinged with gray yet, but the longer length covered for the way it now crept back from his temples. He wore a plain T-shirt, loose on his frame, and a belt cinching khaki hiking pants.

"I had a feeling that was you," he said. I felt his gaze wash over my face, probably taking in its own changes. The fullness of my early twenties giving way to angles as I aged. The dark hollows under my eyes had undoubtedly grown deeper overnight from not sleeping. The fear of not being able to contact Delilah shifting my expression, sharpening my demeanor.

"What the hell were you doing in my house?" I asked, full of self-righteousness.

His eyes shifted behind me for a moment, like he was checking to make sure we were alone.

"Your house?" he responded, a deep line forming between his brown eyes. "I wasn't." Then he spun the cigarette in his fingers, feigning casual. "Jesus, Beck. It's nice to see you, too."

I gritted my teeth. "I swear to God, Cliff, if you've been harassing—"

"Hey," he said, cutting me off, one arm out, inches from my own. He looked up and down the empty block. "I'm not . . . For fuck's sake, I'm not doing anything, and you can't just go throwing out accusations like that." As if the perception were worse than the crime.

I stared down at his hand, the way it hovered between us, faintly shaking. Like he was hiding something. But I realized he was the one afraid—of what I would say, that others might hear. As if I could ruin his act in one fell swoop. "*Really*. Then what the hell are you doing here?" I asked, spreading my arms wide. "On my street. Half a block from my parents' house."

He mirrored my gesture, sweeping his arms across the empty

lot. "Cleaning up. The insurance company is taking their sweet time with it, and all the trash is getting caught against my house in the wind. I could only take the view for so long."

I followed his gaze to the nearest window, where a layer of black marred the edge of the brick beneath it, though the glass had been wiped clean of the soot. A limp garbage bag rested against the base of the foundation, half filled.

"You live here?" I asked, taken aback.

He took a long drag from the cigarette, then nodded. "For the last couple months, at least, yeah. So you'll have to excuse my presence on the same street. It's out of my hands."

He'd managed to get himself to the heart of the place he'd once pretended to belong. A role on campus. A house on the old Fraternity Row.

He cleared his throat. "This is the part where you say, *Nice to see you, Cliff. Sorry for accusing you of breaking and entering. Been a long time. How've you been?*"

I shook my head, jarring myself back to the moment. "I didn't know you lived here. My parents didn't say."

He frowned. "Well, like I said, it's a recent development. Since right before school started. And it's not like your folks are really involved in the college minutiae anymore, are they."

I looked over my shoulder, up the road. "You didn't see anyone else around my place just now, did you?"

He followed my gaze. A lone black sedan was driving toward our position at the intersection, blinker on. "Can't say I was looking," he said. "You house-sitting for your parents or something? Heard they were gone on some long trip."

"In Peru," I said as the black car turned left, an older couple visible in the front seat. "A visiting lecturer assignment." It wasn't lost on me that he seemed to know more about them than they had known about him.

Cliff dropped his cigarette, grinding it into the sidewalk. I got a flash, then, of a glowing ember, and suddenly pictured Cliff out in the night, at this very spot, back in August—watching me in the dark.

"Did you see me out here, then?" I asked, dropping my voice. "During orientation, I mean."

He ran his tongue across the ridge of his teeth, thinking. "I remember I saw *someone* out here. I was just moving in. Didn't have your name front and center at the time."

He turned back to the empty plot. Wood and debris were scattered on the footprint of the foundation, outlined in cinder blocks. At least the dumpster had been removed.

"Were you here when it happened?" I asked, imagining the flames growing, catching.

He shook his head. "Hadn't finished moving in. I was promoted over the summer. The new role came with living arrangements." His hand twitched again. If anyone else would have a visceral reaction to a fire, it would be Cliff. Charlie Rivers and Micah White and Cliff had been friends since high school—maybe before. He'd probably been haunted by that night, too.

And now his view each morning was of a pile of ash and debris. I didn't blame him for wanting it gone.

"Cliff, I'm looking for my daughter. Have you seen her? Staying at the house, maybe?"

He blinked. "Delilah?" he asked, her name like music. Like he knew her. Knew everything I was desperate to uncover. I pictured him up on the desk chair in my room, black marker in hand—

And then he shook his head. "I've noticed a light on when I passed some nights. Assumed it was automated, honestly." A shrug.

Delilah in the house. Asking her father for money. What did she need? What was she running from?

I took a step closer, felt a tightening in my throat. "I can't reach her."

The line deepened between his eyes. Everything in his demeanor tightened—shoulders up, jaw tense. "Since when?"

"Last night. Since the howling." I felt myself tensing, the word like a portal to the past.

His shoulders relaxed. "It's just wind, Beckett. It's not the same anymore." But he didn't look at me as he said it. As if he hadn't once stalked me through the trees in the night, as a joke or not. He peered down at his watch. "It's been, what, half a day? She's probably sleeping off a hangover." He rolled his eyes for good measure.

"But you can check, right?" I asked. "You can check the cameras?" I knew they must've been positioned around campus for security.

"No," he said pointedly, "I can't. Only the campus police can do that, and only if there's an actual investigation."

"Oh, please. I'm sure you know *exactly* how to access—"

The front door of his neighbor's house swung open just before a stocky man in a ball cap stepped out.

"Jesus," Cliff said under his breath as his neighbor locked up behind him. "Just— Let's take this inside."

I followed Cliff up the concrete steps. Over the narrow door was a wide stretch of beige trim where Greek letters used to hang. Inside, the circular foyer gave way to a step-down living area to the right and a closed room to the left. Before me, a stairway led up to a visible balcony. Behind the stairs, the wood floor of the main level stretched down a long, dark hallway.

It was easy to see the ghost of what this place once was. The old fraternity homes here were small, operating more as a base of operation than a housing system. If these walls could talk, I imagined they would tell of decades of parties, of fights, of people stumbling through doorways. If I closed my eyes, I could almost smell the liquor, feel the sticky floor and the humidity of too many bodies pressed together in one space.

I shifted on my feet; I wasn't sure why he'd brought me in here—what he didn't want his neighbor to hear. "Can you . . . I need you to talk to the RA in Delilah's dorm. Her name is Raven something. She definitely knew something she wasn't saying. And I need to track down Delilah's friends—"

His eyes widened. "You can't go questioning students, Beckett. There are protocols, I told you."

"I'm asking as a favor, then. From an old friend."

He pressed his lips together, considering me. It was so much dimmer inside the house than out in the morning sun, and my eyes were adjusting to the change in perspective.

"An old friend," he repeated. "I had no idea."

It was true. We had never been friends. We had been drawn to each other as teenagers and, just as quickly, had fallen apart. Like me and Maggie. And here I was, trying to stake a claim to the past only when I needed it. Eventually we had been on opposing sides of a tragedy. Me, a friend of the suspect. Cliff, a friend of the victims. Whatever sense of obligation once existed between us, it was long gone.

He was messing with me, just like someone was messing around in my parents' house. He had information—something I wanted—and he could finally hold it over me. I could sense the power of it radiating off him, like when he'd caught me in the woods during the howling my freshman year.

"I saw you, you know," I said, and watched as his demeanor slowly changed, the corners of his mouth pulling down first. "In the bell tower. At orientation. Like you were up there watching everyone."

He let out a single incredulous laugh. "I wasn't *watching,* Beckett. The automation system's broken, so I had to set it off manually during orientation. We're still trying to get it serviced, in case you haven't noticed."

I hadn't. I'd heard the bell tower the night we arrived in Wyatt Valley, and I'd heard it during orientation, the noise drawing my attention that way in the first place. But he was right—if I gave it any thought, I hadn't heard it any time throughout this morning. There was nothing to wake the students. No chime marking the hours from nine a.m. to eight p.m. It had been the soundtrack to my first twenty-one years of life.

A dull thud came from somewhere upstairs, and my head jerked up, every muscle on high alert.

"My cat," he said as an orange tabby peered down at us from between the slats of the hall balcony. And then he sighed. "All right, come on." He gestured me toward the closed door on the side of the foyer. "What else are old friends for?"

Behind the door, inside his office, I knew, were things I was not supposed to see. The blinds were kept closed, so the wood-paneled walls seemed even darker, like we were stepping into the past. The two wide-screen monitors side by side on his desk, connected to a laptop—as if he were keeping an eye on things after all. And the photo on the windowsill of a young boy, five or six, with side-swept blond hair.

Cliff took the seat behind his desk. "My son," he said, noticing me looking. "He's with his mother right now." *His mother.* Sounded like a divorce. My eyes drifted to Cliff's bare hand: no ring.

He shifted the photo before opening his laptop, as if warning me it wasn't up for discussion. Maybe I'd read him wrong. Maybe *this* was why he was letting me see what he knew. He was a parent, too. Maybe these were fears he could understand—the nightmare of things that could happen when you weren't paying attention.

He gestured for me to sit in the gray love seat against the wall, but I thought he was trying to keep me back while he entered the log-in information. Now I wondered if it was even his.

"I'm doing this as a favor," he said, in warning. As if there were things he was worried about, too. A threat I had implied: Cliff Simmons in the bell tower. Cliff Simmons accessing the cameras.

A rumor I might be capable of spreading: *Dean Simmons is watching.*

Right now, I didn't even care if he *was* doing something he shouldn't be. Right now, the more he could see, the better.

The glow of the large monitors turned his face an unnatural hue in the dimly lit room. "Like I said," he began, eyes skimming the screen, "I can't access the cameras. I *can* check the card scans. But that's it. Anything else needs to go through campus police."

How many students thought themselves untraceable, not realizing someone could track their every move?

"Here we go," he said, and I stood from the love seat, stepping closer. "She entered Beckett Hall just before midnight last night." He looked away from the monitor, up at me, face stoic.

"That's it?"

He swiveled the monitor so it was facing me. Delilah's identifying details were listed at the top: *Bowery, Delilah. Class of 2029*. He placed his thumb directly on the screen, beside the time stamp from Friday night, so I would know he wasn't lying.

"That's her last card scan," he said. "But if she was with someone else, her card wouldn't necessarily be used."

"She could've also been using her phone to get inside, right?" I asked. It was the first thing she had set up during orientation. A newer technology than we'd had as students.

His eyes cut to me. "Yes, they have the card programmed in their phones, too. This system doesn't tell us which she used."

"What was she doing over there at midnight?" I asked. Beckett Hall was an academic and administrative building. It would've been empty in the evening.

"I have no idea. Studying? There's a library on the second floor." He raised an eyebrow, as if he knew it was unlikely on a Friday night. "Look, she's fine. This was barely eleven hours ago. She's not missing, Beckett."

But I was already picturing her running across campus in the night. Hiding. Desperately holding her phone in front of her to gain access to the locked building. Heading to a place I'd once told her about, to get away—

"Cliff, do you have a key to the tunnels?" I asked.

He stared at me, unblinking, and there was something dark and dangerous hovering between us. "No," he said slowly. "Do *you*?"

I shook my head.

"Half of the entrances are sealed off now anyway," he said, throat moving as he swallowed. "They don't connect all the buildings like they used to."

The dancing beam of a flashlight in front of me, leading the way through the tunnels. Nervous laughter in the dark, footsteps echoing—

I shook off the memory. "Can you do me a favor?" I asked.

"That *was* the favor," he said, deadpan. His gaze lingered. The droll humor bridging the time, softening the moment.

"Bryce Wharton." I'd seen him returning from the woods this morning; I wanted to know if he'd also been out on campus, roaming through the same buildings.

"What about him?" he said.

"Can you see if he was with her?"

He turned the monitor away from view. "I absolutely cannot. Look, if you want the campus police to investigate, they will, if she's really missing. But it seems to me she could be doing any number of things. Come on, Beck, we were that age once." He smiled slightly, and I imagined we were thinking the same thing—the way I once sneaked him into that library off hours, when no one was around. Already kissing him as I pulled him into the vacant study room.

I shook my head. The dropped call. The writing on my bedroom walls. The intruder in my parents' house. "I think something's happening here," I said, raw and honest. "This isn't like her."

He pinched the bridge of his nose, squeezing his eyes shut for a moment. "Okay, look," he began, voice low. "I'm a dean of students. I do know she had some trouble with her living situation. Put in a request to be moved. We couldn't grant it." He raised his arms in an exaggerated shrug. "That's the gist of it. I haven't heard anything since. I assume everything worked itself out."

"She asked for a new roommate?" Maybe that was what Raven couldn't tell me.

"Actually, she wanted to be moved from the entire *dorm*."

God, how bad had it been? I couldn't believe she hadn't told me. I'd felt that same cold shock when the acceptance letter had arrived, realizing there were secrets she had learned to keep from me.

I thought of the calls she made late at night as she was walking home. Like she was afraid to return. Like she was waiting for me to say something, to ask the right question—

"We're at full capacity," he continued. "But she's okay. Freshmen can take a while to settle. I think she's getting along fine in her classes, and I see her eating lunch with a group. Plus, she seems to be pretty comfortable off campus. Reminds me a little of you, honestly."

"You're watching her," I said. I hadn't been wrong about that.

"I've kept an eye on her," he corrected.

"Why?"

"Because she's yours, Beck. Why do you think?" He shook his head with a look that managed to cut straight to the heart. "I'll talk to campus security. If they think she could really be missing and isn't just, you know, being eighteen, you'll be the first to know. I promise." He reached over the desk. "Your phone?"

I handed it to him, watched as he input his number. Like we'd met in a bar and he was connecting us for a hopeful would-be date. But this wasn't flirtatious. I felt nothing but panic.

"So you know where to reach me," he said. It occurred to me he probably had my contact all along: It was in the system, listed under Delilah's personal information.

I jutted my chin toward his computer once more. "Can you get me Violet's address?"

His eyes slowly slid my way again. "Excuse me?"

"Violet Wharton. She's not one of your students. There's no conflict of interest."

He set his jaw. "Joseph Wharton is a big developer in the area, Beckett. I don't need any enemies here."

I leaned on his desk, fingertips tingling. "I *know* it's public information and that she's somewhere up in the Estates. I can search it online when I'm back on Wi-Fi, but I figure it's right there in front of you. I won't say it came from you."

I knew I was pushing it—that I'd far exceeded the limits of any claim to friendship—but he took a deep breath as his fingers flew across the keypad. He took a sticky note, wrote the address down, pulled it off the pad.

"Listen, don't go messing around on campus anymore without permission. I'll liaise with security, get back to you."

He sounded like a stranger. Like he was playing some role again. Maybe playing me.

"You're going to *liaise,*" I repeated sharply, and noticed him flinch. As if I'd broken through, finally cracked the shell. Everything shifted then. A mask sliding over the casualness between us.

He stood slowly. "Let's make a deal," he said in a low voice. "You don't treat me like I'm an idiot, and I won't treat you like you're a liar whose parents sent you out of the country to get you away from the investigation."

I clenched my jaw, stepped back. How easy it was to cut back to the past with a single sentence. But he had it wrong.

"That's not what happened," I said. "The *school* practically kicked me out." *After* my interview with Fred Mayhew.

He rolled his eyes. "I find that hard to believe. That's not how we do things—"

"Oh, were you *here* then? Want me to show you the letter? It's probably at my parents' place in some file. They made me take a leave of absence. I had no *choice,* Cliff."

He put up a hand. "I'm just saying. Old perceptions aren't the nicest, are they. Let's not assume the worst about each other, huh?"

Cliff handed me the sticky note, the corner of his mouth slightly raised. I took the address and slid it into my back pocket, not breaking eye contact.

For all that he insisted about old perceptions, he looked at me like he could see right through me.

Like twenty years of time didn't matter at all.

CHAPTER 13

Saturday, October 4
12:00 p.m.

As I walked back to my parents' home, I felt some long-dormant part of me coming back alive, as if I'd thawed and something else had been set free.

I had always been a person who made quick and finite decisions, who didn't waver. Who knew what she wanted and took the steps to make it happen. Who wasn't afraid to go it alone. All those parts had always been there and had been fine-tuned to their most efficient form in adulthood.

But I had been other things, too. Before I learned to mask my thoughts, to keep my own secrets. Before I learned to hide behind someone else's words, worried what other people might discover in my own.

Maybe we didn't become something in adulthood so much as *unbecome*.

But I felt it all now: the remembrance of who I used to be. The person who did not care for rules, who paid no heed to expectations. Who did not wait for permission or approval.

The one who wanted to be seen, and followed, and feared.

Someone had been in my house. Not Delilah and not Cliff. It was possible my parents had entrusted a neighbor with a key in their absence. Someone who could bring in the mail, provide access in an emergency. I'd ask them when I had a chance to get on email, before I falsely accused someone else of breaking and entering. But I was skeptical.

For now, I assumed that whoever it was had been spooked as much by my presence as I had been by theirs. I had a plan, a series of steps I would take before Trevor's arrival, to make progress, keep busy, prevent my mind from spiraling any further.

Cliff had promised to talk to campus police, but that would take time. And time, I knew, was the critical factor.

It was noon. Ten hours since the dropped call. Twelve hours since she'd entered Beckett Hall.

I closed my eyes and pictured her running through the dark hall, the sound of her footsteps echoing in a trail, leading straight to her—

Bryce was my only lead to understanding what might have happened last night. And maybe even before. Violet was my way to Bryce.

And now I had her address.

The gate to my parents' backyard was still hanging slightly ajar. I secured it and then entered the house through the front door. The screen was shut, but the front door hadn't fully latched behind me in my rush out of the house.

I needed to grab my keys, to keep moving. But something was off in the kitchen. My purse was out on the table, wallet beside it. Everything emptied to dry out, as I'd left it. I'd assumed whoever was in here had noticed my bag, realized someone was home, and quickly left.

I approached the table, drawn closer, tallying the items. Then noticed what wasn't there.

The mask was gone.

I circled the table in case I'd missed something, then dug my hands into my bag, pulling out old gum wrappers, crumpled receipts. No mask.

Whoever had been in here hadn't just noticed my purse and fled.

They'd taken the mask with them.

My ears were ringing with a high-pitched frequency. I had assumed whoever was in here had been spooked by my presence. I had hoped the realization that this house was occupied would be enough to deter their return.

But they'd taken the mask. And they must've realized I'd find it missing.

The mask was proof that something had happened out at Cryer's Quarry. That kids had been running through the night just like we had done years ago.

Proof that, despite what Cliff said, the tradition wasn't dead—that it had merely taken on a new form.

But now the mask was gone. The trail was disappearing as fast as I'd uncovered it.

I returned my wallet and car keys to my bag. I didn't have a key to the house—but someone else clearly did. I couldn't even lock up behind me and return without climbing through a window. And what was even the point, if there was someone out there with a key?

I remembered a trick from when I was in middle school. When I believed my mother had been snooping through my room, looking at my journals—before I'd learned to hide things more carefully. I'd leave a piece of tape on the upper edge of my bedroom door, out of sight. Something someone hopefully wouldn't notice as they sneaked inside. Something I could check before entering again myself.

Now I rummaged through the kitchen junk drawer, which held an assortment of supplies—scissors, scotch tape, open matchbook, pads of paper, pens. I took the tape with me to the back of the house, then stood on my toes, adding two strips to the upper edge of the door. Then I locked it for good measure.

I decided to leave the front door unlocked. I was worried that if anyone was going to call the cops on someone in the house, it would be me climbing through the window off the front porch.

I slung my purse on my shoulder, took the last strips of tape with me out the front, and carefully adhered them to the outside of the screen door, crossing the top of the black metal frame.

It wasn't perfect, but it would have to do.

The entrance to the Estates was a few miles out of downtown, where the roads wove up into the mountains. On the Whartons' designated street, the houses on my right were set just above the road, while the ones on the left were barely visible, built into the sloping landscape below.

The address Cliff had written on the sticky note led me to a house above—part modern, part contemporary, a blend of wood and metal; large black-trimmed windows and a traditional peaked roof. I turned up the steep driveway, weaving through the trees.

A black SUV was parked outside the garage, and someone had planted a shock of colorful flowers in a mulch bed surrounding the front steps. If anyone noticed my arrival from behind the walls of glass, they made no indication of it.

A text message came through as I parked—I guessed there was some sort of cellular service accommodation for those up in the mountains of the Estates. Closer to both God and satellite.

Trevor: *Halfway there. Any updates?*

I responded while I had the chance: *School security is looking into it. Checking cameras. Seeing if they can track where she went.*

Even though I wasn't sure whether Cliff believed Delilah was missing, I knew it was his job to move it up the chain.

Trevor responded immediately: *ETA 2 hours. Call if you hear anything please.*

I peered up at the Wharton place. No signs of movement. *Meet you at the house,* I wrote back. *Save the directions before you hit the town. You'll lose service when you get close.*

And then I stepped out of the car and walked across the Whartons' front yard.

Even the front door was made of glass, so I could see directly inside their open living space as I pressed the doorbell, waiting.

Eventually a man appeared from around the corner, with a slightly hunched posture, so he seemed not much taller than I was, at five-six. If this was Joseph Wharton, he didn't seem nearly as intimidating as Cliff had made him out to be when warning me that this was someone he didn't need to make an enemy of.

The man greeted me wearing a polo, gym shorts, white socks, and a single white earbud in one ear, as if he'd been in a virtual meeting. He peered first at my car and then at me. "Can I help you?"

"I'm looking for Violet?" I said. "I'm Beckett. Our kids are in school together."

He blinked twice, frowning. I guessed he was at least a decade older than Violet, maybe more. His hair was more salt than pepper and overlong at the edges—like that of a tech kid who hadn't realized he'd grown up.

"Sure, sure," he said, beckoning me inside. "I think she's out back."

The inside of the house was as immaculate as the exterior. The open front area encompassed the living and dining rooms, along with the kitchen—and nothing was out on the counters or the sofa. It looked like a page from a catalog. Professional family photos lined the walls, stretching back in time in black and white. Here, I could see the story of Violet's life: two sons, a husband, and a dog; a destination wedding at the beach, barefoot and understated in a form-fitting slip dress and a strand of pearls, smiling at the same man currently leading me through their home.

From inside their living room, I could see straight through the large glass sliding doors to a wooden porch and the trees beyond.

Joseph Wharton slid open the back door, gesturing for me to exit. From the deck, I could see through the iron railings to a small circle of grass with a swing set. Violet stood at the edge of the woods, behind the swing set, perfectly still as the branches swayed above her. She was staring into the trees in a way that unsettled me. That made me think she'd heard something. Like the wind was whispering something to her, drawing her closer.

"Vi!" the man called. "You have company."

She startled, then turned as her husband slid the door shut behind me.

Violet's hair was pulled back into a short, tight ponytail, and she seemed disoriented, not that I blamed her.

"Hi," I said, descending the steps, like it would be perfectly normal for me to drop in on her. *Old friends.* Like Cliff.

"Beckett?" she asked, though it must've been clear by now.

"Sorry, I didn't have your number to call first."

She tilted her head, clearly confused by my presence here. "Just one sec . . ." she began, holding up a hand as she turned back to the woods, waiting.

These were the same woods that eventually bled into town and surrounded the campus, miles in the distance.

"Joey!" she called.

"Coming," a boy called back, his voice faint under the wind.

And then I saw them: a young boy with a stick in hand, walking beside a black Lab not on a leash. Both of them meandering through the trees, back toward home.

Violet smiled, rubbing the boy's mop of brown hair as he passed. "I told you not to go farther than I can see," she said. He looked to be in elementary school, before the growth spurt of gangly limbs that had overtaken his brother.

"I didn't notice," he said. "Sorry."

"Go on inside," Violet said, pushing him along. "And please feed Oscar."

"I didn't mean to interrupt your weekend," I said, watching them enter the lower level of the house, beneath the deck. It seemed Violet and I were staying put, behind the swing set. "It's just, it's urgent, and I didn't know where else to go."

She frowned slightly, though her face didn't move much. She seemed dressed for a day of work around the house, in an oversize camo T-shirt and black leggings. "*What's* urgent? What are you doing here, Beckett?"

My hand went to the base of my neck, where I could feel the rapid-fire pulse, the words I had to say again and again, making them real. "I can't find Delilah," I said.

Her mouth opened as she reached to the space between us. "Since when?"

It was the same question Cliff had asked, like they needed to confirm the details before knowing how to proceed. Decide whether this was worth their panic or their empathy—or whether I was being unreasonable.

"Her call dropped in the middle of the night, and I haven't been able to get back in touch. Not by phone or text or email or social media, which is really not like her. She hasn't been in her dorm. I don't know if I'm panicking for no reason, and I just thought your son might . . ." I swallowed. "I thought Bryce might have some information that could point me in the right direction."

She stared back at me, hazel eyes wide and glassy, then jarred herself back to the moment. "Of course. My God." She nodded vigorously, then pulled her cell phone from the side pocket of her leggings. She held the phone to her ear, still staring right at me. "Hi, sorry, did I wake you?"

It had been only a few hours since I'd seen him running back to his dorm. He must've been jolted from sleep.

"Everything's fine," she said. "But I'm standing here with Delilah's mom, remember we met her at orientation?" A pause. "Right. She's wondering if you've seen Delilah recently. She hasn't been able to get ahold of her." She nodded at whatever her son was saying on the other end. "Can I put you on the line with her?"

She tapped the phone, triggering the video, and Bryce's face suddenly filled the frame. Violet held the phone between us, and she moved closer, shoulder pressing into mine. Bryce was lounging in bed, one arm behind his head.

"Hey," he said, as Violet tilted the camera my way. "Sorry, I haven't seen her, but we're not exactly friends."

His voice was slightly hoarse, and he jostled the phone as he spoke, like he was repositioning himself in bed.

I nodded in understanding. "Thanks for talking to me, Bryce. I spoke to administration, and they mentioned she'd tried to change dorms. It's a small school, thought you might've heard what happened . . ."

He looked off to the side, and I imagined someone else in the room with him. Another freshman boy who might know something. Who might *say* something. Bryce shifted so he was sitting upright, phone held at a more manageable distance. "Yeah . . ." he began, dragging out the word. "She accused her roommate of theft or something? She was cleared, but that obviously didn't go over well." He shrugged. "Hana says she's basically got a single now."

Things going missing from her room. A reason to want a new living arrangement. But Cliff said she'd wanted out of the entire dorm, not only her room.

"Do you know the numbers for her friends? Gen? Sierra?"

His dark eyebrows knitted together. "Sorry, Ms. Bowery," he said, drawing out our last name. "I really don't. Like I said, we don't really run in the same circles."

I nodded, and Violet said, "Thanks, hon," like she was about to disconnect.

"One more thing," I said, hand around her wrist, keeping the phone steady between us. "Security scans showed that she entered

Beckett Hall last night, just before midnight. Do you have any idea what she'd be doing there?"

His jaw shifted, then tightened slightly as his eyes slid to the side—maybe to his roommate, maybe to nothing. "I don't, really. But if she wasn't getting along with her roommate, maybe she went there to study," he said.

"You didn't see her out on campus at all last night?"

"Nah, sorry, we ordered pizzas in the dorm last night. Had some friends over. I haven't been out since my classes yesterday."

My stomach dropped.

He was lying. Lying to his mother or lying to me.

I stared directly into the phone screen, like a dare. Debating whether to say something else, back him into a corner and push.

"We appreciate your help," Violet said, pulling the phone closer. "Do me a favor and call if you hear anything, though?"

"Sure thing," he said to his mother before the screen went black.

Violet took a deep breath in and out, staring into the woods again. "I don't know what to say, Beck. I'm really hoping everything's okay and this is just kids being kids. You know what it used to be like."

I nodded. It was a line people kept repeating to me.

"Let me get your number. If Bryce hears anything, I'll pass it along."

We exchanged contacts, and she led me up the rock steps in the side yard back to my car. At the front, through the large glass windows, I thought I saw a shadow inside—a man, presumably Joseph Wharton, watching from the center of the room, standing perfectly still.

Violet didn't seem to notice. "Listen, Beckett, could it be she just isn't answering your calls?"

"No," I said, "she wouldn't do that."

Violet raised an eyebrow. A jab she was making even now. "Kids do all sorts of things," she said. She grabbed my arm, squeezed. "I'm sure she'll turn up."

I walked for the car, shaken. By Bryce's lie, and the husband in the window, and Violet's implications.

As parents, we're afraid that our children can be stolen from us—by people, by ideas, by careless choices. We don't consider that they might choose to leave.

But they do. I knew this well. Sometimes they do.

CHAPTER 14

Saturday, October 4
2:00 p.m.

The road cut sharply on the descent back to town. I kept seeing movement out of the corner of my eye; I'd brace for an animal only to turn my attention to a swaying branch, a sweep of leaves, tall grass moving against the pavement in an optical illusion.

I pictured someone running through the woods in the night, darting into the street, waving for help. A car barreling forward. The screech of brakes, eyes wide open in terror, hand out. *Stop—*

I shook my head, shook off the thought, tried to stop the spiral. I wasn't seeing clearly.

I needed to eat. Or I needed to sleep. Maybe a shower, to wake up. I wasn't sure which, only that my body was hitting a wall. It seemed supremely unfair that I would require human necessities at a time like this. I swung by a drive-through on the way back toward downtown and picked up some extras for Trevor, who would likely be arriving soon.

My stomach twisted with every glance at the dashboard clock. Almost twelve hours since her dropped call. I might've been panicking unnecessarily when I first left my house. I might've convinced myself I was overreacting at her dorm in the early morning. But Delilah should be up by now, if she were tucked in somewhere safely on campus. She would want food—she was always stumbling down for breakfast before she was even conscious enough to hold a conversation.

She would be desperate to get online even if her phone was broken. Maybe especially then.

She would've seen my messages. She would've known I was looking for her. She would've found a way to reach out, let me know she was safe.

Twelve hours, I knew, was too long.

I passed the turnoff to Maggie's house, then the spot where I'd stood once, tracing the ridgeline. The spot where Delilah also must've visited, to take the picture she'd posted on Instagram.

Maggie may not have heard from her, but Delilah had been right here, so close.

On impulse, I called Maggie again, leaving the phone on speaker. This time she picked up immediately—like she'd been waiting.

"Maggie, I still can't find her," I said, voice tight. I needed help. Trevor. The campus police. Her. "I really think something's wrong."

After a pause, she said, "Bill volunteers with the fire department. He might have more ideas about where the kids hang out these days." Bill, her husband, whom I'd never met.

"Thank you," I said.

"Beckett . . ." she began, then stopped.

"What?"

"It might be nothing, but I heard it last night." I knew what she was about to say. I could hear it, too, in my memory. "It was the first howling of the year."

Cliff might've brushed me off, but Maggie confirmed it.

I was right to be worried. I wasn't the only one thinking it.

As I parked on my parents' street once more, I felt the possibilities of Delilah's whereabouts dwindling in a way that tightened my chest, stole my breath. I closed my eyes and reminded myself that right now, if Cliff kept his word, campus security would be reviewing the cameras at school. If there was reason to panic, they would call.

I approached the front door cautiously, eyes focused on the top of the screen door. I ran my finger along the seam, where the tape was still firmly adhered to both edges of the frame. The screen door hadn't been opened since I'd left. I peeled the tape away, then let myself inside the unlocked front door.

I stood in the foyer, listening—and heard nothing. I believed I was alone, but I checked to make sure no one had entered through the back door in my absence, either: The tape was secure there, too.

In the kitchen, I ate as quickly as I could, then stored the rest of the food for Trevor. But when I stopped moving, I heard something whistling from up the back steps, like a window had been left open.

It had been shut, I was sure of it.

I stared at the dark steps behind the kitchen, then slowly headed that way. My hands braced against the walls of the narrow stairwell as I climbed. The whistling was louder here, coming from the bathroom. I peered inside: The door to the attic entrance was fully ajar.

The sound of the wind was coming from the attic, where it whistled through the gaps, unprotected by the insulation of the house. I shone my phone light inside, as if someone might've been hiding in the corners, then pulled the door shut firmly—the noise dissipating.

I couldn't remember whether I'd left the attic door open in my rush.

Still I could hear the whistle of the wind, shuddering against the windows, taunting me.

I poked my head into my parents' bedroom downstairs, where the bed was perfectly made with hospital corners. Their bathroom right outside, with a window to the side yard. Locked.

My father's office, where I'd accidentally left the window unsecured over orientation.

I pivoted to the hallway outside my father's office—there was one more place to check, to be sure: the basement. Though my mother preferred to call it the laundry room.

I flipped the switch just inside the hall door, and the overhead lighting below flickered once before catching.

The wooden steps were painted gray but otherwise unfinished, with a small railing on either side. When I was younger, I used to get vertigo standing at the top, looking down.

I didn't have much cause to ever be down here; this was my mother's space. The only time I'd venture down the steps was to play around with the old dumbwaiter. It led from the kitchen to the basement, with a cabinet built directly into the cinder-block wall. We never used it other than in jest—sending laundry up and down for the novelty of it.

I always thought there was a darker history here, inside the walls of our house. Why else would someone need to deliver food to a basement? But my father said I had it backward: a chef's kitchen in the basement, food sent to the residents above. I wasn't so sure. There was no evidence of that setup now.

The washer and dryer were tucked against the far concrete wall. Several wooden posts extended from the floor to the ceiling throughout the space, supporting the house. My mother had added stand-up metal shelving for laundry baskets and cleaning supplies, with bins for spare linens and old three-ring binders full of her years of lesson plans. On the top shelf was an antique mantel clock that didn't seem to be in working order.

I retraced my steps to the main floor, flipped the light switch, and shut the door. I was sure: The house was secure.

I heard Trevor's car before I saw it—the hum of an engine crawling slowly along the street. Pausing, house by house, before continuing on. I went out to raise a hand at his dark blue sedan and felt a surge of relief as I walked his way.

His gaze caught mine over the hood as he exited the car, and I could see everything I was currently feeling mirrored back. Dark circles under his light blue eyes; hair, shaggy and unstyled in his rush to leave, starting to turn gray along the sides; athletic clothes thrown on haphazardly, in mismatched shades of charcoal, though I imagined he had showered after his run before hitting the road. He was broad-shouldered and tapered like an athlete still. His expression was pure vulnerability—something I'd seen only once before.

"Thank you for coming," I said, my throat unexpectedly tight. I could feel the tears coming and fought to stop them. Once they started, I knew, they wouldn't stop. I didn't think, just fell into his chest, and his arms wrapped around me in a tight squeeze.

"Of course I came," he said, the words a shudder in his chest as he tucked his head over mine.

Here was the only person who would care as much, fear as much, give as much to find her. Who would immediately get into his car and drive, to look himself.

Ever since Delilah was born, she'd been the conduit between us. She'd run to him for a hug while I'd stand back and watch her circle her arms around his neck, swing off his shoulders, rub her palm against the dark stubble of his jaw.

Until now, I realized, that was as close as we ever got, since I left London—and him. Even in the hospital two days after Delilah was born, when he'd taken a plane across the Atlantic and then a taxi straight from the airport, his hand had hovered over my shoulder before he thought better of touching me. His thumb had moved instead to Delilah's cheek, where she was swaddled in my arms.

Now I felt his arms tense, his posture straighten. "Anything new since our last call?" he asked.

I pulled back from him, shaken. "No, sorry. I've been driving around, checking in with people who might have had contact. I went to the dorm. To another parent. To the dean of students and an old friend." I was talking too fast, the words spilling out, and I could tell he was trying to process, to keep up. "No one's seen her yet. But campus security is supposed to be checking now."

"Good, good," he said, nodding. His eyes looked bloodshot, his gaze slightly disoriented. I noticed his throat move as he looked down the street, straight toward campus, and I realized he was seeing it all for the first time: the mountains in the distance, and the trees stretching toward infinity. All the places his daughter might be.

He took a sharp breath, then reached into his backseat. He swung a backpack over his shoulder, grabbed a weekender bag by the handles. He was prepared, of course. He was always prepared.

Trevor was the person, I imagined, anyone would call in an emergency. Even-tempered, possibly to a fault. He rarely raised his voice, never let emotions escalate the stakes of an argument. He didn't fight—not with you; but, in my experience, not *for* you, either.

He'd been a planner since the day I met him. It was one of the many things I had liked about him, especially because I'd gotten to know him at a time when my life had felt unfamiliar, without form or direction. He had an uncommon blend of responsibility and adventure, with a wide-open heart that he wore proudly on his sleeve, something I found both disarming and endearing. But I never had to guess what he was thinking. I never had to guess which parts of him were real. And he was always planning: to see me again; to show me things around the city. And more: He'd told me his plans for the semester, for the summer, for his career.

Delilah had been the ultimate unexpected twist. I supposed I had been, too. In hindsight, I should've given him some more time, some more grace. But I couldn't forgive his first reaction; I don't think I wanted to. He'd asked me to stay once and only once—before I left for home for Thanksgiving. He wore the same expression as now, like he was all exposed nerves. He'd made a mistake, he said; he could make it work—make us work—if I stayed. But by then I was already showing, and it felt like the offer was made under duress. I needed to trust myself. I was also naive. So very, very stubborn. I said no. And he silently watched me pack instead.

Now Trevor followed me inside the house and placed his bags along the wall beside the living room, just as my cell rang from the pocket of my joggers.

I felt my eyes widen—saw his expression mirroring my own.

My hand shook as I pulled out the phone. *Cliff Simmons*. "It's the dean," I said, answering the call.

"Hello?" I could hear my heartbeat echoing in my skull in the half second of silence.

"Beckett, it's Cliff. We haven't found her yet." I let out a sigh, shook my head at Trevor. "But I'm with the campus police, and they're compiling the footage from last night right now. We'd like to invite you in for a meeting at their office at four-thirty, so we can discuss how best to proceed. Make sure we have all the relevant information. Keep you in the loop."

That was over an hour away. An hour of lost time. "Okay," I said. "Four-thirty, see you then."

"Same place it's always been," he added before hanging up.

I bit my lip as I turned to Trevor, felt my mouth turning dry. "Nothing yet. Campus police are setting a meeting."

"Four-thirty," Trevor repeated, nodding once. "Is there a place I can set up my things in the meantime? And change?"

I nodded to the room behind him. "My father's office. Don't mind the decor."

He picked up his bags again, then his eyes trailed down my body—to the long-sleeved waffle shirt and joggers, which were barely a step above my pajamas. "Have you had a chance to take a breath?" he asked. Probably meaning: to sleep; to shower.

"There's been no time," I said, feeling a tremble in my hands.

He frowned. "There's nothing else you can do before the meeting. I'll make some calls in the meantime."

I nodded, then watched as he slipped into the office, shutting the double doors that didn't quite seal or latch.

He was right. I had to get ready. Shower, change, make myself presentable for the meeting.

Make them show me everything. Make them help me find her.

I showered in the downstairs bathroom attached to my parents' room, where two beige towels hung perfectly side by side. I was lucky they hadn't turned off the hot water.

When I emerged in the jeans and black button-down I'd hastily thrown in my bag in the middle of the night, I heard Trevor talking on the phone in the office.

I pushed one of the doors open, feigned knocking while he quickly waved me inside. He was sitting behind my father's wide cherry desk, the line of masks on the wall beside him like they were peering down at him.

Trevor's laptop was open, and he had a lined notepad beside him, dark writing in list form.

"Bowery," he repeated to whomever was on the other end. "She's eighteen. Five-seven, with wavy dark brown hair."

I approached the desk, saw what he'd been writing. It was a list of nearby hospitals and phone numbers, most already with a line through them.

"Thanks for your help," he said, and hung up.

"I hadn't thought of that," I said.

He drew a dark line through the last name on the list. "Well, it was a dead end. But a good one to be able to cross off." He turned to his laptop, where he pulled up a map, searching for more possibilities in the area.

"How are you online?" I asked, wondering if he had some sort of portable Internet tech with him.

He frowned at me, then gestured to the side of the desk. "I plugged in the modem underneath."

I leaned down and saw the black box with a series of green lights flashing. "I thought my parents called to turn off the Wi-Fi," I said, confused. My mother had made a big show of it when we were here for orientation.

"It doesn't seem like they did," Trevor responded with a small smile.

I let out an exasperated sigh. Both at them and at myself for not checking. I plopped on the futon across from the desk, pulling my legs up to the side, and connected my phone to their local network.

The first thing I did was check Delilah's Instagram again, trying to see into her past, pull any insight from her world.

I opened the last image she'd posted with the mountains in the distance and the caption: *Here*.

I searched through her list of friends for anyone named Sierra or Gen—the two names I heard most often.

Nothing came up for Sierra, but searching the list of followers for Gen pulled up a private account. The profile picture was of a girl holding a bucket hat over a head of very curly hair, her mouth open in feigned shock. A theater kid if I ever saw one.

I couldn't send a message since the account was set to private, but I took a screenshot of her picture. A place to start. Something to pass along to the campus police.

Then I opened the latest email from my parents and sent a reply.

> *Mom/Dad: Did you give someone else your spare key? I'm in town and couldn't find the key out back.*

I debated telling them more but figured it was better to wait. What would they do with the information other than panic, separated by time and distance with nothing at all they could do but ask me for continual updates? Or they'd say: *Beckett, please, you're overreacting.* I wasn't sure which I preferred.

I sent the message, then clicked the next one down, about the memoir. It had been sent last night, after I'd gone to bed. Before my world had shifted on its axis.

So nice to finally hear back from you, Beckett. The project is a firsthand witness account of a crime—unresolved, decades old, in a small town. You understand, of course, the need for privacy and sensitivity. The timing is urgent. We can come to you; pls send your availability ASAP.

By the time I finished reading, the hairs had risen on the back of my neck. The details were vague—vague enough for me to potentially see something in it that might not exist.

Crime, unresolved, decades old. Small town.
You understand, of course—
The timing is urgent.

I closed the message, tossed the phone onto the futon beside me.

Trevor looked up from the laptop screen. "Everything okay?"

"Yeah. Just reached out to my parents." I forced a tight grin.

He came around the desk, sat beside me so that I could feel the warmth of him—something he wanted to say. "The police are involved, Beckett. Let's give it a minute, okay?" He reached a hand for my shoulder, squeezed it gently in reassurance.

As if he could see me on the cusp, about to completely fall apart.

"Yeah," I said. "I'm trying." But I left the room, filled a glass at the kitchen sink, trying to shake the unsettling chill.

Witness account. We had all been witnesses. There were witnesses the night of the howling, and a bar full of witnesses the weekend before. I wondered how many still lived here. How many knew I'd come back.

Maybe it wasn't Delilah being targeted here but me. Maybe she was just an extension of the effort—the clearest way to hurt me the most.

Someone had been trying to reach me. I'd had three emails from them before I noticed. Maybe they'd seen me here in August, down at the Low Bar. Maybe they were still angry. And when they were unable to get my attention, they started targeting my daughter instead—

I imagined a shadowy figure sneaking into the dorm, stealing her things. Taking the key to my parents' house, writing the threatening words on my wall. Following her in the night while she tried to hide out in Beckett Hall—

"Ready?" Trevor asked, from the entrance of the kitchen.

I nodded. "I'll meet you in the car."

After I heard the screen door shut behind him, I pulled another fresh piece of tape from the drawer to secure the house on the way out.

BEFORE:
THE LOW BAR

Adalyn and I met Charlie Rivers and Micah White down at the Low Bar on a Friday night in late October. The revving of their engine caught the attention of the entire room, and we watched them pull up in a shiny black F-150 through the murky front windows.

They were a few years older, and I knew them, of course. I knew them from Cryer's Quarry. From my time dating Cliff in high school.

But we weren't friends. We were people who once coexisted in the same time and place, and even then there was something about them that made me nervous. It was the way they moved together, as a pair, and seemed to think the same thing, an idea ricocheting before gaining force—not unlike the connection Adalyn and I had.

By the night I saw them at the bar, enough time had passed that it was as if we had never known one another at all.

We were seniors behind the gates of Wyatt College, traipsing down the hill for a taste of something different. They were six years out of high school, working construction. They smelled of manual labor—tar and diesel and tobacco and sweat. Their bodies had been chiseled by it all, rough hands and thick arms and sun-scorched skin. They downed mugs of beer like it was water and they were dying of thirst. Cliff had just started working with the crew; his old friends had gotten him in at a time of need.

When Adalyn approached them, pointed toward me by the dartboard, and said, "How about it? You have what it takes? She's got the best aim in the valley," they pretended not to know me. That's how far the chasm had grown.

Even Cliff looked into his drink, then up at me with a head tilt. Well?

I hadn't interacted with him since that night in the woods during the freshman-year howling. But he must've remembered how good I was—must've remembered losing to me often on the dartboard in my backyard.

Micah strode toward me, and I shook his hand, rough and strong. He turned my arm over, pulled it closer, and I watched his gaze trail to my wrist, finger on the pulse of the mountains. He raised one eyebrow as if asking: Who do you think you are?

That night, there was a bar full of witnesses who saw me lose, and not on purpose—my hand faintly trembling while I tried to steady my aim. Who then saw Adalyn double down, raise the pot. Who saw me lose again, this time on purpose, because I remembered that feeling of being around them—something dangerous steadily growing in the silence.

After, a bar full of witnesses saw Adalyn shrug and say she carried no cash, like that should be obvious. They watched her turn away smiling, like it was all a game.

And then they saw Charlie reach out and grab her arm. Her eyes were wide as she turned back and stared at his thick, tanned hand pressing into the pale skin of her upper arm. A reminder that they no longer played childish games.

"What's your name?" he asked.

She kept her expression stoic, didn't show fear—maybe she didn't even feel it. If anything, she appeared surprised. "Adalyn Vale," she said, speaking each syllable slowly, as if talking down to a child.

She didn't understand where she was. She didn't get her place here.

I felt the silence creeping through the room. Felt something else growing in the absence of sound. I took out my single emergency credit card, placed it on the bar counter. "I'll pay the tab," I said.

But Micah shook his head. His gaze trailed down Adalyn's face to her thin neck—I could see her breath coming fast. "We'll take the necklace," he said.

The pearls she always wore, gleaming in the dim light of the neon wall sign, caught on the collar of her green short-sleeved sweater.

For a moment, I thought she would balk or laugh. But she seemed to be waiting for something else to happen—for someone to stop this: the bartender who always flirted with her; the young off-duty cop at the table beside us; me, maybe. She must've been confused. She'd grown up in country clubs where no one would dare grab her arm, treat her roughly. Where a bartender would take her side, and a cop would always come to her aid.

But these were the things she couldn't know: The bartender was also a Rivers; the cop, Fred Mayhew, had been in the same graduating class six years earlier. It was the silence, I thought, that surprised her the most.

And then we all watched as she reached up, fingers under her blond hair, around the back of her neck, for the strand of pearls she'd worn every day since I'd met her. Valuable to her, I knew, in more ways than money.

We watched as she placed the strand carefully onto the sticky high-top table, coiled into a perfect spiral.

We left the bar, but we didn't go home. She stayed in front of the bar window, staring in, like she was waiting for them to look.

"Come on," I said. But she didn't. Instead, she waltzed around to the far side of the truck.

She didn't move fast. Didn't seem to be in a rush. Didn't worry about being caught as she slowly dragged her dorm key along the side, over and over.

I couldn't see it clearly, but I heard it—the scratch of metal in the night as a round of laughter came from inside the bar.

I saw it more clearly the next day. The rev of an engine drew me to the dorm room window.

*A single word—*TRASH*—keyed into the side of the shiny black paint in sharp, angled strokes as the truck slowly crept through campus at dusk.*

CHAPTER 15

Saturday, October 4
4:15 p.m.

The school was a different beast in the afternoon. It seemed like half the student body was outside, playing Frisbee or set up on blankets with their laptops propped open. It was jarring—all these people moving forward with their day. Like they didn't realize how close they were to the precipice of a tragedy.

Trevor's Mazda still had that new-car smell, though I recognized the car from earlier in the summer, at Delilah's graduation. But I guessed that's what was possible when a car wasn't used on the daily to transport groups of teenagers.

The campus police were headquartered at the divide between the upper and lower sections, in a low brick building tucked at the edge of the property. I directed Trevor up the same access road I'd taken earlier in the day, past the construction vehicles idle at the old pit for the student center. Like everything here was best kept out of sight.

We were early, but we didn't wait. Trevor pulled open one of the glass doors at the entrance, then held it for me to enter first.

Though the outside looked exactly the same as it had long ago, the inside had gotten a rehab, just like Beckett Hall. White paint brightened up the walls, and there appeared to be a faux wood tile—a modern light gray—through the lobby, where a floating semicircle reception desk was positioned in the middle.

There was no one behind the desk, but Cliff stood beside it like he'd been waiting. He wore khakis and a blazer with bright white sneakers. They reminded me of Delilah's.

"Beckett," he said, eyes sliding from me to Trevor. He seemed surprised by the presence of a second person.

"This is Delilah's father, Trevor," I said as they shook hands.

"Cliff Simmons, one of the deans." Trevor was both taller and broader, and I noticed Cliff straightening his posture. His eyes then slid to me. "Let me show you to the meeting room."

When he led us to the small room with an oval table and a television screen on the back wall, there were three other people already in the room.

An older Black man in uniform stood first, chair legs scratching against the floor. "Paul Signs," he said, walking around the table to shake our hands. "I'm the head of the campus police. And this is Amanda Christianson, one of our patrollers. She's been out talking to some of the students today."

Amanda appeared younger than I was, with tanned skin and brown hair that fell in waves, similar to Delilah's. Amanda wore jeans and a white T-shirt, like she'd been called in from somewhere else. She seemed like she'd blend right in with the students; maybe that was the point.

Paul gestured to the man at the other end of the table. "We've asked our partner at the Wyatt Valley Police Department to join us to make sure we're covering everything. We believe in open communication. We all want the same thing here."

"Thank you," Trevor said. And then I froze. Fred Mayhew reached out to shake my hand, mouth a tight line, no indication of the history between us.

"We want you to know," Cliff cut in, "that we're all taking this very seriously."

I shouldn't have been surprised that Mayhew would be called in. In a small town, there were probably only so many detectives. But I wished I had prepared Trevor more for this moment. *There's a cop here who thinks I'm a liar.*

"We have no reason to suspect she's anything but fine," Paul continued, "but we're going to exhaust every possibility until we get eyes on her."

He gestured for us to take a seat at the table, then cleared his throat as he opened his laptop. The television on the wall behind him flickered to life, mirroring his screen.

"In the spirit of transparency, we wanted to share the footage we've managed to spot her in. This is from the camera at the front of Beckett Hall."

The time stamp at the bottom of the screen said *11:56.* Just before midnight, like Cliff had confirmed earlier. The camera must've been positioned over the door, pointing down, so that you could see only the concrete pad positioned in front of the arched entrance. It was so dark—everything in shades of black and gray.

And then someone entered the frame. My heart leaped, seeing her. Proof that she was here. I felt the thread between us pulling tighter. The footage was grainy, choppy. It was more of a time lapse of static images than a video feed. She was wearing a sweatshirt with the hood pulled up, so I couldn't see her face. She seemed to be carrying a backpack, but it was impossible to tell if it was her school bag or something else. The video feed jerked forward, and suddenly her arm was reaching for the scanner. And then I saw it: a cursive *D* for Delilah, hand-painted in neon gel on the back of her phone.

Trevor reached out and grabbed my hand under the table. I felt either his pulse or mine in the tight grip.

In the next frame, her head turned, like she was looking over her shoulder for one frozen moment. And in the next, she was gone, the footage eerily empty.

It had all happened so fast. Here and gone. "Again, please," I said, wanting to hang on to her, find something else in the gaps.

Paul scrolled backward through the frames—her image jerky and haunting in reverse—then played it forward again. This time I took my phone out, recording it for myself.

The other member of the campus police—Amanda—frowned at me. There were probably rules against this, but I dared her to object.

"Did anyone else go in after her?" I asked, placing my phone on the table again. I imagined someone chasing her. I imagined her trying to hide—

"We didn't see anyone else," Paul said, though I noticed his careful choice of words. "She doesn't appear to come back out through the front door. Unfortunately, we don't have eyes on the back of the building."

"Have you—" Trevor began.

But Amanda was already nodding, hand held up to halt the question. Her nails, I noticed, were a shiny, deep red. "We've already searched the building, top to bottom, room by room. Had a team do a full sweep before you arrived, just to rule out the possibility that she'd fallen asleep or had some medical episode and was still inside. No one's there." She spread her hands open as if revealing a magic trick—*poof, vanished*.

"And you didn't see her on any other cameras after?" Trevor asked. But my mind was elsewhere, tracing her path in my memory. *Out the back door*—where would she go next?

Paul leaned back in his chair so that the springs squeaked. "We have cameras at the front entrance of most buildings, including the dorms. We haven't been able to identify her entering any of the dorms after, but that doesn't mean she's not there."

"Also," Amanda said, "a lot of the kids were wearing hoods or hats. It was a windy one last night." She dragged the locket pendant of her necklace across the chain, back and forth.

My gaze darted around the table, trying to catch anyone's eye. *The first howling of the year,* Maggie had told me. "Were there a lot of students out?" I asked, also careful in how I chose my words.

"There are always students out on Friday night," Amanda responded in a noticeable nonanswer.

I turned to Cliff, raised an eyebrow—he knew what I meant. Were they out with purpose, running through the woods, trying not to get caught.

Cliff breathed in. "We can tell you that no one else entered the building after her. The building is locked from both sides. You'd need an ID to scan, and hers was the only one used."

He was evading the question. They *all* were. There were others out in the night, I was sure of it. But there had to be privacy rules they were concerned about. I tried to think where else she could've gone other than out the back, into the woods—

"Did you check the tunnels?" I asked.

I felt Trevor slowly turn to look at me.

Cliff set his jaw like I was breaking some unspoken rule. "Yes," he said slowly. "They were locked, but we checked as part of the building security sweep. As I told you earlier, they don't all connect anymore."

No exit. That's what he meant. I felt my throat tightening, a sense of claustrophobia settling in this small office space.

The room fell quiet then, as if they could all sense the history here—between me and Cliff, or me and this place. It felt like there was something else in the room with us. *The sound of a lock clicking; the scent of smoke—*

Amanda cleared her throat. "We've started interviewing students," she said, like she was trying to move the conversation along, get the meeting back on track.

"I heard there were some power surges at her dorm last night," I said.

"Where'd you hear that?" Amanda asked, like this was news to her.

"Lenny. At the dorm."

She frowned. "Must've been an easy fix. He didn't mention it in his statement."

This was the first I was hearing of any statements.

"What did he say?" I asked.

"Mr. Leonard said it was business as usual there. No calls came in from the dorm. He didn't see her. He only saw you."

I flinched, realizing they had probably also tracked my movements while they were looking for her. "Do you have cameras on the woods?" I asked, keeping my voice steady and calm.

She crossed her arms, leaning back. "We do, near the edges of the trails, at the blue-light emergency phones all around campus. Our crew has been checking the footage from last night." She shook her head. "They haven't spotted her."

Which didn't mean they hadn't spotted *others*. It also didn't mean Delilah hadn't slipped into the woods from a different way, out of camera view, like how I'd seen Bryce emerge from an unmarked path in the woods this morning.

"Look," Paul said, opening his empty hands, "we don't believe in a surveillance state here. No one likes to feel they're being watched all the time. There are generally cameras positioned outside the buildings, in case of property damage. And like Amanda said, at the blue-light phones, so we can see who's calling. Other than that, there's no way we can account for every entrance or egress on campus."

I turned then to face Fred Mayhew, who had remained silent till this point. I realized he had been only listening. Observing.

At the moment, I didn't care what Mayhew thought of me—whether he was an ally or a skeptic—but I knew he would understand. He would understand that, in this town, there might be something dangerous and unspoken about my daughter's last name.

"I don't think she's on campus," I said to him. "I think she's somewhere in the woods." *Their* jurisdiction. Not the school's. It was probably why the township police were here at all.

"What makes you think that?" Mayhew asked, readjusting in his seat. He opened a notebook but looked directly into my eyes. The rest of the room had fallen silent.

"She called me last night. Around two a.m. She didn't speak, but I could hear the outside."

He stared back, unblinking. "What did you hear, ma'am?"

Ma'am, he'd said, like he was putting on an act for the others in this room. As if he hadn't used my first name a hundred times before. *Beckett, stop protecting her and give it to me straight—*

"The wind," I said. "And then the call dropped."

"Okay, look. This is what we're gonna do," Paul Signs said, trying to get on top of the meeting again. "We're gonna start here, canvass the school, knock on doors. Talk to more students, see if anyone knew her plans." Then he gestured to Mayhew at the other end of the table. "The Wyatt Valley PD will check around town. They'll ask the owners of shops or restaurants to check their cameras from last night, see if they can spot her."

I knew there were cameras around downtown, but not many—the deli didn't even take credit cards. There might be some doorbell cameras in residential areas. Still, I thought they were starting in the wrong place.

"We could use your help to get a couple recent photos. We have her school ID, but it's best to have some candid shots," Paul Signs said.

Finally the reason we were here. This I could do. I opened my phone, scrolled back to orientation, showed him the photo of Delilah standing in front of Beckett Hall, her arms spread wide. "How's this?" I asked.

"Perfect. And if you have one with her hair pulled back. You'd be surprised how much that can matter in an identification."

I scrolled back further in time, to our backpacking trip from the summer.

He nodded again, taking out his own phone. "Yes. Please airdrop both of those to me. I'll circulate them among the group."

"She's a hiker," Mayhew said.

"Not at midnight," I snapped, sharing the photos with the other devices in the room. She might've been young and reckless, but she was smart. She knew the dangers.

Paul Signs stood suddenly. "We'll ask the students. Check to see if there was some sort of trip planned." He gestured between me and the detective. "Just to cover our bases."

Cliff adjusted his blazer as he stood. "Can either of you think of anywhere else she might've gone?"

"My parents' house," I said. "But it was the first place I checked." I shook my head. "They're away for the semester, but I think someone else has been in there."

"Delilah?" Fred Mayhew asked. He was staring at me in a way that unsettled me.

I paused before answering. "I don't know." *Yes, Delilah. But someone else, too. Someone who wrote threatening notes on the walls. Who chased her from the dorm. Scared her from her family home. Who might still be after her—*

I needed to keep them from viewing me as a paranoid parent seeing the danger around every corner the first time their child left home. "Her roommate made it seem like she wasn't staying in her room anymore," I added. "Delilah has mentioned a girl named Sierra. Maybe check the registry?"

Amanda took a deep breath, then typed the name in her laptop. "No Sierra," she said, as if I were the one who was mistaken. Maybe it was a nickname. A middle name.

I pulled out my phone for evidence. "There's another girl. An upperclassman. Gen with a *G*. I don't know her last name, but here." I turned the screen to face Amanda with Gen's profile picture. It was a place for them to start.

"That would be Genevieve Ryan," Amanda said, softening. "Third year, theater major." As if this were Amanda's main role—to know the names and details of every student.

Paul nodded. "Wouldn't hurt for you to ask around near your parents' place. Knock on some doors. Make sure we're not missing something obvious."

It wasn't a bad idea. Cliff had mentioned noticing the lights on. Maybe one of the neighbors had spoken to her.

As head of security, Paul made sure to exchange contact numbers with everyone. "I'll be the central point of contact," he said. "Call if you think of anything at all. We'll be in touch with any updates."

Trevor and I left the building together, though the rest of the group seemed to be waiting inside. Dissecting the meeting, perhaps. Deciding what they really thought, sharing their opinions of the case—or us. We entered his car in silence.

Trevor looked over at me, and I could see it in his eyes: He wanted to believe them. He wanted to trust them. "Beckett, it's going to be okay," he said, as if this were the one thing he could do.

I nodded, but I couldn't say anything back. I feared he'd be able to hear it in my voice: the uncertainty; the fear, growing with every passing moment.

"You've done a really good job," he said. "They know where to look, how to begin." Trevor started the car, staring back through the window for a moment. I saw his throat move, like it had finally become real for him. "They're moving fast."

I knew this was a good thing, but it didn't do anything to ease my fears.

A weight had settled deep in my gut the moment we stepped into the room. The moment I saw everyone gathered around that table.

They were moving fast because they somehow understood—even in the absence of evidence—that something was very wrong here.

CHAPTER 16

Saturday, October 4
6:00 p.m.

Trevor idled at the T intersection of College Lane and my parents' street, directly in front of the empty plot, yellow caution tape blowing in the wind. He was staring in the opposite direction—through the gap to the dark green hillside of campus and the mountain peaks beyond.

"I want to go into the woods," he said. I knew what he was seeing: the sun dropping in the sky; a stomach-dropping infinity. A thousand places she could be. I'd already checked the quarry trail and another unmarked path this morning. The campus police would likely be checking the ones that branched off directly from campus, especially if they thought she'd gone hiking.

But I knew that feeling—needing to set eyes on something yourself to prove it.

"Okay. We can leave the car here, it's as good a spot as any. We probably only have a couple hours of daylight."

He pivoted to face me, eyes searching mine. "No, I think they're right. You should start knocking on doors. You know this town. They know you."

I swallowed dry air. Trevor knew the basics of what had happened here twenty years earlier. He knew that my roommate had been accused of a terrible crime and disappeared. He knew that the people who'd died were residents of the town and that it had strained the relationship between the locals and the college. He knew the college had asked me to take a leave.

But I hadn't told him about the feeling of dread whenever I looked out my bedroom window to the same view I once loved so much. He didn't understand that between the college and the town, you couldn't be both. You had to pick. This town may have known me once. But not anymore.

I shook my head. "There's no way you should go in alone." I felt a flutter of panic, like I might lose track of him, too.

"We can cover more ground if we split up," he said. "I'll share my location with you, just in case."

"You'll lose signal," I said. "You don't know the woods here—"

"Beckett," he said sharply, his raised tone surprising us both. He was gripping the steering wheel so tightly I could see the veins in his forearms. And then, more calmly, he added: "Please. I have to do this."

He stared at me, and in his haunted expression I could see a piece of Delilah—it was the way she would ask for something, eyes wide, holding her breath, knowing she needed my permission first.

My heart thundered in my chest. I swallowed, then nodded. "We check in," I said, my hand shaking as I opened my phone to share my location with him, too. "Every thirty minutes."

"Got it," he said.

I took a deep breath, then exited the car. "Trevor," I said, leaning back inside, one hand on the open door. What I wanted to say: *Please find our daughter. Please bring her home.* Instead, I looked toward the mountains, eyes narrowed. "The dark falls fast out there. Faster than you think."

I started at the far corner of College Lane, canvassing the homes on what was once Fraternity Row. The houses looked nearly identical from the outside, differing only in their orientation, the types of window coverings, and the items left out on the small front porches.

I knew many of the homes here used to be rented by professors or people associated with the school. I hoped I would run into someone who knew Delilah from campus—who might be able to provide some added insight into what had been happening with her.

I felt on edge, imagining who might open the door and recognize me—or my name. But time was running out. I didn't care what they thought as long as they pointed me in the right direction.

The first home—porch flowers, beige curtains—appeared empty. But at the second home—tricycle on the porch, plantation shutters—I could hear voices just inside.

A woman answered the door with an impatient expression and a toddler on her hip. The boy was in a diaper, face covered in the remnants of dinner. I was probably interrupting bath time.

"Hi, I'm looking for a student from the college. Delilah Bowery. Have you seen her around recently?" I showed her the photos from my phone, scrolling between the school ID and the first day of orientation.

"Sorry, no," she said, shifting the little boy to her other hip. And then, as I scrolled to the last image from the backpacking trip, she leaned closer. "I don't know. Maybe. There are college kids walking down this street all the time. They kind of funnel through on the way to downtown." She jutted her chin toward the corner of the street.

I nodded, thanking her for her time even as she was shutting her door.

By the time I made it to the end of one side of College Lane, about half the residents had opened the door. Some seemed apologetic, while others seemed intrigued, a flash of interest behind their eyes.

This wasn't the first time someone had canvassed the area. But twenty years earlier, when the police went door-to-door showing a printed-off picture of Adalyn, they were looking for a fugitive. Judging by the ages of most people who came to the door now, I doubted they'd been here for that. It seemed an entire new generation had cycled through.

My phone rang with a call from Trevor—our first check-in.

"I'm on a pretty well-marked trail near campus," he said. I could hear him breathing heavily as he walked; I imagined he was trying to cover as much ground as possible. "Still have signal."

"Just finished the first side of the street here. No updates yet."

"Okay," he said. "Talk in thirty."

I checked his location, could envision him hovering in the woods on a trail that must've forked off somewhere between lower and upper campuses.

I crossed the street, making my way down the opposite side, and got more of the same. A pattern of no-answers, even when I could hear people inside. Or, when they did come to the door, I'd get a fleeting glance: *Sorry, haven't seen her.*

Another check-in from Trevor, his marker showing him a little deeper in the woods.

Time was passing, and I was getting frustrated. This was proving to be a useless endeavor—I should've gone with Trevor. The sky was turning a golden hue in the twilight. I sent Trevor a text as I walked up the porch steps at the house next door to Cliff's: *You should start back soon.*

I barely had a chance to ring the doorbell before the front door opened. A short woman who seemed about my parents' age stood in the entrance, brown eyes large behind thick bifocals. I assumed she'd been watching me making the rounds and had been standing by, ready for me. "Can I help you?" she asked, blinking twice.

"I hope so," I said, pulling up the photos on my cell, turning the phone her way. "I'm looking for a student from the college. Her name's—"

"Delilah," she said, leaning closer to my phone. "Yes, I remember."

I sucked in a breath, felt my stomach flutter in anticipation. "You know Delilah?"

She nodded, lips pressed together. "Is this about the fire?" She raised her hand to the side of her gray bun, brushing back any stray pieces.

"What?" I said, barely able to get the word over the lump in my throat. In that single statement, I smelled the smoke, saw the haze rising over the trees—

"The *fire,*" she said, drawing the word into two distinct syllables, head tipped in the direction of Cliff's house and the empty plot beside it.

I was trying to keep up, find my footing. "You talked to Delilah about the fire?"

Her eyes appeared even wider, if possible. "Well, she came around asking about these old buildings and safety codes. She asked if I was home when that house went up. I was, of course. I was the one who called 911." She shook her head, remembering. "I told her she could just ask Dean Simmons. I'm sure he knows more."

"How come?"

She started to smile, then stopped like she realized I wasn't in on the punch line. "Well, he was supposed to be living in that house when it burned down. Signed the lease and everything but hadn't quite finished moving in. He's so lucky he wasn't there, sleeping. Or his *son*—" She shook her head, a visible shudder working its way through her. "It went up so fast."

I felt a chill in the settling dusk—a gust of mountain wind descending from above. "I didn't know that." I'd assumed he'd been moving into the house he was currently in, next door to the fire. Not that he was supposed to be living in that very same one.

I pictured Cliff staring at the empty plot of land earlier today—another *almost*. His son's picture beside his desk. How near a miss was that tragedy? It must've shaken him to the core, taken him right back to twenty years earlier.

I remembered him at the top of the bell tower, looking down. The way he'd poked his head out the door after, looking to make sure no one was watching. I'd assumed he was afraid of getting caught. But maybe he'd been afraid that something was out there. Something after *him.*

"When did you last see Delilah?" I asked.

The woman frowned, considering. "Oh, it was just the once. Maybe a week or so ago." Then she tilted her head to the side like she was finally seeing me clearly. "Is everything okay? You look just like her."

I shook my head. "She's my daughter. I can't find her."

She sucked in a breath, then reached for my arm, warm fingers pressing into my skin like she was trying to hold me here. "I'll keep an eye out. Let me get your number, honey. My son Dill works nights on security patrol up there. I'll see what he might've heard when he's back."

He must've been the man I'd seen leaving this house earlier in the day, when I was visiting Cliff. The man Cliff had seemed like he was trying to avoid.

"Thank you," I said as she retrieved a yellow pad of paper from the console in the foyer.

"Beverly," she said as she tore off a piece of paper. "My name's Beverly Lawrence. I'll be keeping you both in my thoughts tonight."

"Thank you," I said again, retreating down the porch steps.

Delilah, what were you doing here? I tried to picture her walking this same street—knocking on doors. Naively giving her name with a smile: *I'm Delilah Bowery.*

I wondered whom she might've shaken with her questions—or her presence.

Three more check-ins from Trevor came and went while I moved on from College Lane to my parents' street. No one else could be sure they had seen her. No one else mentioned her asking about the fire.

We were due another check-in soon. The dark had fully settled, porch lights turning on automatically, moths fluttering overhead in the glow.

All okay? I texted, waiting for my message to show as delivered. It had stalled, but I didn't know whether it was on his end or mine.

I tried calling, but it went straight to voicemail. I closed my eyes, hoped he had listened to my warning and was on his way back.

I was running out of time, too. It was getting too late for this. The folks who answered the door now appeared irritated; I could smell the remnants from dinner, hear the televisions in the background. I was a disturbance to their typical evening.

At the house next door to my parents' place, a couple around my age answered together, both in pajamas—the man hovered slightly behind his wife, frowning. They hadn't lived here when I was growing up, but I recognized them from my visits.

"I don't think we've formally met, I'm Beckett, my parents live next door," I began.

"Are you visiting?" the woman asked. Confused, like all the rest, about why I was here at her door after dusk.

"I'm looking for my daughter, Delilah."

"Oh, yes, we know Delilah," she said before I even had a chance to pull up the photos. And then she frowned. "Has she been staying at their place?"

"I think so," I said.

The man shifted into the doorframe beside her, suddenly animated. "I told you," he said, looking down at his wife. "I *knew* someone was there. Rang the bell and everything, but she didn't come down."

Because she didn't want anyone to know. Because she was hiding from something.

The sound of a car door slamming closed jarred me. I turned quickly, hoping it was Trevor. But I didn't see him on the street.

I pivoted back to the neighbors. "Did you see anyone there earlier today?" I asked. "In the backyard, maybe?" It was a long shot, but they had a view straight down from their upstairs windows.

They looked at each other, then both shook their heads. "We only ever notice it at night," the man said. "The upstairs light."

My old bedroom, with the writing on the walls.

"I thought it was automated," the wife said, like she was defending her side of the argument.

"Just that random one inside?" her husband asked, both his eyebrows raised in disbelief.

"Thanks," I said, trying to remove myself from their argument. "Can I leave you my number? In case you think of anything else?"

They promised to call with any leads.

There was still no word from Trevor as I descended their porch steps.

I tried to pull up his location, but it had updated last over thirty minutes earlier. Night had fully fallen now. I imagined him somewhere out there, in the woods.

I needed a drink and a bathroom break. I wanted to pull up a map on the laptop, see exactly where he'd been heading.

I was busy looking down at my phone and almost ran straight into Maggie, waiting at the bottom of my parents' porch.

"Oh," I said, hand out in surprise.

"Hi," she said. "Sorry, didn't mean to scare you."

"No, it's okay." I looked at her expectantly. Hoping for a fresh lead; a sighting. A rumor.

She frowned in the direction of campus. "Bill said they're getting a search together. I came to see if you could use some company."

She was here not with answers but to offer her support. The same way she'd turned up here twenty years ago, when she'd heard what had happened in her absence. Back then I'd sent her away. This time I didn't.

"I was just about to stop in for a quick break," I said, leading the way up the porch to my parents' house.

But then I paused.

A cloud of gnats had gathered under the automated porch light. And just beyond, a flutter of tape was moving in the breeze.

Both pieces had been disengaged from the top of the frame.

"Did you open this door?" I asked.

"What?" Maggie said, stopping behind me.

"The screen door," I said, eyes burning. "Did you open it?"

"No, I was sitting on the porch, waiting for you—"

But I was already moving closer.

Someone had opened the screen door. There was a smear of mud on the doorstep. Had they gone inside?

Were they *still* there?

I kept my phone out in one hand while I pushed the front door slowly open, listening.

The foyer light was also on; I couldn't remember if I'd left it this way.

"Hello?" I called.

Nothing.

No, not quite nothing.

A steady *thump, thump, thump* came from somewhere under the floorboards.

Like a metronome keeping time. Taunting me.

Eighteen hours missing. Nineteen. Almost a full day gone.

Maggie tentatively followed me inside. "Beckett, we should call for help."

I stepped farther into the house, moving toward the basement door.

It appeared shut, but there was a faint light coming from the strip below the door. Had I left the light on down there earlier? I didn't think so; but I hadn't slept, and I couldn't remember the specifics of the last few hours.

From my spot in front of the closed door, the periodic noise seemed even louder. I looked at Maggie to be sure she heard it, too. She stared back, wide-eyed, phone in hand.

Slowly, I opened the door, hand on the circular rail, wooden steps descending underground, concrete blocks all around me.

"Wait," she said. "Don't."

But this was always the difference between the two of us. I had to know. Had to see.

One step, two. Another streak of mud, partly wiped away.

I recognized the sound about halfway down.

The dryer was running, contents uneven as they spun.

The concrete floor came into view first. And then a figure, facing away: dark hair, gray shirt, sitting at the center of the room.

Unaware that I was behind them.

CHAPTER 17

Saturday, October 4
9:00 p.m.

A scream echoed through the basement, sending every nerve in my body into overdrive. My heart raced, vision blurred.

For a moment, I thought my mind was pushed to the brink, playing a cruel trick on me. And then the room focused down to a point. To her.

"Delilah?" I called, rushing down the last few basement steps, making sure this girl sitting in the middle of the floor wasn't a mirage.

Her eyes were wide, mouth hanging open from the scream—

"Mom?" she said, hand to her chest.

I crossed the room in three quick strides, knees hitting the ground hard beside her. I wrapped her in my arms.

"Oh my God," I said. My entire body was shaking with relief. She was real, and solid, and here. "You're okay." I said it for myself as much as for her. A mantra I kept repeating in my head, over and over.

But Delilah's body felt stiff in my arms, every muscle tensed.

I pulled back slightly to take her in. Her large blue eyes were frozen in shock. A faint scratch marred her cheekbone, raised and pink. Her dark hair was wet, and the shoulders of the gray shirt—one of my old concert tees from the early 2000s—were damp and dark.

She smelled of shampoo and soap, like she'd just taken a shower, rummaged through the drawers upstairs, and changed into whatever she could find.

I still had my hands on her shoulders, and I worried I was hurting her. I worried someone *else* had hurt her. "What happened?"

"Mom?" she asked, like she was trying to calibrate. Her mouth was slightly open, lips pale and chapped in sections. "What are you doing here?" Her voice was raw, cracking at the end of the question.

"You called me," I said, words spilling out. "You called me in the middle of the night, and the line went dead, but I thought I heard you. I heard the wind—"

Her eyes widened even more. "You came?"

"Of course I came. I couldn't reach you. I left you a bunch of messages but . . ." I shook my head, then laughed once in relief. "Your dad is here, too. He's out right now, searching the woods."

Delilah's mouth twitched like she wanted to smile, or like she couldn't quite believe it. I ran my thumb under the scratch on her face, and she flinched.

"Where were you?" I asked. "What happened?"

She sucked in a gulp of air, like I'd finally broken through, dragged her back to the here and now. "Mom, I was lost. I was *so lost.*" Then she let out a shaky breath, fell forward into my arms, her entire body trembling. "I couldn't find the way out." I felt her words vibrating against my collarbone.

"Okay," I said, feeling her warm breath against my shoulder, tears of either fear or relief dampening my shirt. "You're here now. You're safe."

"I was in the woods . . ." She pulled back, eyes shiny, gaze drifting to the side. Something she couldn't find the words to explain. But that was the benefit of growing up here. She didn't have to explain it to me. I knew what happened during the howling, and I'd seen the mask left behind at Cryer's Quarry.

"I know," I said. I nodded, urging her on.

Her eyes slid back to mine. "I took a wrong turn somewhere. I was way too deep in . . ." She shook her head. "I dropped my phone somewhere out there. And I was scared to go look for it. To go anywhere at all."

Trevor was right to search the woods. Of course he was right.

"It's okay," I said, gripping her around the wrists, holding her here. Proving to myself, over and over, that this was real. That I had her.

"Do you remember this summer in the canyons, when we camped at the river," she began, voice dropped to a whisper, "when it was so dark at night, and the water sounded like it was coming from everywhere?"

"Yes," I whispered back. That night I had dreamed of the water rising, our tents flooding, of all the ways I didn't know how to keep her safe—

"They told us not to leave the campsite," she said, her eyes staring directly into mine. "Not for anything. Not until daylight."

"I remember," I said. They had stressed that the biggest danger was in becoming disoriented, heading the wrong way. Walking straight into the thing you were trying to avoid.

I could see the pieces sliding into place before she even said it. I saw her in the dark, slumped against a tree, curling up on the cool ground—

"I waited for the sun to come up," she said. "It took all day to find my way back." She swallowed, raised her trembling hand to her mouth. "I didn't have my phone." All that time while I was out looking for her, and she was trying to find her way home.

"You did so well," I said. "You must've been so scared." I pulled her tight again, didn't want to let go, felt her arms gripping around my back. She seemed to have nothing on her but the carabiner she used as a clip for her keys, currently sprawled on the basement floor beside us.

I'd been trying to hold it together for so long, and now the relief left my body in a choked sob, tears running down my face. I had her. *I had her.*

"I didn't know you were here," she whispered, her breath brushing against my ear. "I didn't know anyone was looking—"

And then her body tensed.

I looked up. Maggie stood halfway down the steps, hand to her mouth, phone hanging at her side. "The police are on the way," she said. "I called for help."

I felt myself laughing in relief—another release, as I wiped the tears from my eyes. Of course she did. But at least she saved me a call.

"Delilah, this is Maggie," I said, smiling. Then I stood and reached a hand down for her. "Come on. Let's go upstairs."

I heard the siren on its way as I paced the living room, trying to reach Trevor. Finally the call connected.

"Beckett—" he began, voice in a panic, like he'd been trying to reach me, too. He must've been trying when I was downstairs. The cell service in the basement was terrible through the layers of concrete.

"I have her!" I shouted, cutting him off.

"What?" A pause, and I worried I'd lost him again. But then he was back. "Where? Where are you?"

She watched me from the couch, where she was curled up in the corner. I couldn't help the smile spreading across my face.

"Trevor, she's safe! We're at the house! Come home."

I waited on the porch for the police to arrive, so they would know there was no danger inside. As the cruiser pulled up, the couple next door emerged, drawn by the flashing lights. A young officer with red hair and a strong jaw stepped out from the vehicle, moving quickly toward the house.

"It's Delilah," I said. "She's okay." I said it loud enough for the neighbors to hear, too. I knew it wouldn't take long for word to spread here.

The officer frowned at me from the sidewalk. "We got a call for an intruder at this address," he said in a deep local accent that made me think his family had been here for generations.

I shook my head. "We didn't know it was her. She was in the basement."

"She was here the whole time?" he asked, head tilted to the side. A patch with the name Fritz was adhered to his uniform.

"No, she was lost in the woods. She just made it back."

Officer Fritz followed me inside, where Delilah sat on the couch beside Maggie. A tall glass of water was on the coffee table, untouched. The only movement came from the constant fidgeting of Delilah's hands, now absently picking at the dirt stuck under her short nails.

"I ordered pizza," Maggie said, standing. "She's hungry."

"Thank you," I said. I was so grateful Maggie was here, that she could think straight, act rationally. I'd felt guilt at the state of our friendship, but now I was thrilled to have her. I'd been so relieved to have Delilah back, I hadn't thought about what else she'd need. All I'd cared about was that she was safe.

"Delilah Bowery?" Officer Fritz asked, standing at the entrance of the living room.

She nodded from the corner of the couch.

"No one else is here?" he asked, eyes scanning the foyer, the hallway.

"Just us," I said.

He nodded and stepped back outside, but he didn't leave. I could hear him through the screen door, talking on his radio. Like he was calling it in, explaining the situation.

Delilah dropped her head into her hands, damp hair swaying forward. "God, this is so embarrassing. I can't believe everyone *knows*."

She was so young—she might not have realized how close she had come to tragedy. How easy it was to get lost forever out there. How quickly one could disappear.

"Don't be silly," I said, sitting beside her on the old blue sofa, cushions shifting under my weight so that her body leaned into mine. I put an arm around her shoulders. "Everyone's just glad you're okay." I rubbed her shoulder, then squeezed her upper arm, and her body abruptly contorted, hunching over in pain.

She held her elbow in her other hand, but she let me extend her arm so I could see. A deep purple bruise had bloomed on the side of her left arm, inches above the elbow.

I sucked in a breath as she pulled back, tugging her sleeve lower—not quite covering the mark. "I think it was a tree branch," she said. "I didn't know it was that bad."

I pictured her running through the night, twigs swiping across her face, branch catching her as she tripped forward, hands bracing for impact in the dirt—

"We should ice it," I began as the sound of footsteps racing up the porch cut through the night. I stood, hearing voices rising out front. "Excuse me, that's my *daughter* in there—"

And then Trevor threw open the screen door, maneuvering himself past the officer in the entryway. He was breathing heavily, eyes wide, his entire body on edge. Something wild thrumming in the air between us.

He saw me first, our eyes latching. I nodded quickly, watched as his gaze slid to the couch.

"Oh my God," he said, crossing the room in quick strides before falling onto the sofa beside her. He had Delilah in his arms then, eyes closed, a shudder as her head fell into the space between his chin and shoulder.

He reached a hand out for me, as if the last few hours of searching in the dark had shaken him to the core, too. I laced my fingers with his, joining them on the couch.

"Oh my God, Dad?" she said. "I can't believe you're here." And he laughed, letting that feeling of relief flood through the room.

There was a knock at the screen door then, and Maggie cleared her throat. "I'll get it."

I knew we were causing a scene on the street, imagined more neighbors coming out, coming over, wanting to know what was happening.

I let the relief wash over me, wanting to stay in this feeling forever.

A man stepped into the foyer—my eyes trailed up from his black boots and black slacks to his blue button-down and sport coat. Fred Mayhew, in the same clothes he'd worn earlier in the day. His boots echoed on the hardwood flooring.

"You must be Delilah," he said from the entrance of the room with a gentle smile.

Trevor released her then, so the three of us were sitting in a row on the couch, looking up at the detective.

"We sure are relieved to see you," Detective Mayhew said, lowering himself into the wingback chair across the coffee table. "You gave us all quite the scare."

"I didn't know anyone was looking," she repeated softly, like she was in trouble.

But he waved her off. "Fred Mayhew," he continued. "I'm with the Wyatt Valley PD. Just wanted to set eyes on you for myself, make sure everything's okay."

"She's okay," I said, wondering if Officer Fritz had relayed the details accurately. "She was lost. All night." I felt the lump in my throat growing, imagining the long night she must've spent out there, alone. But also: a spark of pride. She hadn't waited to be found. She'd taken action. Played it smart. Made sure she didn't make the situation worse. Then navigated her way back out of the wilderness. Made it home safely to us.

Mayhew whistled once, long and drawn out. I saw him taking her in: the cut on her cheek, the bruise on her arm. Dirt under her nails from a night spent on the ground.

He leaned forward, laced his hands together; silver wedding ring catching the light from the standing lamp. "I know how it can be out there at night. You think you know where you are, and then you're out of range, the maps on your cell stop working, and you can't orient yourself. Even emergency services can be tough to reach."

She nodded once. "I lost my phone in the dark."

He smiled, then widened his eyes. "I can barely find my way to *work* without my phone. And I go there every day."

That got a grin out of her.

He placed his hands on his knees like he was about to stand, then paused. "Where'd you end up finding your way back out?"

She reached for the glass of water. The cup trembled faintly in her hand as she raised it to her mouth, taking a sip. I wanted to reach out and steady it for her. "I don't even know," she said. "I kept heading down until I could hear a road."

I put my hand on her back, imagining that moment. The panic of trees and mountains as far as you could see, and then—signs of civilization, that immense wave of relief.

"I recognized the street. I came straight here. I wasn't even thinking." She cut her eyes to me. "I didn't realize anyone even knew I was gone."

Detective Mayhew finally stood, then took a deep breath. "Eventually this will be a good story you can tell your friends. We might have some follow-up questions later. But I'm sure right now you just want a good night's rest in a warm bed." He rocked back on his heels. "You gave us all quite a scare, kid." Then he winked in my direction. "Guess I'll be seeing you around."

BEFORE:
THE SEARCH

I couldn't find her. The barn was burning and the sirens were crying and I couldn't find Adalyn anywhere. My bare hand gripped the flashlight and the falling snow seeped into my hiking boots as I ran through the woods.

"Adalyn!" I yelled, her name catching in my throat. I bent over to cough.

I didn't know where else to look. I couldn't feel my hands, and the smoke from the fire clung to my jacket, my hair.

They said she did it. They said Adalyn set the fire. It had to be an accident, but she had disappeared into the night.

I thought she wanted me to find her, to explain, but I'd already checked every place I thought she'd go to hide—Cryer's Quarry, the alley behind the Low Bar—until eventually I thought: The dorm.

I sucked in a wheezing breath and turned around, heading back out of the woods.

In the distance, the flames were visible over the trees. I worried the fire would spread in the wind. Take out the hillside, spread to the campus, come for us all.

Other students had started spilling out of the woods, back to safety. A handful stood wide-eyed in the quad, staring up at the glow in the dark sky. They didn't even notice me pass.

My ID was in my back pocket, and my fingers were frozen so that I could barely pull out the card. But eventually I was inside, stumbling down the first-floor hall to our room.

"Adalyn!" I called, struggling with the door. I couldn't escape the scent. Wanted to strip it all off me—

Finally I was inside, but a new chill washed over me.

The room was empty. But the window was wide open, flurries blowing in with the wind.

As if she'd come back here after all but had wanted to remain unseen.

The surface of her desk was bare—laptop missing—and I felt a surge of rage. She'd been here while I was out looking for her, screaming *for her.*

I threw open the closet door and immediately saw the absence: the small purse where she kept her wallet, the large bag stored on the upper shelf.

I started opening drawers—dresser, desk—but there was nothing left behind for me. No clues. No note. Nothing.

That was when I knew it was true. She didn't want to be found. Not by me. Not by anyone.

In the days that followed, the police kept issuing promises on the news: "We're going to find her," they said. But I knew that was wishful thinking. Time kept moving. A day. A week.

In a month, or two, or three, who would really look that hard for a girl who once started a fire in a small Virginia town? The families of the dead—the Riverses, the Whites—were not the type to either demand or afford private investigators who would keep the case alive after the leads ran cold.

I imagined that as soon as Adalyn crossed a border—a state line, a country checkpoint—she was as good as gone.

CHAPTER 18

Saturday, October 4
10:30 p.m.

Delilah seemed shell-shocked.

The chaos of the last day was catching up to all of us. I was crashing hard in the aftermath of the adrenaline rush that had kept me going since the dropped call at two in the morning.

Now my limbs had gone heavy, but my brain was still racing, like it was stuck on the edge of some unknown precipice, out in the night.

We said goodbye to Maggie, cleaned up the boxes of pizza, prepared to spend the night in the house together.

A sharp buzz cut through the room, making me jump. It was the dryer in the basement, the alert old-school and grating, audible all the way upstairs.

Delilah stood quickly, stepping around me, dropping a balled-up napkin on the table.

"I'll get it," I said, but she pressed her lips together.

"I've got it, Mom. It's just the basement." She smiled like she could see right through me. But she was right. I was scared to let her out of my sight again. Terrified she'd disappear the second I looked away. *Everyone has to let go—*

And yet look what happened when I did.

I watched as she headed for the hall. There were so many things I wanted to ask her. I longed for the days when she would come home from school and tell me everything, the words spilling forth without prompting.

Trevor ruffled her hair as she passed, which made her grin like he was bringing the old Delilah back.

I didn't want to ruin it with my questions: *Why were you staying here instead of at the dorm? What were you hiding from?*

There would be time. For now, I just wanted to savor the moment.

The three of us were camped out in the living room for the night. Safe and protected.

Trevor had turned on the television for something to fill the silence—like he was also trying to prevent his mind from spiraling closer to the *almost* that had existed only hours earlier. The laugh track from an old sitcom drifted through the space, familiar and comforting.

It was unspoken but understood—we weren't leaving her tonight.

Delilah fell asleep first, head on the arm of the sofa, while I curled up in my father's recliner. I lowered the volume on the television down to zero, the light from the screen dancing across our faces.

Trevor was prepping a spot for himself on the floor, in the place the coffee table once was. He'd brought a decorative pillow in from the futon and draped a throw blanket across Delilah.

I caught his eye over her head in the flash of the television light. Held his gaze for a long moment. I knew we were thinking the same thing: how close we had come and how lucky we were.

Sometime in the night, or maybe the dark of predawn, I heard the creak of the screen door. My eyes jolted open, and it took a moment to orient myself: *My parents' house. In the living room, on my father's recliner. Delilah safely on the couch beside me.*

I felt my pulse slowing, seeing her there, so close. I watched the steady rise and fall of her chest, keeping time.

But there was a blanket heaped on the floor and no sign of Trevor.

I rose from the chair, walking toward the window. Saw a figure moving down the street, head down, shoulders forward. Like he couldn't sleep and needed to walk it off.

I couldn't blame him. I'd done the same thing my first night here in August. And we'd been through a lot more today.

I watched him until he disappeared from view, then retreated to the chair and quickly fell back into a deep and powerful sleep.

I woke to the sound of my cell buzzing on the coffee table.

I frowned, reaching for the phone. I had two missed calls from an unknown number.

The spot where Trevor had slept was still bare. Maybe he'd relocated to the futon in the office on his return.

But I was nervous, imagining who could be calling from an unknown number. I thought of the memoir email again, and the way they'd implied that it had something to do with an old crime, witness accounts, in a small town. As if it was about this place and me. As if they were watching.

The phone suddenly rang in my hand—a third attempt from the unknown caller. I peered over at Delilah, still asleep, grateful that she slept like the dead.

I slipped out the front door and was startled to find Trevor sitting on the porch in running gear.

He raised a hand in greeting as I tentatively pressed accept on the phone.

A crackle of static. And then: "Beckett? Can you hear me?"

"Mom?" I responded. Her voice sounded tinny and distant.

"Oh, good. We just saw your email. Beckett, we thought you understood, you can't stay at the house while—"

"Oh my God," I said, unable to keep the anger from my voice. "Are you kidding me right now? Delilah was lost!" Finally here was a place to unleash my pent-up stress.

Another crackle of static; when she started speaking again, I had to strain to hear her. "She says Delilah was lost. I'm putting her on speaker." She must've been talking to my father. "Is she okay?" she asked, her voice booming from the speakerphone option.

"Yes, she's fine now. She was lost in the woods for a full night, Mom. So excuse us for using *your house* as a base of operations. Fortunately everything turned out okay!"

"Beckett, we're not mind readers! Oh my God, I can't believe she was *lost* out there . . . All you said was that you couldn't find the spare key."

"Well, I got in," I said.

"Okay, good," my mother said.

"Delilah has her own key," my father said, practically shouting. "The spare should be in the weathervane. Haven't touched it in years."

A chill worked up my spine. If they'd given Delilah a key years earlier, who knew how long the spare had been missing? But there was no point mentioning that to them when they were on a different continent.

My mother cleared her throat. "How long do you think you'll be staying?"

"Not much longer," I said. I was anxious to leave. To leave this place behind, hopefully bringing Delilah with me. Nothing good ever happened here.

"Can we speak with her?" my father asked.

"She's sleeping," I said. "Talk to you later. I'll tell her you called to check in." And then I hung up. It was far more generous than the truth, which was that they had called to check in on *me,* wondering what I was doing in their house while they were gone. Like I was a teenager, not to be trusted with their things.

Trevor peered over his shoulder, ran a hand through his hair, as I tried to shake off the interaction. "So," he began, "I guess it wasn't the best time to mention that I was here, too."

I laughed despite myself. "Probably not. They really don't like surprises."

Trevor flinched, and I knew I'd struck a nerve. The biggest surprise of his life was currently sleeping inside. How easily time could contract with a phrase—bringing us right back.

I tried to lighten the mood, move us past it. I gestured toward the house. "They're probably worried I'll use an antique dish as an ashtray or something. Not that I even smoke."

He grinned. "I do know better than that. But I can't believe the things your father has just sitting in his office," he said. I thought he would've gotten along with my father in another version of our life.

"He always had a good eye. I'm sure he'll come back from Peru with plenty from the markets in town. The good stuff is in the attic," I added with a smirk. "They boxed up the valuables before they left."

I sat beside him on the top porch step, mirroring his posture. Arms resting on knees, staring out toward the mountains.

"What are you doing out here?" I asked.

"Couldn't sleep," he said, eyes unfocused in the distance. "I keep thinking about how close we came. God, we're so lucky." His voice cracked, and I reached a hand over, patted his knee.

He laced his fingers over mine and closed his eyes at the rising sun. "I wish sometimes . . ." He trailed off, letting the thought go unfinished.

I turned to face him, waiting—then rested my head on his shoulder with a sigh.

"I'm thinking of taking her home for a while," I said.

He nodded once. "That's a good plan." He waited for a beat, then two. "It is really beautiful here."

My phone chimed with a text then, and I felt the laughter in his chest. "Are you *sure* your parents aren't watching us right now?" he asked.

"God help me if they figure out how to text from whatever network they're on," I said as I pulled away.

I opened my messages and felt the air rush from my lungs.

Automated Alert: Wyatt College is on lockdown. All students to remain in place until further notice.

"What's the matter?" Trevor asked, leaning close to see.

"There's something happening on the campus," I said.

"What? What's happening?"

I shook my head. "The school's on lockdown."

I heard the sirens starting up in the distance. A faint cry coming closer. I stood from the porch, walking slowly down the steps.

I wasn't the only one. A neighbor stepped out from her front door across the street. Another at the house beside hers.

There was more than one type of siren coming closer—a police cruiser, yes. But also: the horn of a fire truck. And then the cry of an ambulance.

I squinted into the distance until I could see the red and blue lights flashing over the trees.

The screen door behind us creaked open, and Delilah stepped barefoot onto the front porch, eyes hollow. "Mom? What's going on?" she asked, scanning the horizon.

"I don't know," I said.

I felt the sound reverberating in my chest—that adrenaline of fear coursing through my bloodstream. I watched as the vehicles approached, one right after the other. They whizzed by, leaving a gust of wind in their wake—heading for campus.

PART 3

THE FALL

CHAPTER 19

Sunday, October 5
8:00 a.m.

The sirens swept past the house, continuing on. The neighbors next door stood outside, watching the lights turn down College Lane.

In the wake of the vehicles, the leaves were spiraling in the wind, cascading into the yard, sweeping across the street.

Delilah walked down the porch steps barefoot. "Is it a fire?" she asked, straining to see over the row of houses.

But there was no smoke in the sky. And no scent carried on the wind.

She kept walking down the sidewalk, drawn closer.

Lockdown was a drill our children had endured since elementary school. It was a term our generation had come to dread on the most visceral level—and we were only a few blocks from campus.

I held her by the elbow. "Get back in the house," I said.

She stared at me with open vulnerability. "I have friends there, Mom," she said, voice cracking.

And she had no phone. No way to contact them. To know that they were safe.

It was a feeling I knew well.

"Stay here with your dad," I said, catching his eye over her shoulder. "Please stay in the house. I'll go find out what's going on."

I was out the door in my final pair of clean clothes a few moments later.

As I drove along the perimeter of campus, I saw a cluster of onlookers on the other side of College Lane, standing across the street.

At the access road we'd taken to the campus police yesterday, orange cones were set up across the entrance, blocking the route. Behind them, an empty police vehicle was positioned sideways, like a barricade.

I idled in my car, lowered the window. I couldn't see anything past the first curve in the lane. There was another access road on the other side of campus, but when I drove past, that, too, was blocked off—this one with two police vehicles.

I couldn't see any activity on the campus itself.

I frowned, then texted Maggie—it felt too early to ring her, but I wondered if her husband had been called in as a volunteer for the fire department. *Do you know what's happening on campus?*

I stared at my phone, waiting for a response—nothing.

I circled back toward the main gates, where Delilah and I had entered campus on foot during orientation. The gates were closed, as expected, but the two footpaths were occupied by a security golf cart positioned in each opening.

They weren't just trying to keep students in place here—they were trying to keep everyone else out. I wasn't the only parent who had apparently seen the alert and driven over in a panic.

A black SUV was pulled up directly at the gate, driver's-side door hanging open, like whoever was inside had gotten out in a rush. I parked my car directly behind theirs, despite the *Tow Zone* signs.

Violet was standing on the sidewalk just outside the gates in a pair of sweats, like she'd been in bed when she got the alert. A man from security, wearing an orange vest and a navy baseball cap, was standing directly in her path, shaking his head.

"Dill, *please,*" she said. Dill—this must've been Beverly's son who worked nights. It must've been an *all hands on deck* situation.

"I'm sorry, Mrs. Wharton," he said, hands out like he was holding her back. "I can't."

Violet threw up her hands in frustration, the angles of her diamond rings catching the morning light, throwing off a prism of colors. "The kids are stuck in the dorms with no idea what's going on. Let me take him home. That has to be safer, right?"

"It's a lockdown. No one in, no one out," he said, as if repeating his orders.

She spun around in disgust. "You can't keep them prisoners!" she yelled back over her shoulder. "They have rights!"

Then she froze, noticing me standing at the curb. Her hand went to her chest, and she quickly pivoted my way. "Beckett, is everything . . ." She trailed off, looking toward campus again—seeming to put things together: The police. The lockdown. My daughter.

I shook my head quickly. "We found her. She's safe at my parents' place."

Violet grabbed both of my arms at once, like we were closer than we really were. But fear could do that to people, bridging a divide, pulling them together in understanding. "Oh, thank *God,*" she said.

"Bryce?" I asked.

She shook her head, too. "He's fine. But the kids don't know what's happening. He said the power's been out all night. And then this *lockdown* alert . . ." I felt a tremble in her hands before she dropped them.

But I'd felt that same fear, and Delilah wasn't even on campus anymore.

"Do you have any idea what's going on?" I asked.

"No one's saying anything." She threw another look at Dill, who was doing his best to ignore us. "But I'm going to wait right here until someone comes to talk to me."

Luckily I knew other ways in.

I backtracked past the access road and drove another half mile to a gravel parking lot that served as the trailhead. There was only one other car—a rusted silver sedan. From here, if I took the fork to the left, the loop would brush against the far side of campus property, where I could cross over to their trails, bringing me back to the access road from the other side.

The morning felt crisp, gusts of wind starting to blow the leaves from the trees.

When I reached the farthest point of the loop, I veered off into the brush. I knew I'd eventually intersect with a campus hiking path.

I hadn't gone far when I started to notice a commotion through the trees.

A cluster of vehicles was clogging the access road we'd driven up yesterday. The red of a fire truck mixed in with white emergency vehicles. There were a few construction vehicles in the area, too. I must've been close to the location of the student center renovation.

I couldn't see anyone clearly, but I could hear them moving—calling out to one another, issuing directives.

I needed to get closer.

Just ahead, a girl was crouched low to the ground. Her dark hair was parted down the middle, long and untamed. I froze in my path, one foot planted in front.

We stared at each other silently, not moving. I felt her assessing me: *friend or foe; one of them or one of us.*

She looked vaguely familiar, with angular, striking features. I'd seen her before—somewhere in town. The deli, I thought. One of the girls working there who looked like sisters. Maybe Delilah's age; maybe not. Seeing her with hair down and face bare of makeup, wearing leggings and an oversize T-shirt, I changed my mind: definitely younger.

She was clearly shaken.

"I remember you," I whispered. "From the deli."

She nodded slightly, eyes sliding up and down my body as if she was trying to place me. There'd been a name on one of the girl's aprons. "Carly, right?"

She nodded again.

"What's going on here, Carly?"

She turned back toward the access road, hair moving over her shoulders. "I don't know. *No one* knows." Her throat moved as she swallowed, and she dropped her voice even lower. "There's someone in the pit."

Her words sent a chill through my body. I leaned to the side, trying to see through the trees. But all I could see were the vehicles. Somewhere beyond that must've been the empty construction site. *The pit.*

"Someone in the pit," I repeated, trying to make it solid, real.

"My sister found them. She was out looking for her friend."

"Your sister?" I pictured the other girl in the deli. The chipping white nail polish as she rang me up at the register.

"Sierra," she said.

The name I'd so often heard from Delilah. No wonder Amanda with campus police couldn't find any record of her. She wasn't someone from the school; she was from the town.

"Was she looking for Delilah?" I asked.

Carly whipped her head around.

How close I had come in the deli, brushing up against her friends, without even knowing it. Cliff had told me Delilah spent a lot of time off campus; I'd seen the photo on her Instagram account from the entrance of town and assumed she'd been out there alone. But maybe she hadn't been.

"I'm Delilah's mother," I said. "I was looking for her, too. She's okay. She was lost, but she's home with me now."

She stared back at me openmouthed, like this was what she'd been looking for. "The cops wouldn't tell Sierra anything," she said.

"No one would tell her who it is. They're with her again now, at the house."

"She couldn't tell?"

Carly shook her head. "Only that it's a girl. She was lying face down." She held her arms out to the sides, as if reenacting it.

A girl—someone like Delilah.

Just then, a radio crackled, like an officer was patrolling the woods, back and forth, looking for evidence. Looking for us.

I pictured students running through the night. The red mask I'd found at Cryer's Quarry, on the other side of downtown. Kids racing from campus into the woods. Someone sprinting toward the old student center pit, not paying attention, not noticing the way the ground suddenly opened up below, in a yawning chasm.

I waited until the footsteps retreated once more before reaching a hand down for Carly. "It's time to get out of here," I said.

I had no idea how long Carly had been alone in the woods, watching, wondering—imagining all the horrors that had led a girl to the bottom of a construction pit in the middle of the night.

"I'm going to follow you home, just to make sure you get there safely," I told her.

She didn't answer, but she didn't object, either. It seemed like she was in a trance, like Delilah had been when I'd startled her in the basement. I hoped that if anyone had found Delilah wandering the woods like this, they would've done the same—leading her back, making sure she arrived safely home.

I waited until I was alone inside my car before calling the number Violet had given me yesterday.

"Are you still there?" I asked when she picked up.

"In my car," she said, "waiting. Not that they seem to care."

"I found out," I said. A reminder, then, that I was still one of them. "There's a girl in the pit of the student center."

"A girl?" she repeated, like a question.

But then I corrected myself. "A body. They found a body."

CHAPTER 20

Sunday, October 5
10:00 a.m.

Not Delilah. That's all I could think as I followed Carly away from downtown.

Another student running through the dark? How close might Delilah have come, entering Beckett Hall in the middle of the night. I couldn't stop imagining the alternate series of events that might've sent her veering on the path to the right, skirting the edge of campus, thinking she could hide—

What would I tell her when I got back home? I needed the name. Needed to know it wasn't one of her friends. The uncertainty, I knew, would send her spiraling. And she'd already been through so much.

Carly turned into a quaint neighborhood about a mile away, where the landscape began to rise from the valley. The homes were all older here, in shades of yellow and blue and gray, clearly built by the same developer.

She pulled up the driveway of a butter yellow ranch home on a small wooded lot.

There was another car in the driveway—belonging to a parent, I was hoping—and a Wyatt Valley Police Department vehicle parked at the curb, currently unoccupied.

Inside, I imagined, someone was questioning her sister,

Sierra. Asking her to repeat again and again what she saw. Why she was out there. What her intentions were. Twisting things until she started to question things herself. *Tell me again, from the beginning—*

Carly paused on the front porch, like she was listening through the storm door, before finally slipping inside.

Word was starting to spread. There were cars parked all along the old Fraternity Row—which was as close as onlookers could legally park.

I could see people gathered on the other side, watching campus. A police car was visible at the border, like a warning for people to keep back.

There was a media van now, too, idling nearby. It felt like we were on the brink of something.

The school must've issued the lockdown in order to go room by room, taking a head count.

I parked abruptly in front of Cliff's rental house, hoping to find him home. Hoping that word had started to spread through the proper channels.

As I approached the front of the house, I could see that the door was slightly ajar.

I remained on the porch but cautiously pushed the door open a little farther, trying not to draw attention to myself.

The first thing I saw was a young boy sitting on the bottom step of the staircase, hunched over an iPad, blue headphones over blond hair.

And then I heard the voices.

"I *told* you, I can't take him right now." The sound was coming from the side of the foyer, where I knew Cliff's office was located. "Look at what's going on!"

"I have a twelve-hour shift at the hospital," a woman responded. "What am I supposed to do?"

My gaze drifted back to the boy. It seemed like he was fully invested in the cartoon playing on his screen. I was glad he wasn't hearing his parents arguing about him.

"Can't you get your parents to watch him?" Cliff asked.

"Can't *you* get a babysitter?"

"Jane, *please,*" he said, clearly exasperated. "You see what's happening out there."

"But you're stuck at home right now anyway," she said. "And I can't bring him to the hospital."

"I'm stuck at home because there's a *lockdown.* I'm getting calls every few seconds."

"This job isn't worth what they pay you," she said.

"Yes, it is. You can thank me when he goes there for free."

Like me, I thought.

Then I heard footsteps crossing the room. A door swinging open. I backed away from the entrance as her voice grew closer.

"We moved back here *for you,*" she said, "and for what? This isn't the first time. You barely take him on the days you have."

"There was a *fire,* Jane, it wasn't safe—" There was a waver in his voice, an uncertain emotion rising to the surface. Fear.

But Jane wasn't listening anymore. The front door flung open, resounding off the inner wall before she emerged in pale blue scrubs with her son by the hand.

She was prettier than I expected, petite with curly brown hair, almond-shaped eyes, and freckles that made her seem ageless. She pulled up abruptly, noticing me on the top step, then huffed and kept moving, like I was only one more thing to be exasperated by right now.

She lifted the boy up on her hip, and he wrapped his free arm around her neck, peering back over her shoulder with wide eyes.

Cliff appeared in the doorway, a few steps behind. "I'll come by tonight—"

The words died in his mouth as soon as he saw me there, motionless on his steps.

His hand tightened on the open door. "What are *you* doing here?"

I climbed the final step, joining him on the porch as he watched Jane buckle his son into the back of a small SUV. I decided to go with the obvious. "They found a body on campus?"

His eyes darkened, his gaze sliding up and down the street. I understood now that this was supposed to be the quiet part. This was why there were guards at every entrance point on campus. *This* was what they didn't want people to know.

"We can't make a statement yet. *You* can't say anything to anyone." He pulled the door open wider in welcome. Or, more likely, in a need to keep this quiet and contained.

"Who is it?" I asked, stepping inside. I shuddered, imagining all those parents receiving the same text alert and imagining the worst. I imagined each of them trying to contact their child—

"I don't know," he said. "For all their talk of open communication bullshit, they're keeping everyone back, even us. We're completely out of the loop."

"What the hell is going on out there? What happened?"

He took a deep breath, looking me over carefully. "It's fucking chaos, is what it is. I'm only home because there's no power, and we need to have access to the class lists. I've been printing them off. We've got a crew out at each dorm."

"Was it an accident?" I pictured the students running through the night, chased by seniors in masks. How easy it was to slip and fall. I could see the pit on campus being a hazard in the dark.

"They haven't said." He blinked slowly before speaking again. "But they *did* ask us to initiate a lockdown."

My throat tightened. Lockdowns were to protect the students. Lockdowns were to keep people safe from an active, present danger.

"They're worried someone pushed her. And that they're still out there," I said. A threat that remained in the area.

He didn't confirm but didn't deny. I understood why he wouldn't want his son around, even if he were working from home.

It was the same reason I was desperate to keep Delilah away from this place.

We wanted to shield them from danger, even if we couldn't prove it was here.

I looked toward the open door of his office. "Aren't there cameras around that area? Wouldn't they see?"

He shook his head. "Not at the construction pit. The building's demolished."

"But around it. There are other buildings nearby."

He frowned, crossed his arms. "The power's been out since late last night."

A chill worked its way through my body, like there was something darker at play. The power out at night and a dead body by morning.

Maybe it had nothing to do with the night of the howling. Maybe it was more recent—a student walking across campus in the dark.

"How long are you going to keep the kids up there? Violet's already been at the gates, demanding action."

He sighed. "Until the police advise us. In the meantime, you seem to know just as much as I do." He shifted his jaw like he was trying to pop a joint. "Is Delilah still at the house?"

"Yes," I said.

"Then," he said, guiding me toward the front door, "you have nothing to worry about, do you."

I didn't argue as I exited his house and walked down the front steps. But he was wrong.

I was worried that something was after her—looking for her.

I worried that someone had died in her place, out in the dark of the night. That she was still in danger. Not just in an implied threat from the words on the wall. But someone tracking her, close by.

My fear only grew as I pulled up the street.

Something was happening at the house.

There was a police cruiser parked at an angle in my parents' driveway, the rear tires sticking out in the street. Trevor stood on the porch, arms crossed, speaking to an officer in uniform.

"Hey," I called even before I'd finished climbing out of the car. "What's going on?"

My heart raced, every nerve on high alert. Had something happened to Delilah while I was gone?

I didn't know the man in uniform, hadn't seen him before. He was stocky and older, not much taller than I was, with a round face and soft expression.

"Hi, ma'am," he said, taking a step closer. "I was just telling your husband here, I'd like to have a word with Delilah."

My stomach dropped. I shook my head, climbing the steps. "She already talked to your colleagues last night," I said, standing beside Trevor.

"Yes, we're just working on a timeline. We need a little more detail. Trying to close out the paperwork on this one today."

He said it soft and sneaky. Like it was protocol.

"She's sleeping," I said, and I felt Trevor's body tense.

I hoped she stayed inside. I hoped she didn't hear us out here.

"It would be helpful to know the details of where exactly she was. For safety training."

"She was lost," Trevor said. "How would she even know?"

I raised my hand to Trevor's back, pressing firmly, to get him to stop. He didn't know what was happening here. And wasn't that the point? This man was coming to us before we found out.

The officer stared back, waiting. As if he expected me to be more accommodating. Invite him in, like my parents might've done.

But there was a dead body on campus and a police cruiser at my house.

My daughter had been missing for nineteen hours—unaccounted for during that period of time.

She had been lost in the woods, but her last name was also Bowery.

I knew what they were doing here. I knew exactly what they were looking for.

CHAPTER 21

Sunday, October 5
12:00 p.m.

We waited on the front porch, watching until the police cruiser was out of sight.

Trevor turned on me suddenly. “What the hell is going on?” he asked, a tinge of anger in his voice. He knew I’d lied to the officer about Delilah sleeping. He knew I’d wanted to stop him from talking about Delilah in the woods, even though he was telling the truth.

“Inside,” I said, pulling the screen door open, scanning the downstairs. “Where’s Delilah?” I asked, poking my head into the kitchen. I didn’t want her to hear this. Not yet.

Trevor stood in the middle of the foyer, arms crossed. “Upstairs, with my laptop. Probably checking her email.”

I couldn’t stop pacing. “I can’t believe this. I can’t believe *them*.” It was the past, rising up. My name alone, putting her in danger again.

“Beckett,” Trevor said, grabbing my arm as I passed by so that I had to stop, ground myself back in the present. “Talk to me, please.”

I glanced toward the kitchen again, where the steps led up to the bedroom—and Delilah.

My eyes slid back to Trevor’s. “There’s a body,” I said, my breath shuddering. “They found a body at the school.”

Trevor flinched, his face going pale, mouth open in that state of frozen shock I'd seen only once before, when I'd told him I was pregnant.

Finally he shook his head. "What do you mean, *a body*? Whose body?"

I felt my back teeth grinding together in frustration. "I don't *know*. A girl was found in the construction pit of the old student center. We passed the spot on the way to the campus police yesterday."

Silence. And then: "What the hell is happening, Beckett?"

"I have no idea. No one's getting on or off campus right now. The lockdown makes me think they're looking for an active threat." I swallowed, gaze sliding away.

Trevor didn't respond, but I could feel him looking at me closely, trying to understand what I couldn't say.

"I just want to get Delilah away from here," I said, voice softer. It was my basest instinct, to protect my child and avoid this place. And now look. The police were here, checking her story for cracks.

He dropped his voice to a whisper. "Listen, she asked about ordering a new phone. I looked into it, but the nearest store is an hour out of town. Why don't I take her there now, get some food while we're there. It'll get her away from here for a while."

I nodded. "That sounds like a good plan. And, Trevor?"

"Yeah?"

"Please don't tell her yet." She'd been through enough in the last twenty-four hours. "Not until I know more."

I took a shower while they were preparing to leave, mostly to avoid Delilah's questions. I was terrible at lying to her, and I didn't want to have to do it now. I'd made it a promise—the one foundation of my parenting. I may not have told her everything about this place, I may have avoided the topic of my past, but I wouldn't lie to her, either.

By the time I emerged from my parents' bedroom, Trevor and Delilah were gone, but they'd left Delilah's spare key on the kitchen table, beside my cell phone. At least I had a way to lock up now.

My phone was flashing with a new message. I was hoping it was Maggie with information from her husband.

But it was from someone not in my contacts—sent not from a phone number but from an email address. The name—*FordGroup*—sent a chill up my spine.

It was the same email account that had been contacting me about the memoir. I'd ignored their last message, asking for a meeting. But I'd given them my number in our first email exchange, and now they were using it. Escalating.

I opened the message, and all the hairs rose from the back of my neck in a slow wave.

We see you've come to us instead. Welcome home.

Welcome home. Like the text I'd received the very first day I returned to Charlotte, after driving away from the Low Bar.

Welcome home, like whoever it was had been waiting for me to return.

If I'd had any doubt whether the messages were referencing what happened here twenty years earlier, it was officially gone. They were watching, and they knew I was here.

I searched the sender's address for any clues and decided to channel Trevor, making a list.

There were pens in a ceramic container on my father's desk, and I was sure he kept pads of paper somewhere in the office. My parents were pretty old-school with technology, as evidenced by their shared email address and the unplugged modem—like they were concerned about strangers using their Internet connection while they were away.

The larger bottom desk drawer contained hanging files of research papers and clipped articles. Inside the one above that, stacks of papers stapled together. I riffled through an assortment of spreadsheets that appeared partially printed but overwritten in ink, with addresses all over the country. I assumed this was his holiday card mailing list. There was also a folder labeled *Accounts* with a checkbook tucked into the corner. I cringed, thinking about the window I'd left unlocked, all their financial information within reach.

Finally I found what I was looking for. Unused pads of yellow paper and spiral-bound notebooks under a stack of unopened mail. I moved the envelopes aside—they seemed to all be from the same sender, a mortgage company.

I did a double take.

I'd thought my parents owned this place outright. It was the reason they had never left, even in the high market—so they could live easy in their retirement, however they chose. Was that just what they'd told me as an excuse for why they were still here, in the place that had sent me away?

They loved it here, despite all that had happened. They loved it here enough to stay, even though it was a place they knew I would never return. Maybe they'd made a choice, too.

Here was a place you could feel the history existing all around you, both in the buildings and in the landscape. They'd met here, brought me into existence here, built a life here. It was the beginning and end of their world. During his tenure, my father had even been entrusted with the college archives—a keeper of its history on the third floor of Beckett Hall. How could they ever leave a place like this?

I slid a pad of paper out from under the stack of mail and started writing down every possibility I could find for companies with the name FordGroup, but it was so generic. There were endless options related to finance groups, legal teams, and automotive clubs, but none seemed to be related to Wyatt Valley or the college.

On a whim, I googled the full email address, hoping it would bring me to a website listing. But the search result came up empty. As if the account had appeared out of thin air.

Whoever had sent the message knew far more about me than I knew about them. I was tired of being on the outside, desperate for information.

Impulsively, I sent a response: *Who is this?*

And then I stared at my phone, waiting for something to happen.

I was holding my breath, sitting perfectly still, which was how I heard it through the office window: a creak of the gate to the side of the front porch. And then the shudder of the old wood slats catching against the uneven ground.

Someone was out there in the backyard *right now*. I remained perfectly still. Thinking: *I've got you.*

Quietly, I rose from the desk and left the office, planting one foot carefully in front of the other as I walked down the hall. I passed the entrance to the basement, the kitchen, and then my parents' bedroom. I stopped in the middle of the hall, staring at the door—waiting. Anticipating the slide of a key or the twist of a handle.

The seconds stretched out, but nothing happened.

Eventually I moved into my parents' bedroom, where their windows looked directly into the backyard. But I could see nothing moving within the small, fenced space.

I backtracked to the hall and then carefully exited through the rear door, phone in hand. The yard was overgrown, and several skinny trees lined the perimeter, but there were no hiding places out here. The yard was empty.

I followed the slate path around to the side of the house, where the gate hung slightly ajar. As if whoever had opened the gate hadn't been sneaking in but sneaking out.

As if they'd been inside the yard, watching, all along.

BEFORE:
THE LAST HOWLING

We woke to the sound of the wind in the morning, slowly gaining force. I rolled over in bed, but Adalyn was already awake, watching me from across the room. She lay on her side, head on the pillow, smile stretching wide. "It's here," she said. "Our last howling!"

By the afternoon, the snow had started to fall. I could see my breath in the air, misty in the gray. The school was buzzing with anticipation after the long stillness.

The countdown was on. It was our senior year. It was time to prepare.

We'd been talking about the plan all month, waiting for this moment: Take the shortcut through the tunnels. Get to the old president's house first. Defend the perimeter.

All we needed was the key.

I bumped into my dad in the cafeteria line during lunch. "Whoa, there," he said, readjusting his glasses.

"Can I borrow your ID card?" I asked. "I left mine in my dorm, and I'm locked out."

"Sure thing," he said, removing the lanyard from around his neck. His faculty ID hung beside the key to his office, along with another for the archives.

"You're a lifesaver," I said, spinning for the exit.

"Beckett," he called sternly.

I slowly turned around.

"I need that by next period."

I smiled. "I'll bring it right back."

At the end of the day, Cliff Simmons stepped into my path as I walked across the center quad, like the wind had blown him in, too. A ghost from my past. Someone I used to know.

I jolted back, confused.

I didn't know what he was doing here. "It wasn't me," I said, taking a step back. "I didn't touch their truck."

I'd seen the truck creeping across campus earlier in the week, Charlie and Micah in the cab, looking for us.

"I'm not here because . . ." He trailed off, eyes narrowed, looking off to the side. Like he wasn't supposed to be here and was afraid of being caught.

Then he took a step closer, lowered his voice so I had to strain to hear him over the wind. "Tonight," he said. "Be careful. They're coming."

CHAPTER 22

Sunday, October 5
3:30 p.m.

For the rest of the afternoon, I couldn't shake the feeling of being watched. Trevor and Delilah eventually returned with several bags from the mall out of town and an assortment of groceries from our local shop.

I was shocked by the vision of Delilah. There were bruises forming on both of her knees, too, so that she looked younger, like she did as a kid, scraped up from falling off the school jungle gym. The sneakers were her own—once bright white, now a little worse for the wear. But the soles were squeaky clean, like she'd been desperate to wash the night off them.

I remembered the streaks of mud yesterday, when I'd arrived home. The smudge at the front door. Another at the basement steps.

So that was the noise in the dryer—the uneven thud of her clothes, with the shoes caught in between. I hoped my mother didn't notice any damage to the dryer when she was back.

After Delilah dropped her bags in the foyer entrance, I gave her a hug, on instinct.

She tensed for a moment before giving in to it. "Is this going to happen every time you see me now?" she asked.

The fact that she was making a joke was a good sign. But it was also a sign that she probably hadn't heard about the body on campus.

"Maybe," I said. "Probably."

"Phone acquired," Trevor said, holding up a small paper bag in his left hand in triumph. "And food." He held up his right hand, three plastic bags straining against his fingertips.

I took the plastic bags and carried them into the kitchen. Delilah brought her phone into the living room while the two of us unloaded the groceries.

Trevor raised an eyebrow at me over the rustling of the plastic bags—a question he didn't want to ask when she was in earshot. *Anything?* he mouthed.

I shook my head. There were no updates. No answers. Not from Maggie and nothing online, either—I'd checked.

Trevor cleared his throat as he removed a carton of milk from a bag. "I didn't know . . ." he began. "I wasn't sure how long I should stay." As if explaining the amount of groceries he'd purchased—clearly more than for the day. "But until we know what's going on, I thought . . ." He trailed off again, waiting.

I paused at the counter, then turned to face him.

It was a question for me. An unspoken agreement. A line we always carefully walked and one I couldn't be bothered to keep up with now.

"Can you take tomorrow off?" I asked, another vague question.

He nodded, then opened the refrigerator, storing the perishables inside. "Yeah, of course. No problem. I already told my boss I had a family emergency, it's just . . . I don't have anything to wear. Probably should've picked up some more clothes at the mall while we were out, but I stuck to Delilah's list. The phone took precedence over fresh boxers."

I laughed, the sound foreign in the house. Maybe that was all we needed to break from the grip of the spiral. I hadn't been able to free my mind from its high-alert level since her dropped call. "I'm out after today, too. I can run a load tonight to see us through."

"I *do* know how to do my own laundry," he said. "I'm something of an expert in that regard." He smiled the same crooked smile he'd given me the first time we met, then he extended an open hand—waiting for me to pass him the juice.

But I was struck motionless. I'd gotten a sudden flash of another life. Another *almost*. Something I'd veered sharply away from. Something I might've missed.

I had dated a handful of men since him, more casually than seriously, which, I had come to learn, was primarily a fault of mine—that I was, to quote from my last significant breakup two years earlier, *bad at committing*. But that wasn't true. I was excellent at committing. I made decisions quickly and often; I bought a house at first sight; named Delilah in a single glance; fell in love in a heartbeat—in no time at all. It just hadn't been with them.

I stepped back quickly from the counter, needing air.

It was the proximity. The intimacy of being together in the house I'd grown up in. The vulnerability of the last day and the fact that my defenses had been all but stripped bare.

"Are you okay?" he asked, leaning against the counter.

I nodded, stepping back. "Can you finish this by yourself?" I asked. "I need to talk to Delilah before she gets that phone up and running." I was sure word was starting to spread.

"Yeah," he said, shaking his head slightly, like he was confused. "I know how to do this stuff, too, believe it or not."

I leaned against the entrance of the living room, preparing myself. Watching as Delilah sat hunched over the new phone, working through the setup process. She didn't have it completed yet, but I needed to prepare her.

"Hey," I said before joining her on the couch.

"Hey," she answered. Her hair had fallen in front of her face, so I couldn't see the scratch—or her expression.

"Delilah," I said, tucking one leg up, shifting to face her. "A girl was found dead on campus in the student center pit."

She stared up at me in shock—or fear.

"Your friend Sierra was out looking for you. She's okay, but she found the body," I added. I gestured to Delilah's phone. "I wanted you to hear it from me first. That's what the sirens were for this morning."

Her hand was trembling as she raised it to her mouth. "I don't . . . I need to . . ."

I grabbed her wrist, tried to refocus her attention. "Delilah, there's nothing you can do right now. We're not allowed on campus." I gestured to her phone. "You can check in with your friends from here."

She fell silent, her expression, for the first time, completely unreadable to me. Almost two months here, and as I had feared, this place had changed her, transforming her into someone quieter, more secretive. Someone who didn't tell me that she'd accused her roommate of theft; that she'd basically moved out of the dorm; that she'd been struggling.

It was time to hear what had been happening—not just over the last few days but since she'd arrived on campus. "Delilah, what happened at the dorm with Hana?"

She stared back at me but didn't answer. Like she was trying to figure out what I knew and how I knew it.

"I know you've been staying here," I said, my voice quiet, like I was in on the secret. "It's fine. I get it."

She shook her head, eyes widening. "I'm *not*—"

I lifted a hand, to stop her defense. To keep her from telling a lie that she'd have to walk back later. "I went by the dorm yesterday when I couldn't find you. Hana told me you don't stay there anymore. And your grandfather said he gave you your own key . . . You're allowed to be here. You're not in any trouble for it."

But that seemed to be the least of her concerns. "Mom, I'm *not*. I just told my RA that I was spending time at my grandparents' place in town so they wouldn't worry."

I shook my head, trying to recalibrate. "Where have you been staying, then?" I asked.

A friend—Gen, in another dorm. A boyfriend. That butter yellow house where Carly and Sierra lived. I waited for her to say it—whatever she didn't want me to know.

She tipped her head up and groaned at the ceiling. "You're not going to understand," she said dramatically.

"Try me," I said.

She pressed her lips together, debating. When the words came, they were small and quiet. "The theater."

My eyes widened. "You've been staying in a *theater*?"

"I *knew* you wouldn't understand."

I had to stop myself, bite my tongue. Wait for her to explain it.

She shook her head, waves falling over her shoulders. "It was an accident at first. I was doing my work there one night in the back room after a meeting and fell asleep on the couch. I have a key to the back entrance from stagecraft, and it's close to everything, and there's a bathroom and shower in the dressing rooms . . ."

I felt the rage rising. My daughter was staying in an empty building, alone. And no one knew where she was. "Why?" I asked.

"It's just so *loud* everywhere else. And it's so quiet there."

I actually *could* understand that. Delilah and I were both only children. When I first moved to the dorms, I'd been so excited for a roommate. Ready to share the experience with someone my age. I had welcomed the noise and the chaos. But on weekends, sometimes I'd sneak back home for the quiet. For the space. For the privacy. Eventually Adalyn followed me back here, too.

But Delilah still wasn't telling me everything. I had learned, as she got older, that I had to ask the right questions.

"Delilah, I know you put in a request to move dorms. I know something happened there."

She looked away, took a deep breath. "Someone was messing around with my stuff. Just little things at first, like the sign on the door. Or if I left my shower shoes outside. But then it was things *inside* the room." She looked to the ceiling again, like she was trying not to cry. "I thought it was my roommate. It was obviously only my things that were taken. So I reported it."

I nodded. I'd heard that much.

"But then it started happening when Hana wasn't even around—when I knew she was in class. If I took a shower and got back to the room, I could *feel* it. There was always something small missing. Nothing I could prove. The book I was reading for class. The photos on the wall. Like someone was messing with me. It freaked me out."

Her eyes were locked on mine. I was shaken just listening to it.

"So I figured it had to be someone with a key, right?" she said. "I thought it was the upperclassmen in my dorm, some sort of hazing. But last week, they took my laptop."

"Your laptop?" I said, unable to keep the emotion from my voice. "You should've reported that to the police, Delilah, that's a *crime*—"

"Mom, I'm handling it!" She seemed angry, but at *me* instead of the situation.

I tried to slow my heart rate; tried not to jump three steps ahead and lose her in the process. "Why didn't you tell me?" I asked.

Her eyes were shining, like she was trying desperately to hold back the tears. She was so much like me that way—I knew, if they spilled over, they wouldn't stop. "Because you didn't even want me here! I know that, Mom. I know that. You would've wanted me to come home."

"I could've helped—"

"I didn't need your help. I asked Dad for money and got a new laptop from the campus bookstore. I bring it with me now, or keep it in the theater, where no one would even know to look."

She looked pleased, vindicated. Like she'd successfully *handled it.* Meanwhile, there was someone in her orbit who had clearly escalated things beyond any claim of hazing.

I tried to steady myself before responding. I channeled Trevor, calm and contained.

"You haven't been staying in the room upstairs," I said, trying to keep the doubt from my voice. "Not at all?"

She shook her head. "There was no Wi-Fi. I wouldn't even be able to get work done. Why would I stay *here*?"

"So you didn't see—" I abruptly cut myself off.

She tilted her head. "See what?"

Like she was daring me to say it: *Hey there, Delilah. I can still see you. Did you think you could hide?*

"I think we should go," I said impulsively.

"Go where?"

"Home. Back to Charlotte. Once we can get back on campus and grab your things." *It's not safe here. Not for either of us.*

"I knew it!"

"I want you to be *safe*—"

"No, you don't want me *here*."

"Someone was killed on campus, Delilah!" I shouted. A mistake, I knew, as soon as I said it.

"And we don't even know who it *is*!" she yelled back, her entire body shaking.

Trevor stood in the entryway then. "I agree with your mother on this one," he said, in a united front.

"Seriously?" she said. "*Now* you want to get involved?"

I saw him flinch, just as I spoke her name, loud and sharp.

Her phone chimed suddenly, setup complete. Then it started buzzing with a string of messages finally coming through. Somewhere in there, I knew, would be mine, desperately trying to make contact. I was glad to see a collection of people checking in on her. To know she hadn't been totally alone here.

Delilah stood, pulling at the bottom of my old shorts, then disappeared toward the kitchen. I assumed she was heading up the back steps to my bedroom—where, I imagined, she would start making calls. Checking in with friends. Making sure it wasn't one of them. Trying to get a grasp on any rumor spreading through the school—or the town.

"She didn't mean it," I said to Trevor, hurt still evident on his face.

He pressed his lips together. "No, she did."

For now, she was done with this conversation. Done with the both of us.

I knew there was more: things she didn't want to say; something she wasn't ready to share with me.

Or maybe she really hadn't noticed the writing upstairs. How much time did she spend reading the lines on the walls anyway?

But I was stuck on what she'd told me earlier.

Someone with a key, she'd said. I tried to work it through. It wasn't someone with just a key to her dorm room. It had to be someone with a way in here, too.

CHAPTER 23

Sunday, October 5
6:00 p.m.

There was nothing we could do to make Delilah leave. She was stubborn. She was also eighteen. She had her own scholarship. An adult, whether I wanted to believe it or not, responsible for her own decisions.

Maybe she was right anyway. What good would running do? It only prolonged the problem, held the dangers at arm's length, always threatening to reemerge years later—as if you could never be free of them.

She came down before dinner less upset and maybe a little contrite.

All of her friends had checked in by then—*not them*—though she didn't seem able to relax. But this was good news, and Trevor asked if she'd help with dinner. A way to take her mind off things. A feign—or a fight—for normalcy.

Trevor's macaroni bake was apparently Delilah's favorite when she visited him in the summers, something that brought to mind comfort and childhood.

I watched as they worked side by side in the kitchen—Delilah making the side salad, plopping the bread in the oven—like a view into a part of her life I'd never had access to before. I knew

Trevor was a good father. Knew it from the way she spoke of him, the stories she told, the pictures he sent, the questions he asked. I knew it even before she was born. It was never a question in my mind.

But I hadn't gotten to see it. Not like this.

They had a rhythm that was different from the way Delilah and I interacted, another cadence to their conversation—but still something comfortable and familiar. Here was a person she would trust with her secrets.

"Mom, wait till you try this," she said, spoon in hand at the counter.

The scent had brought me back nineteen years, to the first time he'd cooked for me. "I already have," I said.

Trevor paused only briefly, eyes shifting from me to Delilah. "I have very few tricks up my sleeve, kid."

We ate together at the kitchen table, with Delilah's phone for company. I always hated it when she brought her phone to the table for a meal, but right now we were letting everything slide. The truth was, we were waiting for updates, too. And it was highly likely Delilah would hear through the grapevine first.

I jumped with every text. Watched as she read each message, trying to gauge her reaction.

Abruptly, she dropped her fork, then turned the most recent message my way. "The lockdown was lifted," she said. "They're letting people in again."

"Okay, that's good," I said, looking to Trevor for reassurance. That had to be good. They must've gotten answers, and they hadn't come back here looking for them.

The body must've been someone local, I decided, if the school was opening again. A girl from town, running through the night, trespassing. A tragic accident. But something they could claim, once more, was *not their fault*.

We were cleaning up from dinner when the sound of the dryer buzzing carried from the basement again.

I was first down the stairs for the laundry, but Trevor was only a few steps behind, apparently incapable of letting me handle this one task for him. Not that I should be one to speak; I'd probably do the same if the roles were reversed.

"She seems better, right?" he asked, now that we were out of earshot. As if that were the real reason he'd followed me.

"She does," I said. "What did she talk about on your trip to the mall?"

"What do you mean?" he asked, peering up the steps to the partially open doorway.

"I feel like there are things she's not telling me," I said. I thought she'd stayed in the room upstairs, but she'd denied it. And yet I'd seen the toothpaste and the wet towel hanging askew. The next-door neighbors had seen lights on at night upstairs. "I didn't even know she asked you for money."

I was realizing that she hadn't been telling me things for weeks. She'd gone to her father instead.

He took a slow breath, like he was thinking before he spoke. "She hasn't said much. But I'm not pushing." Which was probably a better move than my attempt to extract information. "We listened to the radio most of the way. She wanted to know why you called me down here. And, for your entertainment, she asked how long we planned to babysit her."

I rolled my eyes. Only an eighteen-year-old would fail to see why her parents had both come to search for her when she went missing in the woods. Or why they'd stayed when someone had died in an accident on campus.

"Did you know she was struggling here?" I asked.

He scraped the side of his shoe against the concrete floor, frowning at the dirt he left behind. "Not in so many words. But she'd been reaching out more often, with fun facts." He looked up at me, a small smile growing. "Like, did I know you were named for a building here."

I looked off to the side before the past could grab hold of me again. *Like Samuel Beckett?*

"I didn't, for the record," he said. "As you know."

When I looked back, he was grinning.

"Who wants to admit that they're named after a building where their parents both worked?" I asked.

"And," he continued, "did I know why you left the college."

I didn't respond. Felt time contracting again—but farther back. To snow-peaked mountains and the bite of winter wind; the crunch of boots and the feeling of cold deep in my lungs—

"I told her I did know that one," he said, "but that she should really ask you about that."

I shook my head, surprised. "She didn't."

She knew enough: There had been a horrible accident, and my roommate was involved. There was so much attention, the school asked me to leave. Maybe my parents had told her more. I was sure she could read a more salacious version online. Lord knows I had.

But whenever I shared our story, it started in the after: *I went abroad, and then you were born*. The history of her life began out there. *I* may have existed because of this place, yes. *But* you *exist,* I wanted to tell her, *because I left.*

I'd opened the dryer, felt the heat escaping, when Trevor spoke again. "She also asked—not for the first time—why we didn't work out."

"Huh," I said, still facing away.

When I turned back, he was standing close, with a crooked grin. "Yeah."

"That's something she hasn't asked me in years." Maybe she was comparing our stories, deciding whose was stronger—or who was at fault. "I told her we were very young," I said. Which we were, in more ways than age.

I'd been twenty-two and hadn't yet learned to treat people well, with a grace of time. I couldn't slip happiness into focus then—my imagination kept reaching back instead of forward—and I didn't believe he would choose me if he knew me better.

And he'd been twenty-three, incapable of seeing a life different from the one he'd planned.

"That's generous," he said. "I told her the truth. That I didn't handle the news of her right."

I cringed, imagining her hearing that and trying to process. The truth was, he was always better at the concrete than the hypothetical. Had to see something in person, hold something tangible and real. She never would've known that if he hadn't told her. By the time she was two, he was living back in the States, and he'd asked if he could visit for birthdays and holidays. And then he'd started asking for more: a weekend, a week, a month. They had a different type of relationship than Delilah and I did, but it was a real one.

"I didn't respond the right way. I know that," he added—like he needed to tell me, too.

"I didn't give you the time to," I said.

I had been afraid also. For weeks. Afraid that I'd be a terrible parent. That I wouldn't be able to decipher what she needed. That she would always be a mystery to me. But our relationship had been nothing like I'd feared.

Until recently, I'd thought she told me everything.

"I can't shake it, Trevor," I said. "This feeling that she's still in danger." I was sensing it everywhere: in the creak of an open gate; the writing on the wall; the police asking questions about her whereabouts that night, like she was a suspect instead of a child.

I wanted him to tell me it was all in my head. That I was stuck in a spiral. I thought I'd believe him if he said it.

"Me, too," he said, frowning.

But then he stepped closer and placed his hand on my wrist, taking my pulse with two fingers on the line of the mountain ridge. He closed his eyes like he was keeping time. I felt the blood racing through my veins, like something was still coming.

"But she's okay," he said. "She's right here."

And so was he.

"By the way," I said, turning my arm so the tattoo faced up, "this isn't a heartbeat."

He laughed, rubbed his thumb along the peaks and valleys.

"It's the mountains," I said. "It's here."

"Okay," he said, his breath low and husky, pulling my arm closer. "I see it now. Beckett Bowery, named for a building, with a tattoo of home."

I moved my hand to the side of his face, felt the warmth of his skin as I ran my thumb against the stubble, down to his jaw. I watched as his eyes drifted shut for a moment, and I closed the space between us, pulling his head down to mine—transported, once more, in time.

I knew things now that I hadn't known then. There would never be a right time. Never quite enough time.

But he was right: Here we were, right now, in the present.

The door creaked at the top of the stairs.

"Hellooo?" Delilah called, her voice echoing down the stairwell. "I think someone's here!"

"We'll be right up!" I yelled as Trevor stepped back, laughing under his breath. Fitting, I thought, that the moment would be broken by our eighteen-year-old daughter.

Trevor handed me a laundry basket from the metal shelving as I gathered the clothes from the dryer.

"Not to point out an obvious question, but why is there an antique clock in your basement?" he asked.

"Trevor," I said, partly exasperated, "that clock is the least strange thing about this place." I gestured to the single cabinet set into the cinder-block wall beside the steps. "Go upstairs and I'll send your laundry up the dumbwaiter." I was fighting to stay in this moment—for the normalcy of it, or maybe the promise of it.

His eyes widened, following my gaze. "You're kidding," he said.

"Creepy, right?"

"Where does it go?" he asked.

"A corner of the kitchen. Trust me, you'll know it when you see it."

Though the dumbwaiter door was made of the same wood as the rest of the cabinets, it was clearly set apart, opening directly into an empty space in the drywall.

Trevor's steps echoed on the wooden stairs as I brought the laundry basket over to the corner of the basement. The dumbwaiter had been built directly into the cinder-block wall, like it was a part of the original home structure.

The automated press-and-hold button was on the outside, in a simple up/down mechanism. The system ran from the floor to the ceiling through a hollow shaft directly in the unfinished bones of the house.

I opened the cabinet, but the dumbwaiter wasn't visible. Only the dust, seeming to hover in the gap. I pressed the button to bring the device down, and a dull buzz filled the space as the box slowly lowered into position.

I released the button as the dumbwaiter box came into view.

Something was already inside.

I dropped the laundry basket to the floor, staring into the box, my heart racing.

A phone. Neon gel writing on the case; a single word, hand-drawn: *Delilah.*

CHAPTER 24

Sunday, October 5
7:30 p.m.

I stared at the phone, unable to move. Reaching back in time to the moment when I'd found her in the basement, sitting on the floor, facing the dryer. Hair wet, keys on the concrete beside her. She must've taken a shower, thrown her clothes and sneakers in the wash. And she'd tossed her phone in a hidden space, hoping it wouldn't be found.

Something had happened in the night. Something she hadn't told me.

My hand was trembling as I picked up the phone and slowly turned it over. The screen was shattered—a central point of impact, with cracks spreading outward.

She said she'd lost her phone in the woods. She said she'd dropped it down an embankment. She said—

"Beckett?" Trevor called, standing at the top of the stairs.

I spun around, hiding the phone behind my back on instinct. "Sorry," I called. "The dumbwaiter's not working. I'll be right up."

The stairs creaked as he took a single step down. I could see the blue of his sneaker, the bottom of his pants. The stillness of his body. "He's back," he said in warning.

He's back.

He must've meant the police.

"Hold on—"

I couldn't think straight. My vision had gone blurry at the edges. What were they doing back here at night?

What were they looking for?

I pressed the button to the side of the dumbwaiter, raising the empty box. Then, before I could question it, I dropped the phone into the shaft below before lowering the dumbwaiter back into position.

I emerged from the basement to find Fred Mayhew on the other side of the screen door. "There she is," Trevor said as I placed the full laundry basket on the floor of the hallway.

I hoped Delilah was upstairs. I hoped she stayed out of sight. So I could say: *No, she's not available to talk right now. No, you cannot come in. No, you cannot look around.*

"I was hoping to catch you here," Mayhew said, straight-faced. "May I?" He gestured to the screen door.

His eyes were bloodshot, like he'd been up all night. He'd left his sport coat behind today, and the sleeves of his button-down were rolled up, as if he'd been working with his hands.

I wondered if he'd been at the student center pit all day.

"What's this about?" I asked.

"Is there somewhere you and I can sit down and speak privately for a minute?" he asked.

There wasn't, really. Just my father's office, where one of us would need to sit awkwardly behind a desk with a series of masks staring down from overhead. "We can talk out front," I said, though it wasn't exactly private.

But I didn't know where Delilah was. I didn't want him shifting the conversation to her in a quick bait and switch.

He was older now, and he had gotten better at this.

I joined him outside and sat on one of the two white rocking chairs in front of the living room window. Mayhew dragged the other chair so it was facing me. In the dark, the porch light threw long shadows to the side.

"I heard you were at the scene today," he said, lowering himself into the seat. He rocked forward, resting his hands on his knees so he was leaning even closer. "Heard you were watching."

I didn't answer. Maybe that's why he was here—wondering what had taken me over there. How I'd known where to go. Wasn't that a rule for finding a suspect? Look at the people who come back to watch. Everyone knew: You couldn't return to the scene of the crime.

"I wasn't the only parent there." Violet and I were just the closest to the campus.

"What did you hear from Carly Mathers?" he asked, changing directions. As if he wanted me to know there would be no secrets. He knew exactly where I'd been and whom I'd talked to. That I hadn't been just on campus; I'd been lurking in the woods. Watching in secret.

"I heard that her sister, Sierra, found someone in the student center pit," I said. "Do you know who it is?"

He stared back at me, silent and still. This was not the strategy he'd used when interviewing me in the past. Back then, he'd pushed and pried and dug. He hadn't mastered this tactic of uneasy silence. He hadn't quite learned the value of time—to wait for someone else to crack in discomfort and fill it.

He breathed in deeply, rocking back slowly like we were old friends casually chatting on the front porch. "There was a student ID on the body," he began. "We haven't officially confirmed it, but we have a name."

I nodded, needing him to continue. Delilah's friends had all checked in. Still, my stomach twisted, waiting.

Fred Mayhew folded his thick hands on his lap, leaning forward again.

"Strangest thing," he said. "The name on the ID is Adalyn Vale."

I stopped breathing. Whatever I had been waiting for, it was not this.

A girl—that's what Carly had told me. Which had made me think young, student-age. And that's what she'd been the last time I'd seen her, twenty years earlier.

Racing through the dark, black mask pulled down over her face, only her blue eyes visible in the beam of the flashlight.

I pictured it anew: That trail in the snow, ending at the road at the edge of campus where she disappeared. The men's size-ten boots, no longer helping her escape—but catching her.

Someone who had been angry. So angry for what she'd done. Hurting her and then hiding her away. And letting a legend grow in her absence.

Had she been there all along? On campus, hidden inside the student center—dead?

The town was full of suspects. People with motive.

I thought of Cliff—the only one left. He'd been close to the victims through high school and after.

Then I thought about all the other people Micah White and Charlie Rivers had grown up with—their friends and family. *This* man, even, smugly sitting in front of me, with all the protection in the world. Before he was a detective, Fred Mayhew was the young officer who once sat in the Low Bar the night Adalyn was forced to turn over her pearl necklace. I remembered his inaction then.

He'd picked a side, too.

We all had.

Who would know where to hide her, how to bury her?

I took a slow breath, to recalibrate.

This had nothing to do with Delilah. The phone in the basement meant nothing. This had to do with the past. With me. With him.

"Where was she?" I asked, my voice razor-thin.

"What do you mean?" Mayhew asked.

"Where was she buried?" Under a floor somehow? In a hidden

basement room, maybe, that had been unearthed? Or had she been in the soil found along the perimeter, under the spot where students walked each day?

The construction vehicles must've uncovered the spot just before the weekend. But it was only in searching for Delilah that Adalyn had been actively found.

He tipped his head to the side, looked straight into me. "She wasn't."

"I don't understand."

The silence stretched again, like he was waiting for me to say something. To reveal something. He'd been waiting a long time.

"*If* it's her—and again, we need to confirm—she's been living another life for the past twenty years. Best we can guess, she died sometime in the last forty-eight hours."

CHAPTER 25

Monday, October 6
1:00 a.m.

I couldn't sleep. From my spot on the futon in the office, the wind pushed against the windows in a low whistle. *It's Adalyn.*

Wasn't that what the kids at the school said now, under the sound of the howling? *It's Adalyn.* Like a whisper, a séance drawing her back.

Hadn't I felt it? The past existing right beside me here? I had never been able to shake the feeling that something else was coming. I'd just been preparing for the wrong thing.

Detective Mayhew had said they couldn't be sure yet, but they seemed sure enough to tell me. Adalyn's parents had died in a car crash five years ago, so there was no next of kin to identify her, no DNA available for a quick match. But they were working their way back in time from the details in her wallet. A license under another name. A photo that looked similar enough. And she'd had the old school ID with her—like proof. Something she had held on to for twenty years, for the moment she returned.

I imagined her name spreading through town in the wind, in whispers, on phone lines, in text messages. *It's Adalyn.*

I had done it myself after the detective left. Said the words to Trevor and Delilah first, where we were all together in the living room: *It's Adalyn.*

I needed to speak it out loud, make it real. I saw Trevor reaching for context in the silence—she was a stranger to him. *My old roommate,* I added.

Delilah must've known enough. Her eyes widened, but she remained silent. As if there were too many questions to know where to begin.

Trevor, like me, first assumed she'd been dead since that tragic night. And I had to explain it all over: *Died sometime in the last forty-eight hours.*

I had emailed my parents. Channeled my mother, quick and to the point, with no emotion: *Adalyn Vale was just found dead on campus.*

In my mind, I tried to reconcile the twenty-one-year-old I'd last seen, with someone who had aged two decades. An entire second life in between. All I could picture was a before and after. The beginning line of her story—and the very end.

She must've been out there for twenty years, living an entirely different life. She'd gotten away with it. She'd gotten *away.* I didn't understand why she'd come back. Didn't she know? You couldn't return.

Fred Mayhew assumed I knew more than I did. It seemed like he thought I'd been in contact with her since she'd been gone. But I hadn't been. Despite what he thought, I hadn't seen her since that night in the woods. I hadn't helped her. I wouldn't have.

Now I pictured her as a shadow, lurking around campus. Seeing Delilah, someone who looked just like me. Sneaking into her dorm, messing with her until she had to move. Following her. Writing threatening messages on my bedroom wall.

I pictured a horde of kids running through the woods, celebrating the first howling of the year—a tradition that must have reemerged sometime in the years since. I pictured Adalyn joining—she always loved a game.

And then I pictured Delilah out there, too.

I had to wait until the middle of the night, until I knew I was alone. Delilah was upstairs in my old room. I'd set Trevor up in my parents' room—I had no interest in staying in there myself. I'd taken up residence in my father's office. As if I alone could keep watch from the front windows of the house.

I thought of those footsteps in the house that I'd heard when I was up in the attic. Realizing it was not Delilah. Wondering now if it had been Adalyn, so close.

Wondering if she'd known I was here, too.

The house had fallen silent, save for the wind pushing up against the windows, whistling through the gaps. If I put my hand up to the base of the glass pane, I could feel it: a hiss through the window seal.

I tiptoed out of the office and stood in the hall, listening. I didn't turn on a light, hoping to remain undetected. And when I let myself into the basement, I closed the door behind me before flipping the switch.

At the bottom, the concrete floor was cold against my bare feet. I paused before continuing, making sure I didn't hear anyone overhead.

I opened the cabinet for the dumbwaiter, then pressed the button to raise the box. The hum of the gears felt louder in the silence of the night. Slowly, the hollow space underneath was revealed, the spot where I'd panicked and stashed Delilah's phone.

I leaned inside the cabinet opening and used the flashlight on my phone to peer down into the dumbwaiter shaft. At the base, the neon of her name on the phone case caught the light; it rested on a layer of grounded rock and soil.

I had to get inside.

I raised the dumbwaiter box even higher, to make sure I had space to stand beneath it—and in an attempt to alleviate the impending claustrophobia. Then I shone my light around the pulley system, checking the gears, making sure I avoided anything that could hurt me.

This was an old apparatus. All I could picture were the accidents waiting to claim the curious and naive: electrocution, a chain snapping, the box falling from above. Another missing person, this time trapped in the walls of the house.

I flipped my mother's laundry basket upside down to use as a makeshift step stool. Then I eased myself backward onto the small cabinet ledge, twisted my legs around in the narrow space, and dropped inside.

The base felt gritty, ancient, like I was standing on top of some untouched history.

I crouched down carefully, picking up Delilah's phone. I'd barely had time to look at it earlier, hadn't tested if it worked. I held the power button, trying to get it to boot up, but nothing happened. No light from the shattered screen, no sound of it coming to life.

The phone was in her clear case, which looked splotchy with dried watermarks. Exposed to the mud and the elements from a night in the woods, like she claimed.

I placed the phone on the cabinet ledge, preparing to launch myself back out, but it wasn't as easy from this side, without the step stool. I couldn't get enough leverage to push myself up. I tried bracing my feet against the concrete wall on the opposite side of the shaft, but it was a little too far. A decade or two earlier, I was sure, I would've climbed out of here easily.

As it was, my heart was pounding, and the claustrophobia was making the enclosed space seem even smaller. My phone didn't get good service in the basement, but I knew noises carried. If I called for help, someone in the house would hear me. I just didn't want to have to explain what the hell I was doing down here.

I positioned myself backward, braced my hands on the ledge, and kicked off the bottom in an attempt at a jump.

Finally I made it up, scooting myself onto the ledge. But in the process, the angle of my foot had dislodged a piece of metal on the floor of the shaft, sharp against my heel. I shone my light down there again. A curl of silver. A small jagged edge.

I dropped down into the shaft once more, pulling a chain free. On the other end, a fine layer of grit slid away, revealing the shape underneath. A key.

I recognized it immediately.

A skeleton key. Attached to a necklace.

I couldn't get enough air. Felt the four walls closing in, the space narrowing. The feeling of being trapped, with no way out.

I was holding the key from the original construction of the tunnels, the one my father once oversaw as part of the archive collection, a living history of the school.

"Is that you?" A groggy and disoriented Trevor was halfway down the steps. "I thought you were . . ." His sentence trailed off. He watched as I scrambled to climb back out from the walls of the house—like an animal or a ghost.

"What the hell are you *doing*?" he asked.

I needed to decide fast. Could I trust him? No, *did* I?

Trevor reached a hand to help pull me out.

But I lifted the phone from the ledge and watched as his eyes moved from me to the neon script of his daughter's name.

Delilah must've hidden it here as soon as she was back.

I stared at him, waiting. Begging him to come up with a different explanation.

Something that didn't end with Delilah lying to us. Hiding her phone. Coming straight here to wash her clothes, her shoes, her hair.

Destroying the evidence of what really happened out in the woods that night.

BEFORE:
THE KEY

"What's the matter?" Adalyn asked when I returned to the dorm, dusk settling. She was plaiting her hair, tying the braids tight.

"That guy Cliff, we had a thing back in high school. Briefly," I added at her shocked expression, even though that wasn't exactly true.

Her eyes met mine in the mirror. "Look at you, full of secrets."

"I saw him today," I told her. "He was looking for me. Adalyn, those guys in the truck, they're coming tonight. They're going to track us into the woods."

It was a warning, a gift. The only words Cliff and I had spoken in years: They're coming.

She turned to me, bemused. "Are you scared of them?" she asked. As if I were something to study, like my mother would do. As if my humanity were a curiosity, my emotion a data point.

I hadn't learned to mask my thoughts from Adalyn.

I hadn't learned to hold on to my secrets in the silence.

"I don't think we should go tonight," I said.

She frowned briefly, then picked up her black wool hat, turning it so the eyeholes were facing her. "I think," she began, "that they *should be scared of* us.*"*

"They're not." They were not the type, which was the problem.

Both Cliff and I understood. The howling was a game for not just the students but the folks in town, too. Now there was a different undercurrent. The stakes had escalated. Her necklace, their truck. I'd seen their vehicle crawling through campus. They knew who we were—where we were. It was their move next.

"Did you get the key?" she asked, maneuvering away from my comment. I pulled it out from under my sweater, where it hung around my neck. The ornate, looping design fed through one of my silver chains. I'd used my father's access to sneak into the archive room in Beckett Hall during lunch. I'd opened the case. I'd taken the key from the school. From my father, the keeper of its history, the holder of its past.

Adalyn smiled wide, then cut the final hole in her hat, the snip of the woven wool crisp and satisfying.

I felt a rush of fear and adrenaline as I watched her pull it slowly over her head, unrolling the fabric to conceal her face, two blond braids extending from the bottom. So that, out of the dark mask, all I saw were a pair of blue eyes and her berry pink lips.

And then the shape of her mouth as she whispered, "Are you ready, Beck?"

CHAPTER 26

Monday, October 6
9:00 a.m.

We were tucked behind the closed door of my father's office, the phone resting on the desk between us like a ticking bomb.

"She said she dropped the phone in the woods," Trevor said, not for the first time, going back to his core point from the middle of the night, before we retreated to our separate rooms, pretending to sleep, trying to work it out on our own. Now he was showered and overcaffeinated and pacing the tiny square of the room, making me even more anxious. My eyes trailed him back and forth from my spot behind the desk. There wasn't enough room in here for his pent-up energy.

"She said she *lost it,*" I whispered. She'd been very clear on that point. She'd said it to me and to the police.

"And it was just . . . in the dumbwaiter?" he asked, voice rising.

I nodded, peering at the closed door behind him, hoping Delilah hadn't come down for breakfast yet, eavesdropping on the conversation. No matter how he tried to spin it, there was no way he could map a way out, bring us to a safe and comfortable understanding.

"Maybe we missed something. Maybe she was . . ."

But we were talking ourselves in circles.

I stood, then abruptly swiped the phone off the desk. "I'm going to ask her."

Trevor stopped pacing, stared at me silently. Like this was something he hadn't considered.

"She'd tell us if she wanted to," he said. Like he didn't want to push her into revealing a truth he might not be ready to hear. This was the first time I could recall him ever verbally disagreeing with my parenting decisions.

"Trevor, someone is dead. *Adalyn* is dead. I think she was harassing Delilah, stealing her things, making her feel unsafe in the dorms, and this house, and—" I stopped myself before I went too far down the track.

"And *what*?" he asked quietly. His hands were shaking, and I didn't know whether it was from the caffeine or the horror of the unfinished sentence.

He reached for me then, his hands circling my wrists. "Please," he whispered, resting his forehead against mine. "Please tell me this isn't happening."

I took an unsteady breath in. "We really need to ask her," I whispered. "We can't help until we know."

He stepped back, releasing me.

I strode through the house to the narrow stairs behind the kitchen. "Delilah?" I called from the place my mother used to call my name. "Are you up?"

I waited, like always, for the sound of her footsteps above, rapid and frantic, realizing she had overslept. But there was only silence. "Delilah!"

I felt Trevor standing in the kitchen behind me. "Beckett," he said gently. I turned, saw him standing beside the round table, holding a piece of paper in his hand. He frowned, eyes skimming the page. "She went to school."

"She *what*?" I asked. I strode across the room, took the note from Trevor's outstretched hand.

She'd written lengthwise across a sheet torn off the grocery list pad in my parents' junk drawer: *Needed clothes. Went to campus. Classes are in session today and I can't miss. —D*

"You've got to be kidding me," I said through clenched teeth.

She could've easily knocked on the office door before she left. Could've called through the house to find me—Lord knows she'd done that enough. She could've called or texted us a heads-up. I knew the fact that she didn't was only because she didn't want me to tell her no. Delilah always believed in asking for forgiveness instead of permission.

I felt my stomach drop, my throat constrict. How dare she just leave a note at a time like this—

And I was embarrassed that Trevor saw this—how she so obviously didn't want to talk to me first. That he was witnessing my failings as a parent up close. And that maybe Delilah and I didn't have as strong a relationship as I'd always believed.

I'd thought I knew her better than this. I'd thought our relationship was better than this.

I took a deep breath. "I'm going," I said, leaving the phone behind on the table.

He reached for my elbow as I pivoted for the exit. "Beckett, think about this," he said. "Slow down for a minute."

But I'd already thought it through. I'd already decided. I needed to get onto campus anyway. There were things I had to check; something I had to know.

I stared up at him, wide-eyed.

"Don't go in angry," he said, releasing me.

"I'm not angry, Trevor." No, that was covering for something else. "I'm terrified."

Same as him.

"Give me a second to get ready, and I'll come with you," he said.

But I needed to be there alone. The skeleton key didn't belong in this house. It was something Trevor didn't understand—and it was dangerous.

"Stay here in case the police come back," I said. I pointed emphatically at the cell phone. "Do not let anyone see that. Do not let anyone inside. No one."

There was a noticeable security increase at the school. Golf carts driven by personnel in orange vests, patrolling the roads and sidewalks. Campus police, in uniform, a visible presence. A reminder—or a promise—that the students were safe.

At first I couldn't believe that school was in session. Someone had died at the edge of the property. But Adalyn wasn't a student, and there were tragedies everywhere. It was Monday. Parent weekend was rapidly approaching. It was best to keep the students occupied rather than to let them sit in their rooms with the knowledge of what had happened; with the realization of how close they each might've come.

They needed routine.

The only place I could park without a tag was in the visitor lot on lower campus, designated for admissions. It was close to the start of the admissions tours, in the back lobby of Beckett Hall.

Luckily, I had arrived on campus a few minutes before the start of the ten a.m. classes. There were so many students walking across the academic quad that it was easy enough to blend in.

From the walkway, I looked to the top of the arched doors and saw a small black device pointing down. That must've been the camera that had caught Delilah entering the building just before midnight.

I knew it was taking freeze-frame pictures of everyone as they passed. I knew the photos would be stored for security to piece through if anything should happen.

I kept my head down and slipped in at the back of a larger group stepping inside. Voices echoed through the front atrium, carrying snippets of student conversation.

They think she was running from something and didn't see the hole—

Someone pushed—

No way, definitely an accident. There were no lights out there—

I broke away from the group, lingering at the edge of the atrium, sliding along the curved wall. The entire room was brimming with people and conversation and activity. Some groups had clustered together, sipping coffee, leaning close in conversation, while others moved down the hall in single-minded focus.

I scanned the crowd for a familiar face. No Delilah. But I wasn't here for her yet anyway.

No one seemed to notice me. I traced the perimeter, dragging my hand against the texture of the cool curved wall like I'd done long ago. But now the walls were smoothed over with plaster and fresh paint. I stopped at the outline of the old tunnel door, which blended into the wall so well that only the keyhole was visible.

The silver chain I'd found in the dumbwaiter shaft was currently wrapped around my wrist, the skeleton key clenched in my palm. I leaned sideways against the door like I was just passing time. Then I slipped the key into the lock.

I had to know if it still worked. So many years had passed since I'd last seen it. The key had disappeared with Adalyn twenty years earlier—or so I'd thought.

I peered around the atrium once more; the campus police had said there were no cameras inside, only at the main entrance of each building.

No one else in the room seemed to be paying attention.

I turned the key to the right and felt the bolt click open, the seal of the door give slightly, in a breath. Quickly, I turned the key back, sealing the door, securing the bolt.

Was it possible that Delilah had found this key somewhere? Was that why she had sneaked into Beckett Hall in the night? To access the tunnels that I'd pointed out to her at orientation?

I pictured Delilah entering Beckett Hall at midnight. Cliff had said most of the entrances were sealed off, but not *all.* Not this one. Was this a way for her to avoid the cameras? To slip through campus unnoticed.

It was the simplest explanation. What else could she have been in here for?

Not the library. She said she'd been staying at the nearby theater, where she could enjoy the quiet she craved. What was worth the trip here just before midnight?

My hands shook. The phone in the dumbwaiter. The skeleton key stashed below. My parents' house, full of evidence—

I had to get the key back where it belonged. It wasn't safe in that house, and it wasn't safe in my possession.

The atrium had started to empty out, a stream of students heading down the hall. I followed them past the admissions door and the other administrative office where Cliff must be.

I continued with the flow of bodies, veering up the old steps with the iron rails that were probably original to the structure. Half the students filtered out at the second-floor landing, where my mother used to teach. But I continued on to the third, where my father's office used to be—beside the archive room.

The doors up here all appeared the same: dark, heavy wood, with inset glass that provided a view into the room beyond.

A buzzer sounded from somewhere in the halls, something dull and grating—not quite the chiming of the bell tower but a marker of time for class. I watched as the rest of the students disappeared behind various wooden doors, the hallway falling empty.

I peered through the glass window into the archive space, a small room with a domed ceiling and wooden four-person tables with green wired lamps for studying. There was a single student in there now, headphones on, bent over his laptop with an old book open beside him.

Inside, shelves were stacked with record books and blueprint scrolls. And framed on the walls: the sketch of the original campus; the picture of the first all-boys' graduating class, in black and white; a portrait of the first college president. And then there were the drawers that you could slide open but were covered in glass, like in a museum. Inside which this skeleton key had long been kept.

My father always carried the key to the archives on a lanyard around his neck, along with his faculty ID card and office key. The day of our final howling, I'd asked to borrow it from him during lunch. He'd handed it over without blinking. But I'd gone to the archive room instead, unlocked the case, and taken the skeleton key so we could use the tunnels as a shortcut to the ruins of the old president's house.

I was sure no one would notice before I returned it; people rarely sifted through the archive drawers. I'd planned to slip it back behind the locked glass the next day, but I never got the chance.

Now I opened the door, and the scent brought me immediately back: old books and wood polish, leather binding and handmade paper. *This* was the scent of my childhood. I'd loved to explore while my parents worked, had been a permanent fixture on campus.

The student in headphones didn't look up from the table as I passed, heading to the back, where the drawers were built into an antique-looking dresser.

I pulled the handle of the bottom drawer: A layer of thick glass protected what lay inside, with a locked metal latch where it connected with the wood. It was something I pictured whenever I was in a pharmacy, peering at the medicines kept in locked cases.

I ran my fingers along the surface. Below the glass, each item was labeled with a nameplate. The original school bell, dark bronze and cracked; the deed for the land purchase—and then I froze. The nameplate said *Tunnel Key,* but the space below wasn't empty. There was another key in its place. Something that looked similar to the original: ornate looping, tarnished silver, a ridge of teeth.

But the color was off. The pattern different.

It wasn't the real key.

The real key was currently in the purse slung across my chest. The only explanation for this replacement was if someone else had noticed the original was missing.

My breath caught in my throat. There was only one person who would've understood how those men had gotten into the tunnels.

My father.

He knew I had lied when I asked for his lanyard, or he'd figured it out soon after.

He'd known, and he'd said nothing. To cover for me, he'd found a way to replace it with a good enough replica that nobody would look twice.

I wondered if he'd known immediately, when the police started questioning the security guards about their keys, asking how the men *could've possibly gotten into the tunnels*. Or whether he'd discovered it years later, as he was showing a guest around the archives, the final piece of a puzzle clicking into place—

"Excuse me!" A deep voice reverberated through the circular room.

I spun from the cabinet, caught. A young man wearing a ball cap and a campus security vest stood at the other end of the stacks. Dill, the same guard Violet had been trying to talk her way past yesterday. He was Beverly's son—a local. Like my parents said, most of the people who worked here were. "You aren't allowed in here."

But there was no sign. No lock. Nothing to indicate I'd done something intentional. "Sorry, I was just looking around."

"You can't be in the buildings unless you're a student," he said.

"I'm a parent," I said.

He seemed unmoved. The keys on his hip jangled as he took a step closer. "That doesn't matter. Right now this is a closed campus . . ."

They must've been trying to keep journalists off the property. Or people wandering in from town for a closer look.

"I'm going," I said, hands held up. "I'm just waiting to meet my daughter."

Dill insisted on escorting me out. As we walked down to the first-floor hall, I caught sight of Cliff Simmons through the window of his department office. He turned at our movement out here—like I was a shadow in the corner of his eye.

Our gazes locked for a moment, his head swiveling slightly as I passed, his expression turning dark. Without breaking eye contact, he reached for his office phone and slowly raised it to his ear.

CHAPTER 27

Monday, October 6
11:00 a.m.

I sat on a bench in the middle of the academic quad, waiting.

I was able to pick Delilah out easily as she emerged from the half-sphere theater entrance. She was met by another young woman who seemed to have been waiting for her outside. I wondered if this was Gen for Genevieve.

She was back in her own clothes—jeans frayed at the knees, a deep maroon T-shirt, black Vans. Khaki bag strapped to her back. As they walked this way, they appeared deep in a comfortable conversation.

Our eyes locked, and I lifted a hand in a half wave. Like my heart wasn't pounding; like my head wasn't full of questions. *What were you doing in Beckett Hall at midnight? Why was your phone hidden in the dumbwaiter?*

What aren't you telling me?

My eyes slid to the person beside Delilah as I stood from the bench. I felt my smile fracture. Dark hair, wavy like Delilah's. Jeans, T-shirt, a badge clipped to her waistband. She was older than she looked from a distance.

It was Amanda, from the campus police department.

"Hi," she said, reaching out to shake my hand. "Amanda Christianson," she reminded me.

"I remember," I said, eyes sliding to Delilah, trying to get a read on the situation.

"We're so happy to see her back safely," Amanda said. She smiled at Delilah, pink lip gloss shimmering, which seemed garish given the death that had occurred on the other side of campus. "We'll chat more later, okay?" She squeezed Delilah's elbow once before leaving.

I watched Amanda go, waiting until she was out of earshot. "What did she want?" I asked.

Delilah blinked rapidly, hitching her backpack more firmly on her shoulders with both hands. "Um, to make sure I was okay?"

But I knew better. "They're taking statements, Delilah. Someone's dead, and they're talking to everyone."

Delilah had covered the scratch on her face with a thick layer of makeup, but I could still see a faint pink line underneath.

"They think she fell," Delilah said, shifting on her feet, eyes trailing the students who were milling around us between classes.

"No," I said. "They don't." I shook my head. "You can't talk to them alone." I was furious that they were talking to students without their guardians present, but they were all presumably eighteen and over. We had no right to their conversations. The campus police could talk to Delilah all they wanted, pick at her story, tear the foundation to shreds.

Delilah rolled her eyes. "She was just seeing if I needed anything, Mom. Really, that's it."

I was aware, then, of the cameras on the buildings around the quad. And the fact that Dill in security and Amanda in the campus police had already noticed me here. I was very careful with my choice of words. "No one asked you about what happened?"

"No," she said, readjusting her posture. "Is this why you needed to see me in person in the middle of the school day?"

I shut my eyes, shook my head. "Delilah, we need to talk to you. In private."

"What about?"

"It's really better if we do this at home."

"Mom," she said, voice loud and definitive, "I get why you and Dad came. I do. But I don't need a babysitter. You can't stay at the house forever and expect me to be there, too."

"Someone's dead," I said, louder than intended. Her eyes widened, and she looked around like I was embarrassing her. "It's about the phone."

She tilted her head to the side very slowly. "What about the phone? Because I didn't text you before coming to school? You were *busy,* whispering in the office with Dad." She shot it at me like an accusation. A secret for a secret.

"No. I'm talking about the phone in the basement."

We stared at each other, a stalemate. "I don't know what you're talking about, Mom."

"Delilah, please. I found it, okay?"

But she was shaking her head, stepping back. Looking around the quad like something here could save her. Maybe Trevor was right—that this wasn't the way to approach it. There was a better way. A quieter way. A way that wouldn't create this chasm of distance between us.

"I have lunch plans," she said, backing away. "And I'm not going to skip a half day of classes. Do you know how that looks? Everyone already knows I was so lost that the cops were looking for me, which is mortifying enough."

"You can't stay here tonight," I said. She was being unreasonable. Stubborn at the worst possible moment.

"Mom, really. How is this not the safest place to be right now?"

Because at home, I could keep watch.

"Delilah, it's really important that we talk before you say *anything else* to anyone."

That seemed to get her attention. A tiny line formed between her eyes. She looked over her shoulder once. "I'll come after classes," she said.

"Okay, I can pick you up—"

"I'll walk," she said, like I had crossed the line. But with consolation. She was coming.

I drifted back to the parking lot in a daze. They were questioning the students, and these kids had no idea the webs they could get caught in. The lies that would haunt them. They'd been out in the howling, and they would lie about it because the school had banned it. And they would trap themselves in their lies, unable to find a way out.

I waited until I was safely in my car, with the engine running, to call Violet.

The phone rang for so long I thought her voicemail wasn't set up, but she eventually answered.

"Violet, it's Beckett, I'm at the school. Listen, it looks like the campus police are interviewing the kids."

"Geez," she said, blowing out a long breath. "They sure move fast when the college is involved, don't they."

"Are you going to let your son give a statement?" I asked.

A brief pause, like she hadn't considered that. "Well, he's nineteen. He doesn't really need my approval to answer a few questions."

She might think differently if she knew her son had been out there in the howling, too.

"I think they should have a lawyer present, at the very least. Do you happen to know any local folks? Would your husband have any connections?"

She let out a high-pitched laugh. "Joseph has a business lawyer, sure. But a *criminal* attorney, Beckett? I really don't think that's necessary here."

"He lied to you, Violet."

There was a long pause on the other end. Better that she hear it from me than the police. "Excuse me?" she said.

"Bryce. He lied about being in all night when we called him. I saw him that morning."

She cleared her throat, and it sounded like she was moving. Like she wanted to keep this conversation away from whoever was nearby, listening. "You saw him where?" she finally asked.

"Coming out of the woods. I think they were all out in the howling."

There was a long pause before she responded. "No one does that anymore."

But I'd seen the mask at Cryer's Quarry. Just because the old tradition was banned by the school didn't mean the students listened. If anything, it probably increased the allure. "They do, Violet. They're doing it again." Maybe not at the same place, with a fire marking home base, but they'd been out there in the woods. I'd seen evidence of it. I'd ask Delilah to confirm it tonight.

"Where?" she asked. "Where exactly were you?"

"I was on campus, by the dorms. I followed the path—it leads straight to the Low Bar. I think he was out at Cryer's Quarry. I think they all were." I paused. "I think that's the new location of the game."

She sighed. "Thanks, Beckett. I'll talk to him. These kids. They're going to be the death of us."

"One more thing," I said. My heart was thrumming. "I'm not sure if you heard. The person who died, they say it's Adalyn—"

A knock on my car window made me jump. Cliff Simmons stood just outside. I had no idea how long he'd been standing there.

"What?" I heard through the phone, before I mumbled a quick, "Sorry, I have to go."

I ended the call and lowered the window an inch. "Can I get a lift?" he asked.

I gestured to the passenger side. I knew he'd seen me inside Beckett Hall. I guessed he'd watched me on the cameras, heading this way.

In the enclosed space, Cliff reeked of cigarettes and peppermint, like he was trying to cover the former with the latter. There was a nervous twitch to his hand.

"Where to?" I asked as I backed out of the parking spot.

"The deli. I've got an order waiting."

"While I'm happy to do you this favor, can we cut to the chase? It's not really that long a drive."

He twisted in his seat. I could feel his eyes searching my face. "I talked to Dill, who you met up with in the archives. What were you doing up there, Beckett?"

Like he knew what I was looking for. Maybe he'd checked himself, wondering if the key was missing. Remembering how I'd led him through those tunnels long ago. Looking for proof that I'd been involved.

"I spent half my childhood up there in those halls," I said.

"Yeah, I remember. You let us *all* know it growing up."

I let his comment slide. "I hadn't been up to my father's office in twenty years, believe it or not. Call it nostalgia."

He snorted in response. "Sure, let's call it that. You know, nothing was really keeping you away all this time. Other than your parents, of course."

I paused at a four-way stop sign. "Ha. My parents would've loved if I moved back, trust me. They wanted me to, you know. When I was pregnant with Delilah."

He narrowed his eyes like he didn't believe me. "The school keeps good records, Beckett. I checked, you know. They didn't put you on any leave of absence. *You* initiated a transfer request."

I shook my head. "*No*. We decided to do that *after* the letter arrived . . ." But the words died in my throat. I felt the wind knocked from my lungs as I pictured my father up in the archives, afraid and checking for the tunnel key.

He would have had access to the school's letterhead.

Maybe Cliff hadn't been wrong when he'd said my parents had sent me overseas to prevent the police from questioning me more. Maybe they were afraid of what I would say. Maybe my father knew, if the police pressed too hard, they would stop checking the keys that had been issued to the security guards and end up in the archive room, looking for me.

A car honked behind me. I shook off the memory and drove through the intersection. "I know what this town thinks of me, Cliff. We both know there was no way I could've stayed here."

I felt him turn to stare at me. "Did you know I had to leave, too, Beckett? Except I didn't have quite the same opportunities as you. I never did. You and I, we were never going to have the same life after high school. I always knew that."

"I didn't know . . ." I hadn't seen what had happened to others in the aftermath. I hadn't checked. Hadn't asked. I'd left everything and everyone behind, very careful never to look back.

"Uh-huh. What do you think it was like for me? I grew up with those guys, knew their families. They all knew I told the cops that Charlie and Micah were coming after you and Adalyn that night. It didn't help their case against the school. Made it seem like I thought they deserved it . . ."

"I'm sorry," I said, voice small. Because I was. Because I hadn't looked back, hadn't seen the fallout, hadn't seen what other lives had been ruined in the process.

He had picked a side, too. He had chosen. The school or the town. I shouldn't have been surprised—deep down, he'd always wanted this life instead.

"I was supposed to be with them that night," he said, his eyes haunted. I'd always assumed he was the one who had driven them and dropped them off on campus. That he'd found his moral line, and that was as far as he could go.

I felt trapped—in the car, in the past.

We'd both been changed by the proximity—the *almost* of it all. My hands were trembling on the steering wheel, and I gripped tighter, hoping he couldn't tell.

But he noticed; I felt his gaze on me. Maybe that was the point of this: To see my reaction. To hold me in one place and shake the truth free.

"They had friends," he continued. "Parents. Siblings. A fiancée. Trust me, I'm no one's favorite person around here since I moved back. But in twelve years, if I'm lucky, my kid will get to go here for free. Just like you. And have a different sort of life from me."

I swallowed. I didn't know what else to say. "You made a different life for yourself." We both had, in our own ways. A second life, unrecognizable from the ones we once expected for ourselves.

"I tried to stop them, you know. I begged them not to go." His voice turned raspy, tight with emotion.

"I believe you," I whispered. Like I'd tried to stop Adalyn.

I imagined him in the truck, saying: *We can turn around right now. You don't have to do this—*

I'd thought I could protect Adalyn if I was with her. I'd thought I could keep everyone safe.

I turned onto Main Street, the deli in sight, grateful for the break in conversation. There was a patrol car parked in front of the Low Bar, in the spot Charlie's truck once was, where Adalyn had taken a key to the side of it. The bar door was propped open, and I could see an officer in the doorway, talking to someone inside.

When I went to turn into the deli parking lot, I saw that another police car blocked the entrance there.

"They must be interviewing everyone," I said, idling at the front curb.

Cliff frowned, peering at the two police vehicles, diagonal from each other. "Be right back," he said, before heading into the deli.

I sent a text to Trevor while I waited: *Sorry, got held up. Be home soon.* But it got stuck sending—I was probably in another dead zone.

I peered in my rearview mirror and saw the officer just outside the entrance of the Low Bar now, talking to a man in jeans and flannel, pointing up. I thought it was that same young bartender—Wes. The one who gave Mayhew his daily updates. I twisted in my seat to see more clearly.

The passenger door flew open, and Cliff slipped inside, white paper bag in his lap. "Something's happening there," he said. "Half the department is in the deli, talking to the employees. They didn't even charge me for my order."

I gestured to the scene through the back window of my car. "Looks like they're checking for footage," I said.

Like they'd promised to do when we were searching for Delilah.

The paper bag rustled as he folded the top down, sealing it tight. "Can you drop me back home?"

As if the police presence was making him nervous. Here and on campus. Something he couldn't seem to escape.

We drove the rest of the way in silence, as if something had shifted between the school and the deli. There was a small construction vehicle at work on the empty plot beside his, digging out the brick of the foundation. Progress at last, days before the parents were set to arrive in town again.

"I didn't even know she applied here," I confessed. "Not until it was too late."

He tucked the paper bag under his arm, then stared out the side window, straight through the empty plot to the rise of campus. "Didn't you read her essay for the scholarship? It started with something like: 'My mother is a ghostwriter. She tells everyone else's story but her own.' She talked about the words on your bedroom wall." He smirked. "I remember that wall. She wrote about the feeling that your history was all around her here but still unreachable. That her father is an art historian. And that you're both complete mysteries to her."

I turned to stare at him, understanding what he was saying. She was looking for the story of her own history. She was digging into the past to understand her origins.

I wondered if somehow she'd managed to draw Adalyn back in her searching.

"Do you think she did it?" Cliff asked suddenly, voice low.

A cold sweat broke out on the back of my neck. *"What?"*

"Adalyn. Do you think she set the fire." He gestured to the empty plot. The place he was supposed to be living before the fire swept through. He'd just started moving things in, he'd said. It must've been his seared photos in the dumpster. Here, then, was the reason Cliff had been so shaken.

"I don't know."

"First it was the house. Then the bell tower." He squinted into the distance. "Dill's keys went missing at the start of the year. It was a whole fiasco. Now all I can picture is Adalyn sneaking into his house and taking them."

Now I did, too. Adalyn sneaking into Delilah's dorm. Sneaking into my childhood home. Taking the key from the weathervane when my parents were away; taking Dill's security keys while he slept.

"Someone's been harassing Delilah since she started school," I said. "Stealing her things. Writing threatening notes. But it doesn't make sense. Why her?"

"Why her?" he said. "And why me? Don't you see a pattern?"

The fire. The deaths.

In a way, we had been the only ones to escape.

Adalyn was messing with everyone. She'd become the ghost in the story the kids had always talked about. Was she angry and back for revenge? But it had been nearly twenty years. She'd managed to live an entire second life. She'd escaped. She must've known the dangers. And now she'd died because she'd come back.

"I blamed my parents for Delilah coming here," I said. "When they retired, I really hoped they'd decide to move."

There was a long pause when I could feel Cliff looking at me. "They didn't *retire,* Beckett. They were fired."

I jolted, leaning away. "No, they weren't." They had retired back-to-back, one right after the other, five years earlier.

"They made an agreement to go quietly, but make no mistake, it wasn't their call," Cliff said.

"That's not . . ." I began. But what did I know about their lives, really? Only that they said they weren't suited for retirement. They took gigs, wrote papers.

But also: Their house had been remortgaged. They needed money.

Maybe they hadn't gone willingly into the night.

"It happened before I started," Cliff said, "but I heard the stories. Something about your father selling pieces, using the college's name."

I shook my head, confused. "That doesn't prove anything," I said. But my mind kept going to the boxes in the attic and the ones they'd packed for Peru. The clock that had caught Trevor's eye in the basement, that needed fixing up. Their desire to have me out of the house.

"Maybe not," Cliff said. "But whatever they were presented with must've convinced your parents it was better to see themselves out the door instead of mounting a defense. The school, as always, was happy to sweep it under the rug to protect its reputation."

He finally opened the car door, as if that's what he'd come to tell me all along.

CHAPTER 28

Monday, October 6
1:00 p.m.

My father, leaving a fake key to replace the missing one. My father, with a house full of antiques he was selling boxed up in the attic. Addresses in his office. The Wi-Fi unplugged, like he didn't want my mother to receive any emails before he saw them. My father, fired.

Men's size-ten boots, footsteps in the snow—

Maybe he'd managed to keep some secrets of his own after all.

I wasn't paying attention, so I barely noticed it at first as I walked back to the house from my parking spot. Movement visible through the slats of the back gate, which was currently hanging partly open.

Someone was in there again. I cautiously approached. It could've been Trevor, but I was on edge.

I kept my phone out as I pushed the gate open, ready to place an emergency call. It was broad daylight. Trevor would hear if I called for help. The neighbors could see down from their upstairs window.

I rounded the corner and saw a man standing on the walkway to the back door. He must've caught sight of me in his peripheral vision at the same moment, because he pivoted quickly, hand shooting toward his hip.

Fred Mayhew's eyes must've been as wide as mine. He lowered his hand slowly, then looked from me to the house.

"What are you doing here?" I asked.

"No one answered the door," he said. "The gate was open. I thought you were back here. Thought I heard you."

But he'd been staring at the back door like he was making sure no one was home before entering. His sunglasses rested on top of his head like he was preparing to try the handle.

"No," I said. "I just got back."

I let the unspoken hang between us. He was trespassing. I wondered if he'd been crossing lines from the start. If he had a way inside, too.

He cleared his throat, took a step closer, like he had every right to be here. I supposed that would be his story, if questioned. *Heard something in the back. The gate was open. I came to check—*

"I was coming to speak with you. Catch you up, actually," he said. He gestured toward the back door. "Should we take this inside?"

I crossed my arms. Trevor had listened to me—not letting anyone inside.

"No, thanks," I said.

"Fair enough." He grinned, amused by my refusal to invite him inside.

But I had a long memory, too. I gestured for him to get on with it.

"I guess here's as good a place as any. You'll probably hear this soon enough, you know how this town can be." He smirked slightly. "The preliminary cause of death looks to be a strange one, not gonna lie. Asphyxiation."

The word felt so clinical and cold. So finite.

Not an accident. I pictured a man's thick hands around her pale neck. Mouth open, gasping, before she was dumped inside the student center pit—

"But the bizarre part is that it looks like everything inside her wallet had been soaking wet. All stuck together and damp, not drying right."

My mind was buzzing. I couldn't make the pieces fit. Couldn't see where he was leading me. It hadn't rained. She was found at the bottom of the construction pit on campus.

"Look, we're waiting on the official report, but they're pretty sure she drowned."

I shook my head in surprise. It didn't make sense. There were many ways one could drown: head held in a bathtub or a pool.

"She didn't die there?" I asked quietly.

He smiled slightly again, pointed two fingers at me and then back at himself. "Me and you, we're on the same page. We searched the area pretty well but couldn't find any place she could've easily drowned. Not many pools around here."

He paused. Using that same technique from our last meeting, the silence and time—waiting for me to fill it. But I wouldn't. I had learned my lesson about talking too much long ago.

He looked around the backyard, at the tall fence surrounding us, the neighbors' windows peering down. Like he was checking that we were really alone. He took a step closer, lowered his voice. "We got a lucky break. The owner of the deli called about a car that had been parked in their lot for days."

The hairs on the back of my neck stood on end. I'd seen that car, too. I'd seen it parked at the path leading to Cryer's Quarry when I was searching for Delilah.

"Turns out it was rented to a woman whose name matches Adalyn's current ID. Anna Brown." He took a deep breath. "We're checking the footage all around that area, but we're really focused on the quarry as the scene of the crime right now."

I pictured the clear blue water, the rocky, uneven terrain. The red mask floating at the edge.

"We know your daughter was out in the night," he said.

"She was lost," I said. It was the story she'd given, and I needed it to hold. It had to hold.

I tried to stop the spiral, but I couldn't. The watermarks on Delilah's broken phone. The bruises on her body. The scratch across her face. Wet hair and muddy shoes. I pictured a fight, a struggle, the gasp before the dropped call—only the gasp was not hers.

An accident. It had to be an accident.

My eyes burned. This was my fault. The police knew she was out there only because of me. They knew she was unaccounted for during the night of Adalyn's death because I'd begged them to look for her.

"But the body wasn't there," I said, a life raft to cling to. What did he think she had done? Dragged it all the way through the woods, cutting through downtown back to campus?

"The body's a real head-scratcher," he said, like it was all a game. Like there wasn't a dead woman in a morgue somewhere who had lived a very real life for forty-one years. Like he wasn't currently threatening my daughter's future.

"If it were me," he continued, "I'd need help. I'd need a car. I'd call someone I really trusted."

I regretted being outside like this now—in a position where he was currently blocking the exit from my yard.

"I don't know what you're getting at."

He raised an eyebrow like he could see right through me. "The power was off on campus, like whoever was moving the body wanted to make sure none of the cameras caught them. I can think of a few people who would know how to access the power hub for the school," he said.

"I can think of an entire town's worth," I countered. All of us, as kids, messing with the students during the howling— But it didn't make sense. "Why would anyone want to move the body onto campus?"

He shrugged. "Maybe they were hoping she'd get buried by the construction and no one would notice. Maybe they were planning to drag her into the woods and underestimated how hard it is to carry something like that. I don't know. Criminals don't always think straight." He shifted on his feet. "Usually they panic, honestly. They do something wrong. Make mistakes. You can count on it. It's how they get caught, every time. It's not like you see in the movies, is it?"

I felt my pulse racing, a cold sweat on the back of my neck.

"This is some story, Detective," I said, folding my arms to keep the tremble in my hands from showing.

"Meanwhile, any matter of evidence could've been cleaned up at Cryer's Quarry. While we've been chasing our tail around a location that was definitely not the scene of the crime. Luckily, there are now double the number of potential witnesses who could've seen someone up on campus. Or down at the quarry." And then he grinned. "We have one who puts you there, Beckett."

I heard an echo of his claim, twenty years later. *Someone saw you, Beckett—*

"Who puts me *where*?" I asked. It wasn't possible. I was sleeping in the living room, with Trevor and Delilah beside me. I was out cold. There was no way someone saw me on campus.

"On the trail to Cryer's Quarry," he said.

My ears were ringing. "I was looking for Delilah."

"So you keep saying."

"I went to the dorms first," I said. "Ask Lenny. Or her roommate. Or the RA." I'd been panicked and desperate. I had not been helping my daughter cover up a crime.

Fred Mayhew shouldn't have been here. I knew this. He should have had me down at the station, on camera, so I would know what was happening. His methods may have changed, but his motivation remained the same. He wanted to catch me off guard, trip me up, trick me into a confession before I realized what he was doing. Like he was picking up where he'd left off twenty years earlier.

I started walking, wanting out of this enclosed space. I needed him to stop talking so I could think straight.

He followed me to the gate, then stopped at the driveway, peering at my parents' car in a way that unnerved me.

"Just so I understand the timeline, you called your ex-husband here around—"

"He's not my ex-husband," I said. "He's Delilah's father."

"Okay, you called Delilah's father here when?"

"When I couldn't find her after looking on my own." I tried to remember the specifics. They would be able to find this out easily with phone records. "Around ten a.m. on Saturday, I think."

He nodded sagely. "Looks like you've both been busy running around. I have a kid, two years old. But I get it, the things I would do for her, if she ever needed it."

Just then the front door beside us opened, and the woman I'd met on Saturday night stepped outside. She waved and started to walk in my direction before she noticed Fred Mayhew with me. Instead, she headed for her car at the curb, but I noticed her adjusting the rearview mirror once inside, watching our exchange. A rumor that would start spreading quickly. *There were cops at the Bowery house—*

"Well, I'll let you get back to things," Mayhew said, sliding his sunglasses down. "You know how to reach me if you want to chat."

A warning that the circle was closing, with us at the center.

I closed my eyes and thought, with the same force as always: *Not her.*

I waited until I was sure his car was gone—watching it to the edge of College Lane, where it turned past the construction vehicles and Cliff's house.

And then I let myself inside.

"Trevor?" I called. "It's me."

But the house was eerily empty.

I poked my head into the dark basement, called his name, listened to it resound in a dull echo. Then I headed to the back of the kitchen, where I called for him up the steps. Nothing.

I peered around the kitchen, confused. On the table, Delilah's note still sat there. And written just below was an addendum: *Went for a drive.*

I frowned, checked my phone. My message still hadn't been delivered to him, even though I was back on Wi-Fi. He was likely off grid somewhere. I checked for his location and saw that, at some point between his search in the woods and today, he'd turned off the "share" feature.

Where the hell was he? I tried calling him, but it went straight to voicemail.

I was panicking, and I needed to talk to him. I needed him to have a *plan*—

Instead, in his desire to *go for a drive,* he'd left the back door unlocked on his way out, since he didn't have a key. So close to where the detective had been standing.

Maybe Fred Mayhew hadn't been lying. The gate could've been left open if Trevor had exited that way. You had to pull it shut firmly behind you to latch it.

Trevor didn't seem to understand what he'd done, leaving the house unsecured like that.

Adalyn was dead, and our daughter was a suspect. This house was full of all manner of evidence—from her phone, to the skeleton key currently tucked inside my purse, to the boxes of artifacts packed up in the attic.

I stormed up the back steps, finally with a purpose. I wanted to drag the boxes out of storage, ask Trevor's expert opinion. Have him tell me exactly what I was looking at. Discover what my parents were really doing—if Cliff had been right. That my father was selling off the valuable pieces of his collection in a way that had raised a red flag with the school.

I ducked into the bathroom and once more entered the attic through the narrow door. This time, I bypassed the boxes of memorabilia and went straight for the back, to the pyramid of artifacts.

Carefully I carried them out one by one and left them on the floor of my old bedroom, where I'd be able to see things more clearly.

By the time I was done transporting all the boxes, my body was coated in a fine layer of dust, and I needed to change.

I went back for the very last item, in case there was something valuable wrapped in the old blanket I'd seen earlier, tucked against the wall.

But when I pulled the blanket away, I found a duffel bag underneath.

I crouched down and slowly unzipped it, expecting to see old winter gear that they'd stored offseason. Instead, I saw a layer of neatly folded T-shirts and a bag of toiletries on top. As if this was someone's luggage.

I took the bag out to my room as well and started emptying the contents onto my bed, my heart pounding.

Other than clothing, I found a toothbrush and a body mist—something slightly sweet, the same scent that had lingered when I'd arrived. There was also a small makeup bag with foundation, mascara, and pink lip gloss—a shade that brought to mind the lip print on the cup left in the kitchen the day I'd arrived.

Maybe Delilah had been telling the truth when she'd said it hadn't been her up here.

No, I was sure now: It was Adalyn. It was always Adalyn. Adalyn, who knew where the spare key was hidden from long ago. Who must've found this house empty and decided to stay, sleeping in my bed upstairs. It must've been her light the neighbors had seen in the night.

At the very bottom of the bag was a large padded envelope, the seal ripped open.

I peered inside only to see a stack of white envelopes bound in rubber bands.

I dumped them onto my bed and froze. Each envelope was stuffed with money.

It took some time to count it all.

By my best estimate, at the time of her death, Adalyn had close to fifteen thousand dollars hidden at the bottom of her duffel bag.

CHAPTER 29

Monday, October 6
4:00 p.m.

Trevor had been gone for at least three hours by the time he returned. I'd been waiting for him, pacing the house. Everything was spiraling outside my control, and I couldn't pull it back together. I couldn't see the way out.

I swung open the front door while he was still halfway up the porch steps. "Where have you been?" I asked. "Delilah's going to be here soon."

He remained silent until he was fully inside the house, the door firmly locked behind us. "I was out for a drive," he said with eerie calmness.

"Yeah, I got your *note,*" I said, unable to temper my tone. "You can't just leave the door unlocked. The *police* were here earlier, and I found Adalyn's things in the attic . . . I think she was staying here."

Trevor's eyes went wide.

"Everything's drawing the police back here. If they looked inside," I continued, "if they saw—"

"I took care of it. It's gone," he said, hands deep in his pockets. It looked like he hadn't slept. Neither of us had, and the cracks were showing.

"*What's* gone," I said.

"The phone. It's gone. So it doesn't matter how it got here anymore."

My eyes widened. "How could you not tell me first?" When, really, what I meant to say was: *How could you not* ask *me first?*

Of course he had a plan. A plan that didn't involve me or my input.

"I didn't want you to know. I didn't want you to be part of it." He swallowed. "To be guilty of it."

"The police are watching us," I said, hand going to my mouth. "They basically told me that. They could've been following you."

The wrinkles around his eyes deepened. "No one was following me."

"They already think . . ." And then I stopped.

"They think what?"

I chose my words carefully. "The police think Adalyn was killed in the quarry and someone moved her. More specifically, they seem to think one of *us* moved her."

He laughed once, loud and harsh, then turned away, slipping off his sneakers. "Okay, well, that's *clearly* ridiculous."

But all I could hear was the pounding of my own heartbeat in my head as I watched him move through the house with ease. He'd just disposed of a phone. He'd just disposed of something that could've been evidence. He'd already crossed a line—and one that surprised me. How well did I really know him? I knew the man he was nineteen years ago, but hadn't we all been changed by time?

I knew he was a good father to Delilah. That she adored him. That she called him when she needed help—

I thought of her reaching out to Trevor instead of me when she needed money. I thought of him out in the woods near campus when he was looking for Delilah. The way I lost track of him. The panicked sound of his voice when I finally reached him.

And then he'd been gone in the middle of the night, when I woke. The same night the body had presumably ended up on campus.

"Trevor," I called, and he slowly turned around. "Did you see something? Did you do something?"

He shook his head slightly. "I don't understand what you're asking me right now."

"Did something happen? Did she ask you to help her?"

He flinched but moved closer. "Are you actually being serious? How could you think I could do that . . ."

He trailed off; maybe he understood why I had asked him. Because I could imagine doing it myself. Maybe that was my fault with Trevor all along. I had always expected him to see things from my point of view, with no explanation. I'd never told him the full truth, my full story. Wouldn't let myself believe in a future with him.

He stared back at me silently. Maybe he was truly seeing me for the first time.

"You went off-grid," I said. "You disappeared for so long. And when I reached you, you sounded panicked, like maybe you saw something—"

"Yes, I was panicked!" he said, clearly upset. "My daughter was missing, and I was out in the woods. I kept calling her name, kept thinking I heard something. *Someone*. I kept following the sound, and it almost got me lost, too."

There were other people out there. I knew this now. Sierra had been out there, searching the woods. Presumably there were others, too.

"Where were you later that night, when we were sleeping?" I whispered.

He dropped his head, then slowly raised it again, his eyes haunted. "I was walking. And then running. And trying to figure out how I'd let my entire life get away from me." He took a step closer. "I was thinking about how close I came to losing everything I'd ever cared about."

I shook my head quickly, trying to undo it. Trying to take back the accusation. "I'm sorry," I said.

"So, to answer your question, Beckett," he said simply, "I did not put a woman's body in a car and dump it in the student center pit so that it could be found there."

A knock at the front door cut through the silence lingering between us. Trevor swung it open, obviously expecting Delilah, but it was Maggie standing on the front porch, running her hands through the ends of her auburn ponytail, like maybe she'd heard everything we'd said.

"I'm so sorry. Is this not a good time?" she asked.

"It's fine," I said, grateful for the break in the tension. "Delilah's on her way."

Maggie looked tentatively between the two of us, then took a step back, like she'd already changed her mind. "I was coming to tell you . . . I wasn't sure if you knew yet . . ."

"Adalyn?" I said, and she nodded.

"It's not the type of thing you want to put in a text." Something caught her eye off to the side then. "There she is," she said, smiling as Delilah slowly strode up the street, the empty plot behind her. "I'll leave you to your family time."

"Wait," I said as Maggie started to turn. "Do you think it's possible that Adalyn set that fire? Cliff seems to think he might've been the target."

She frowned, and her eyes slid to the site of the fire. "You didn't hear this from me. But Bill says the report is very inconclusive. Insurance doesn't want to move on it." She raised one shoulder in a noncommittal shrug. "So I guess it's possible."

Apparently the plan, as orchestrated by Trevor, was to eat dinner and feign normalcy, listening to Delilah's day.

"I moved back into the dorm," she said, twirling pasta on a fork. "There's so much security around right now. It seems like the safest place."

I froze, a bite of chicken Parm hovering on my fork, halfway to my mouth. "I really think we should go back home for a while," I said. I needed to get her away from here. I needed to get us all away from here. I understood the impulse my parents must've felt, faking a letter from the school to get me to go—

"I'm not leaving in the middle of my first semester, Mom," she said calmly, flexing her adulthood in front of me. "It's not really up to you."

Hadn't I done the same, always claiming *I don't need your help* to my parents. To Trevor.

Delilah and I stared at each other, at an impasse.

"The police came back this afternoon," I said. If she wanted to be treated as an adult, it was time for an adult conversation.

Delilah slowly looked up from her plate. "Why?"

I dropped my fork, couldn't force myself to eat another bite. I wasn't sure how Trevor and Delilah were managing.

"Apparently they think Adalyn drowned," I said. "And they think someone moved her after."

I watched Delilah's eyes go wide, watched the fork start to tremble in her hand. My stomach sank. I knew then. I knew something horrible had happened out in the woods that she didn't want to say.

"Delilah, we found your phone," I continued. I looked at Trevor, who was staring back, hollows under his eyes, waiting. It seemed so ridiculous to have this conversation over spaghetti and chicken Parmesan. The whole situation seemed absurd.

"Where?" she asked in barely a whisper. Like she was testing us.

"Hidden in the dumbwaiter," I said.

She shook her head fast, repeatedly. She leaned back in the chair. "I didn't do that. I didn't. I lost my phone—"

"Delilah, please." I closed my eyes, couldn't take the lies.

"Do you not believe me?" she asked.

"It really doesn't matter," I said in a painful nonanswer, sounding like my mother again. "It matters if the police believe you. And they don't. Delilah, they don't believe your story."

She looked terrified; but then so was I. When I pictured her sitting on the basement floor now, I could see only the remnants of a struggle. I saw someone scratching her face, her skin caught under their nails. I saw an accidental call before the phone slipped from her pocket, colliding with a rock—shattering. I saw her fall to the ground, knees bruising, as someone else fell to the water.

I saw her run. I saw her rush to destroy the evidence.

Most of all, I was scared that she was like me. That my traits had only grown stronger in her. A penchant for darkness. A capacity for secrets. A split-second decision that could send your life into a tailspin, never to recover.

She looked quickly from me to Trevor, eyes welling with tears. "I did lose my phone. I lost it sometime during dinner that night or after. I'm not sure. I was out in town with Sierra, and when I got back, I couldn't find it. I spent half the night searching for it before I remembered I could track it. I tracked it from my laptop to its last known location."

I felt a buzzing in the room. Felt something just under the surface, about to emerge.

"Where?" I asked.

"It was this place behind the deli that I'd been to with Sierra before."

"Cryer's Quarry," I said.

"Right. I thought maybe it was part of the game." She swallowed, and my gaze went blurry. "Part of the howling. We could all hear it that night. It was all anyone was talking about. The old tradition that used to happen until the fire . . . I thought it was happening again." Her eyes flicked to me and then away.

"You went out there *alone*?" I asked. Of all the things I thought I'd taught her about the night and the woods.

"There were plenty of people out on a Friday night," she said, ignoring my horror. "I knew the area. But I couldn't find the phone.

All I had was the mini hiking flashlight on my key chain, and it's not very bright. But I thought I saw . . ." Her gaze drifted into the distance somewhere over our heads. "I thought I saw something in the water."

A body. Adalyn.

I stayed silent, entranced. Like I was out there with her. Her eyes slid back to me. "And then I heard someone else there. I called out to them for help, but they didn't answer. They kept coming closer, but they wouldn't say anything. I started backing away, but they were still coming. So I ran."

It was a story I could see emerging in the gaps of her first one.

"I heard them out there, Mom. They were looking for me. I hid all night. When I got back in the morning, I was going to go to the police, but there was nothing *there*. There was no one in the water."

Just a mask floating at the edge.

"Why did you *lie*?" I asked.

She threw her arms out to the sides. "Who would believe me? There was nobody in the water when I got back. I panicked and spent a night in the woods because I thought someone was chasing me? It's mortifying enough that everyone knew I was lost. I thought it was part of the tradition. Part of the hazing."

But it wasn't. She'd witnessed something out there. A body that had started in the quarry but ended up on campus. And someone knew Delilah had been there.

"Did you find your phone out there?" I asked, unable to reconcile the shattered phone in the dumbwaiter.

"No, I didn't find it. If I had, I would've called someone."

The tears were streaming down her face, and I couldn't read the nuance. Whether she was afraid of what was happening or that I'd see the truth underneath.

"I didn't put it there," she said, gulping air. "I don't know how it got here."

There *had* been someone in the house after I'd arrived here. When I was looking for Delilah upstairs and I first went into the attic. Someone had let themselves in with a key. It hadn't been Delilah.

And it couldn't have been Adalyn—she was already dead.

I'd heard them below me in the kitchen—opening a cabinet.

It was possible. It was possible to believe Delilah.

But it didn't quite add up.

"They're going to tear this story apart," I said, cold and clinical.

"Beckett—" Trevor said in warning.

But everything was on the line. "The campus police tracked you, Delilah. They have you on video, scanning yourself into Beckett Hall, just before midnight." Two hours before the call dropped.

She shook her head adamantly. "That's not possible. I was never there."

I pulled out my phone, showed her the video I'd taken of the television screen as they replayed the Beckett Hall security feed for us at the campus police headquarters.

She looked up. "Mom, that's not me. I swear. It's not me."

I zoomed in on the image, looked again, twisted the phone. Brought it close to my face. I sucked in a breath. It was grainy and choppy, and I couldn't tell how the person moved or I would've known from the start.

The hood of her sweatshirt was up. All we could see clearly was a woman's arm reaching out with Delilah's phone—the door letting her in. *Is that you, Adalyn?*

"Why didn't you say?" I asked, both relieved and horrified. "Why didn't you just say that the first time!" I was angry now, because we didn't have to be here.

"What should I have said: that I followed my phone to Cryer's Quarry, and I thought I saw something in the water and got scared? That I hid all night, but in the morning, there was nothing there? I thought I must've been wrong. That it was all part of the game, and people were messing with me. You think I was going to tell the cops that?"

"It doesn't matter how it sounds. You can't lie!" I said, trying to impart something so important—how you don't get into a stranger's car, or touch a hot stove, or run into the street. You can't lie to the police. You can't change the story.

It was the first domino to fall, and nothing else you said would be believed.

You were not to be trusted.

You were an unreliable witness, an unreliable narrator.

"I didn't think it mattered," she said. "I didn't know anyone was dead until after."

I looked to Trevor, waiting for him to know the next step. See clearly what to do. But he only stared back, shell-shocked.

"I'll tell them I was scared," she said. "I *was* scared."

I didn't know how to help her. How to tell her the truth.

I channeled my mother and just said it: "No one cares that you were scared. You're an adult now."

She flinched, clearly hurt.

Eighteen. It was such an arbitrary distinction. I wanted to apologize because I hadn't prepared her—not for the things that mattered. I should've told her: *You could stay silent, say nothing. You could disappear. But you could not lie.*

She crossed her arms over her chest, looking at me very closely. "You should talk. You know what they say about you around here?"

I felt a hot rush to my cheeks. "Yes, I do."

"It would've been nice to know that *before* I got here." She turned to Trevor, one arm out as if presenting me for judgment. "My mother wasn't just Adalyn's roommate. She was suspected of *helping* her."

She left the comment vague enough to be generous. So that I could pretend I had been suspected only of helping Adalyn disappear and not of helping her in a game that led to the death of two men.

I should've told Delilah the truth long ago. Maybe that's where everything shifted off-kilter. Not back in August, when we arrived.

Not in the spring, when she was first accepted. Maybe it was before that. To the first time I told her the story of her life and where she came from.

"You're right," I said. "I did something I deeply regret once, Delilah. Something I can't ever take back. I didn't mean to, but it happened. I got stuck in a lie. And as you can see, I've been stuck with it for twenty years. Which is why I know what's going to happen next."

BEFORE:
THE PLAN

The plan seemed so simple. Flawless in its ease.

We knew they were coming. Cliff had warned me that they were coming to campus to find us—to track us.

It was Adalyn's idea to let them.

The freshmen were starting to slip into the night, but we were waiting by the access road. It was the same place I'd heard the rev of the truck engine earlier in the week, when they had prowled through campus, looking for us.

The snow was falling. I wished I'd brought gloves. I could see my breath in front of my face, feel the cold in my lungs, the scratch of wool against my cheeks from the mask.

Footsteps raced behind us in a brisk crunch of snow. I spun in time to see a senior in a mask sprinting into the woods—in chase.

"Maybe they're already here," I said. We could've missed them. They could've changed their plan, come on foot.

They could've changed their minds.

And then suddenly: headlights.

"Got you, assholes," Adalyn said.

Adalyn stepped into the street first, black mask pulled down over her face, blond braids escaping out the bottom. The headlights blinded me as they crested the hill, so I had to put a hand up to block the glare.

The truck stopped. We waited there for a beat. Then two. And then the passenger door swung open.

They were here, like Cliff had promised.

"Ready?" Adalyn said. "Go."

Adalyn ran, and I took off after her.

The clock had started.

I glanced over my shoulder as we raced down the snow-slicked path toward the academic buildings on the lower campus. Two men were out of the vehicle, long shadows stretching toward us as the truck backed down the road, leaving them there.

Adalyn was skidding down the path in front of me, laughing, and I was desperate to keep up. I could hear my heart inside my skull: Go, go, go—

We had enough of a head start to make it to the entrance of Beckett Hall before they caught up—but not by much.

"Keep it open," she said, and I made sure it didn't latch behind us before racing to the tunnel doors.

It took so long to unlock the tunnel entrance, and all I could think was: Faster, faster. *I could hear them outside the building now.*

Then the click of the lock resounded in the atrium, and I pushed the door open. She slipped the key around her neck and grabbed my wrist. "Let's go."

It was a simple plan, to contain them.

We thought it was the safest thing, to keep them out of the game and out of the night. To keep them away from us.

To win.

Adalyn laughed as she ran, but I felt terror even then. What did she imagine two grown men were doing chasing two undergrads through campus? They were twenty-four years old. She had carved the word TRASH *into a brand-new truck. What did she think would happen if they caught us? I could feel it: This was no longer a game.*

We were in the dark of the tunnels, and no one would find us if something happened. No one would get to us in time to help. We were on our own.

I'd thought I could protect her if I stayed with her, but I was starting to panic. There was no safety here. I had let her lead me straight into danger. Worse, I had given her the key.

The beam of Adalyn's flashlight bounced along the wall in front of us. "It's a dead end," she said—but I knew it wasn't.

"Left, go left," I shouted, lungs burning.

They were faster than we were, and they were getting closer.

But they didn't know how the tunnels worked. While the outer tunnel doors required a key to lock or unlock from either side, the inner doors didn't work the same. They locked automatically as they swung shut behind you.

They would lock you inside if you didn't have the key.

The plan was painfully simple. At the next fork, she'd keep going, heading toward the exit at the storage barn beside the ruins of the old president's house—home base—and turn the lock. I'd stay behind, tucked around the corner.

All I had to do was wait for them to pass and shut the door.

CHAPTER 30

Tuesday, October 7
8:30 a.m.

I woke to find Trevor standing at the living room windows, mug in hand, peering out. It looked like he'd aged five years in the last three days. "I think someone's out there," he said. "In a car. Watching."

The police, keeping an eye on us. The circle tightening.

As I joined him at the window, he handed me a mug he'd had waiting on a coffee table coaster for me.

"Do you believe her?" he asked.

"Yes," I said. "But it doesn't look good."

He dragged his hand down his face, pulling at the skin. "I should've kept it," he said. "It could've proved something. Fingerprints, maybe."

I shook my head. "It was in the water. All it would prove is that someone wanted her to take the fall. You were right to get rid of it."

I opened my phone, checking to see if Delilah had contacted me in the night. There was nothing but her single text letting us both know she was back in the dorm, going to sleep.

I checked my email next.

I had two new messages: one from my parents and the other from FordGroup—an email this time, with an attachment. I held my breath as I opened that first.

There was only one line: *I know what you did.*

The photo attached, I didn't understand. It was a picture of the mountain ridge. The series of peaks that were so clearly visible from the road on the way into town, near Maggie's house. The same view I'd seen on Delilah's Instagram page with the caption: *Here.*

As if they wanted me to know they were watching us both.

I peered up to find Trevor looking me over. "You okay?" he asked.

I nodded, then opened my parents' message—a response to my short note that Adalyn had been found dead.

We were able to get your mother on a red-eye last-minute. I just dropped her off. Here is the ticket info.

There was no note as to whether I was supposed to get her or not. I checked the ticket details. She had already landed in Charlotte, was due on her connection into Richmond by eleven.

"What's the matter?" Trevor asked.

I looked up and grimaced. "My mother is coming."

I barely had time to shower and throw on my jeans and button-down from our police meeting days earlier.

I grabbed the keys while Trevor passed me a bagel sandwich he'd made me for the road. "Thank you I love you oh my God," I said without thinking, racing for the door. And then I turned back. "You'll take care of her, right?"

He stared straight at me, nodded once. "Of course I will. You know I will, Beckett." Something in me loosened, relaxed.

I realized it was the only reason I could leave right now. Because I believed him.

The Richmond airport was a two-hour drive out of the mountains toward the coast. It was smaller and commuter-friendly, and I easily found parking before her landing time.

Made it, I texted Trevor, hoping all was okay in the valley. I worried about being this far away. But there was nothing I could really do until the cops came to us with more details.

Trevor texted back: *I got a few referrals, making calls now.* That was the plan for today. Make sure we protect Delilah. Starting with finding a good lawyer.

Another text from Trevor arrived: *I also stripped all evidence I was sleeping in your mother's bed.*

I smiled, then tucked my phone away and headed toward the pickup area.

One short landing delay and a long wait for baggage claim later, my mother emerged, squinting in the midday sun. She looked exactly like someone who'd been traveling through the night, in purple velour sweatpants and a matching zip-up hoodie. It was a little hot for that now, but by the time we made it back to the mountains, she'd probably be perfectly comfortable.

"Mom," I called, raising my arm.

She veered my way, pulling a large suitcase behind her as if coming home for good. I opened the trunk of my car and took the luggage from her while she stood there, wide-eyed, disoriented.

"I didn't know you were coming until I landed," she said, motioning to her phone. She blinked rapidly, as if I were an apparition.

"Well, I didn't get Dad's email until this morning. So it was a little last-minute." I was glad she had at least gotten my text. I hadn't been sure her cell would even be back online when she landed in the States. It seemed like they'd shut everything down for the international trip.

We started driving in silence. I didn't know where to start. *How was your flight? I think Adalyn Vale was staying in your house while you were gone.*

"Beckett," she said after we merged onto the highway heading west, "tell me. Tell me what's been going on."

I told her more in the course of thirty minutes than I had in the last five years. About the dropped call that had brought me back to her house in the middle of the night. Delilah lost, then showing up in her basement. The evidence that someone else had been staying in her house. And Adalyn Vale turning up dead on campus.

Then I told her more: about the police and how they didn't seem to believe Delilah's story. And then, as the first set of mountain ridges came into view in the distance, I told her about the money I'd found in Adalyn's things.

"Okay," she said very calmly, resting her head on the back of her seat like she was about to take a quick nap. "Okay."

"That's *it*?" I said, twisting in my seat. She'd flown across a continent through the night to tell me everything was *okay*?

She gestured toward the road like I was about to drive us both off it. "This isn't the time, Beckett."

"It's not the—" I cut the wheel at a sign for a rest area, picnic tables at an empty overlook. I slammed on the brakes, jerking us to a stop in a diagonal parking spot. "It is very much the time, Mom. In fact, I can think of no better time."

"This isn't helping right now," she said. "Let's get home first and we can talk there."

"There's a police vehicle currently stationed outside your house, Mom. So I'd rather talk now, if you don't mind." My hands shook as I twisted around for my purse in the backseat. I reached inside and pulled out the silver chain, the skeleton key dangling between us in the car. "I found this in the house," I said. "I think Dad hid it and replaced it with a fake in the archive room."

Her face paled, and her hand went to her chest. "Where did you get that?" she asked. For the first time, I seemed to have rattled her.

"The space under the dumbwaiter," I said. "It was partially buried. I have *no idea* how it ended up there. But it seemed like it had been there for a very long time."

She stared at the key, then threw open the car door and climbed outside, like she was desperate for air.

I followed her to the edge of the overlook, where a long, hazy mountain ridge was visible in the distance. Maybe ours, maybe not.

"It wasn't your father," she said, turning to face me. Begging me to see it, asking me to understand without her going any further.

"Tell me," I said as a series of cars whizzed around the bend behind us.

"There was a fire. We heard the sirens," she said, looking out to the mountains instead of at me. "We didn't know where you were, and I had this terrible feeling." She swallowed, hand to her throat. "I was in a panic. I threw on your dad's boots at the front door."

Men's size-ten boots, footsteps in the snow.

I swallowed, the lump in my throat practically burning. "What did you do?"

The wind blew through her short hair, and she finally looked me in the eye. "I ran toward campus. And there she was outside the gates, just standing at the edge of the road, like she was in a daze. She had a bag with her. She'd *packed.*" My mother shook her head. "I had to get close before she even seemed to notice me. Close enough for me to see she had the key hanging around her neck. She smelled of smoke. Reeked of it. And I knew. I knew something terrible had happened."

And it was. Terrible. Absolutely horrific. The worst thing I could imagine.

"She took the key. I couldn't get back in—" I pressed the back of my hand to my mouth. What if I'd said this years ago, decades ago. Confessed her sins and mine in the process?

My mother stared back, like she'd been waiting for this moment all along.

I'd emerged from the tunnels at Beckett Hall and had to make my way back through the woods to home base on foot. "Did she tell you what happened?"

"She said she'd lit a torch too close to the building. It brushed the wood, and it went up so fast. I couldn't tell whether she meant to. She seemed shocked that she'd done it, discovering what she was capable of."

That's what everyone said after. That she'd watched it burn, eyes reflecting the flames. The power of what she had done seeping through her.

"She said she was in trouble. I brought her back to the house."

"Why did you help her?"

"Why do you think?" she asked, leading me to the right answer—as if afraid to say it herself.

A truck barreled around the curve, brakes squealing before catching traction, drawing our attention.

"She held up that key. Said you got it for her. Said there were people down there, and you locked the other way out."

"I didn't. I didn't lock a door." But that was semantics. I'd closed it, and in the end, that was the same thing. I shook my head, walking back the lie. "I didn't know what she was doing until it was too late."

"I wanted to kill her," my mother said. Her voice shook. "For the first time, I understood the base impulse. That desperate desire. I wanted her dead."

But it was different to want than to do.

"I told her to change in the basement, to leave the clothes in the dumbwaiter, I'd take care of them later. And when everyone was searching the woods for her, I drove her out of the mountains, north. She used a phone at a roadside restaurant to call her father's work. She told me he was coming. And that was the last I saw of her."

I waited for her to say more, but she'd stopped. Apparently that was the end of the story.

"But that was nearly twenty years ago," I said.

"I really thought I'd never see her again," she said, frowning. "So much time had passed. And then five years ago, she came back."

Five years ago. The police had mentioned this. "Her parents died."

She nodded. "She couldn't get her inheritance. Couldn't get any more money. Couldn't make enough on her own as a person with no history. They hadn't planned for it, hadn't left her a way to access their funds. Unless she went back to her old life."

"She couldn't. She wouldn't."

Her eyes widened. "It doesn't matter if she would or not. The threat was out there."

Her old life meant the police. Meant the truth coming out. Meant me.

"She had a license but not a passport. Her world had limits, borders. But her parents found a way to support her. She had managed for years. And then it was gone. So now we pay her as much as we can. Support her like a child. Had to sell some things so that we didn't lose the house."

"Dad was selling his collection." I tracked the timing. "He got fired over it?"

"That first year, yes. We needed cash quick and maybe didn't do things carefully enough. The fact that his items had been part of an exhibit gave everything legitimacy." She sighed. "The college said it put them in a tough spot. That he had overstepped for his own financial gain."

And then, without his job, they were really in a tough spot. Had to mortgage the house. Take extra work wherever they could.

"The money in the house, that was from you?" I asked.

She nodded. "Every fall, she comes for the money."

"You knew she was coming?" I asked, horrified. They could've prepared me. Could've *warned* me.

"We didn't know *when*. We have no way to contact her. No phone, no email. Our only stipulation was that she couldn't come in the summer, when Delilah might be there, visiting. It was too close. We agreed on the fall. We never know when, but she always shows up."

As inevitable as the howling after a long stillness, I thought.

"We had no way to tell her we'd be away. We left the money for her. Knew she would find her way inside."

It was why my parents needed me gone before they left for their trip. They were preparing for her arrival. And it was the reason they didn't want me at the house when I emailed them about the missing key. "You knew she was there when I asked you about the spare key."

"I *worried* she was there," she corrected.

"The neighbors saw the lights on," I said. "She was staying this time. I don't understand what she wanted other than the money."

She must've wanted her life back. Decided that she'd served enough time. She must've been in town, watching, planning. She might've escaped, but how free was she, really? How free were any of us from the past?

"Should we go now?" my mother asked, and I almost laughed.

I started walking back to the car. "Sure, we should go," I said, and then, since we were putting it all on the table, "Someone's been sending me notes. In my email. To my phone. Ever since I dropped off Delilah. The first said *Welcome Home.*" Even now, it sent a wave of nausea through my body. "But they've gotten worse. More specific. Like they want me to know they know."

"Could it have been Adalyn?" she asked, as I opened the car door.

"I thought that at first," I said, slipping inside. "But the messages keep coming."

We continued the drive in silence, stuck in our own thoughts.

Whoever killed Adalyn might've had the key to my parents' house, might've figured out where she'd been staying. By the time I'd asked my parents about the spare key, Adalyn was dead.

"One more thing," I said when we finally pulled up to the house. "I forgot to mention. Trevor's here."

CHAPTER 31

Tuesday, October 7
3:00 p.m.

The house was too small for the three of us, though my mother was doing her best. She thanked Trevor for coming. She sat with us in the kitchen as we made a plan: There would be no more texting. No trail. Anything from now on could be used as evidence.

Trevor was heading to meet with Delilah, to talk to her about the lawyers—and what she should do in the meantime. My mother was taking care of things at the house. The money upstairs. Anything that might lead people to the reason Adalyn would have come here.

I needed space, and air, to think. Away from the history in the house, binding me to the past—and to Adalyn. I drove over to the deli to pick something up for Trevor, as thanks for earlier. Good coffee, fresh sandwiches. We'd been going nonstop for the last few days.

The parking lot behind the deli had been reopened now that Adalyn's car had been towed away. The lot was pretty busy for an hour before closing. Maybe the proximity to the scene of the crime was increasing the allure.

I was glad to see Sierra back behind the counter. I introduced myself now as Delilah's mother. "Thanks for looking for her," I said. "It means a lot to know that you were out there. I'm sorry about what you had to find."

Sierra tucked her dark hair behind her ear. "Delilah had been with me that night," she said, "before she went missing. I was worried something had happened on the way back to campus."

I nodded, then paid for the food. At least this was someone who could corroborate the first part of Delilah's story.

Sierra handed me the change and the bag of sandwiches. "I saw her around, you know," she said. But I didn't know what she was talking about. "Adalyn. I recognized her photo on the news today. I just didn't know it was her."

On my first day back at the house, I'd seen a white bag in the garbage that looked identical to the one I now held. I couldn't believe Adalyn had just gone walking out in the open here. Maybe she'd grown accustomed to it, at ease in her second life—but not satisfied in it.

The news had started to dig up pieces of her second life, but there wasn't much. A string of rental homes. An inconsistent stream of jobs. It certainly wasn't the life the Adalyn I'd known had once expected for herself.

"She stopped at the deli almost every day, and I had no idea. This whole town talks about her like she's a legend, but no one even realized she was here, walking up the street. She wasn't even hiding!"

"How long was she here?" I asked.

"A week, maybe two? I used to think she must really like our coffee. But looking back, I think she was following Delilah."

I imagined Adalyn arriving at my parents' house, driving through town, and seeing someone who looked just like me—my daughter. A double take. An entire second generation here, while she'd been living an unstable life, with no roots and no history. No name, even, to leave behind.

Delilah must've been such a stark reminder of what she'd missed out on, what she'd lost. The freedom she'd traded.

"Her car was found in the back lot," Sierra whispered, eyes wide.

I nodded, a chill rising up my spine.

"I took Delilah on the trail back there. Wanted to show her the quarry before it got turned into a park and we all have to start paying for it."

"I didn't know that was happening." I'd seen the new private-property signs but hadn't realized the new owners were planning to monetize the site.

She shrugged. "Well, that's the plan, not that anyone's happy about it around here. But now I wonder if she was watching us back then, too. If she was always following us."

A visible shudder rolled through her, transferring straight to me.

"She's gone now," I said. "It's okay."

I didn't understand why Adalyn would taunt Delilah. Delilah was still practically a child. And Adalyn would've been forty-one. Surely she had better things to do than to make my child's life a living hell.

I thanked Sierra and headed for the door. Half the tables were taken, people eating sandwiches, drinking coffee, and chatting.

I passed an older woman at a table by the window and recognized her as Cliff's neighbor. "Hi," I said, pausing over her table. "Beverly, right?"

She placed her hand on my arm. "Oh, I was so glad to hear Delilah was okay," she said, gesturing for me to sit.

"Thank you. Can I get you something?" I asked.

"Oh, no, I've had my share." She smiled. "The construction on the street is driving me crazy. I'm just waiting it out here until five. I'm glad they're finally taking care of the mess, but I can't even hear myself think." She laughed. "I guess the Whartons finally got sick of seeing it, too."

"The Whartons?" I asked.

She nodded. "Joseph Wharton. He owns most of the street. It was one of his houses that burned down. His insurance company has been dragging its heels."

Cliff rented from Joseph Wharton. No wonder he had been nervous about turning over information about their family. He'd told me as much: that Wharton was someone he didn't want to make an enemy out of.

"I didn't know that," I said. "I know his wife, Violet."

She smiled. "He's a nice man, for a landlord. Brings his stepson around in the summers to teach him the ropes. It's nice to see a kid like that working. Not a common sight nowadays."

I was confused. I didn't know about any stepson. I'd been inside their house, seen their family photos. "Stepson?" I asked.

"Bryce, I think is his name," she answered. Then she nodded to herself. "Yes, Bryce. Joseph sent him out to make a report this summer when we had a plumbing issue."

I shook my head. "I thought he was a Wharton."

She looked out the window, thinking. "Oh, I think he did change his name when Violet married Joseph. Like I said, it's nice, the way they work together."

"I didn't realize. Good for Violet. He sounds like a good man. Seems like he's given them all a good life."

"Well," she said, leaning closer conspiratorially, "it's her who had the money anyway, from what I hear. Good for *him,* is more like it. They've done very well for themselves together since, though."

I shook my head. Violet had not come from money. I knew her growing up. Knew where she came from.

"How did she come into money, do you know?" I asked. I had no idea what Violet did for work. Maybe it was an inheritance. Maybe she had a second secret life that I'd known nothing about.

"The settlement," Beverly said. She gestured behind us, into the distance. "From the school."

I shook my head again, not understanding.

She sighed like she realized she'd have to spell it out for me. "She was engaged to marry Charlie Rivers when he died in that terrible accident years ago. The family made sure everything went to her, especially since she was pregnant."

I felt my shoulders tense, my spine go rigid. "Charlie Rivers is Bryce's dad," I said. I needed her to confirm it.

She nodded. "There's another boy, too. A Joseph Junior, I think . . ."

Her wedding photo with the simple, spare jewelry—I wondered suddenly if it was the same pearl necklace that Charlie had taken from Adalyn, if he'd given it to Violet . . . or just left it behind.

And if it *was* the very same one, I wondered if Violet even knew where it had come from. If she knew it was the beginning of everything.

I stood, excusing myself. We had met Bryce on the very first day of orientation. Delilah had shaken his hand. Did he realize right away who she was? Was it when he saw her last name? Or was it when she started digging around, looking into her own history?

My ears were ringing. Bryce had been working in Dill and Beverly's house. Cliff told me that Dill's security keys had gone missing.

Bryce would have access everywhere with them. The dorms, the buildings, the tunnels.

What had he been told about the people who had come before him?

He must've hated Delilah. Hated everything she represented. And now she was back, at the same school, with no idea of the history she'd stepped into.

I barreled out the door, back toward the parking lot, and almost ran straight into a man in uniform. A shock of red hair against the sun in the sky. The scent of cinnamon gum.

"Whoa," Officer Fritz said, hand out to brace me. And then he took a step back, looking me over. "Surprised to see you here, ma'am. I was under the impression you'd gone and left town today."

So, they were definitely watching, like Trevor had said. They must've followed me all the way to the edge of town.

"No," I said. "Just went to pick up my mother from the airport. But I'm back."

I smiled at him, then continued on my way. I had nothing to run from this time.

I had nothing left to hide.

I was sure I had the answer. Bryce, with his own ID card for the school and a set of security keys. Not Adalyn but Bryce taking the things from Delilah's dorm. Hearing through the grapevine that she was staying at her grandparents' house, even though that wasn't true. Sneaking inside an unlocked window he'd found, writing a threatening message on the wall.

Had Adalyn seen him snooping around there? Had she known who he was?

She must've noticed him. I wondered if they'd spoken. And then I wondered if maybe she caught him inside.

I parked in the admissions lot again, then wove along the path to Beckett Hall. This time, I didn't care if I was seen. Class was currently in session, but the doors were unlocked. A security guard I didn't know was stationed inside the door.

I gestured down the hall. "I have a meeting with Cliff Simmons," I said.

He nodded me along but watched my path. There would be no sneaking around this time.

Adalyn had been the one to come in here just before midnight. What was she doing? Where did she go from here? How did she end up dead at the quarry a few hours later?

I paused at the office for student life, about to knock on the glass pane to get Cliff's attention.

But I was done asking for permission here. Instead, I turned the handle and let myself inside.

Cliff looked up from his desk, quickly minimizing a student schedule.

I frowned at the access he had. The way he could know where anyone was if he so chose.

His eyes went to the open door behind me, as if confirming we were alone before speaking. "What do you want now?" he asked, leaning back in his computer chair.

"Bryce Wharton," I said. "He has Dill Lawrence's missing keys."

Cliff shifted forward quickly, elbows on his desk. "How do you know that?" he asked.

"Because I talked to Dill's mother, Beverly. She told me Bryce used to come around to their house in the summer, working for Joseph Wharton."

Cliff shook his head, brushed his overlong hair back from his face. "That doesn't prove anything," he said.

"No, it doesn't *prove* anything." But it was something. I tapped my hand on the surface of his desk. "Did you know he's Charlie Rivers's kid?"

Cliff stared at me, something growing in the silence between us. The long reach of the past coming back for us both.

"I did," he finally said. "But he's been raised a Wharton."

I dropped my voice, leaned closer. "You asked me earlier: why you and why Delilah." I left the rest unspoken. "Ever thought that might be the answer?"

The reason was the same, but the person was different. Not Adalyn but Bryce.

Cliff continued to stare, but I couldn't read into his expression: whether he thought I was way off base; whether he agreed.

I took a deep breath. I'd said what I'd come to tell him. "I don't suppose you'll let me see that," I said, gesturing to his computer.

He blinked slowly, then leaned back, the chair squeaking with the shift in weight. "If you're looking for your daughter," he said, "she'll be coming out of the theater soon."

I could see snippets of Adalyn's path in the night. Starting at my house, where she might've seen Bryce Wharton leaving threatening notes.

Hey there, Delilah
I can still see you
Did you think you could hide?

Maybe she noticed Bryce following my daughter. Maybe she wasn't after Delilah herself. Maybe she was trying to find out who this kid was. Maybe she was trying to protect Delilah.

Maybe she felt she owed me something after all.

As I left Cliff's office, another possibility emerged. She could've taken Delilah's phone to access Beckett Hall—not for the tunnels, not to hide, but for this.

The information she could find. About Bryce. About Delilah. Their phone numbers, their email addresses. Bryce's class schedule. His dorm room. Trying to discover who he was and what he was after.

I waited outside the theater, watching as a group of freshmen spilled out in a bunch. Delilah was near the front, and I raised my hand to her. She hitched her bag onto her shoulders and headed my way.

"Did you talk to Dad?" she asked.

"No, not yet—"

She held out her new phone. "I showed him. Mom, there were other people out at the quarry that night. I know it. No one will admit it around here. But there have to be witnesses."

"How do you know that?"

"From the old messages that came through when I set up my new phone. I got one that proves there were other people out there that night. I just hadn't seen it. It came from an unknown sender that said: *Home base—Cryer's Quarry*."

"Okay, good, that's good. That's a really strong piece to give the lawyer."

I pictured Adalyn with Delilah's phone. That message popping up on the lock screen. *Home base—Cryer's Quarry.*

A game like the one we'd played long ago.

Would she have gone? Was that what had drawn her there? A game in the night that she'd been craving ever since she left? Was it a chance to find Bryce?

Finally I saw him. Bryce emerged from the theater last, lurking around the edges of a group.

He was watching her—watching *us*. Now I could see Charlie Rivers in him. His dark hair swooped to the side. His height. The lanky build, not yet filled out like his father's had been from manual labor. He was living a different sort of life.

I leaned closer, dropped my voice. "Delilah, I want you to listen to me, but don't react."

Her shoulders stiffened on instinct.

"I don't want you anywhere near Bryce Wharton. I want you in your dorm room tonight with the door locked. Promise me?"

She scrunched her forehead, confused. But she nodded. "Yes, I promise." Then she took a step back. "Okay, I gotta run. I have a group project. We're meeting in the library."

She took off across the quad, but I stayed exactly where I was.

Bryce was standing in the same spot, even though the rest of his group had moved on. He made no attempt to hide that he was staring.

I didn't move until he turned away to head in the opposite direction.

He was only a kid. I knew that.

But kids, I knew, could do grown-up damage. They could cause just as much pain as we could.

CHAPTER 32

Tuesday, October 7
5:00 p.m.

When I returned to the house, I heard Trevor and my mother in the kitchen, deep in conversation. I didn't want to break whatever fragile truce they'd made, so I quietly deposited the bag of sandwiches on the countertop.

"Hey," Trevor said, looking up from the table, eyes shining with humor. I could only guess how their conversation had gone.

He cleared his throat, then pushed back from the table. "I'm going to stay at the hotel on Main," he said. "The one you sent me the link for, for parents' weekend. I moved it up. Extended my reservation for the rest of the week."

"Okay," I said, eyeing my mother, wondering if she'd pushed him to leave somehow.

I followed him to the front door. His bags were already packed and waiting inside the office. "Did she ask you to go?" I asked.

He smiled. "No. But it seemed like the right move, considering everything else she was coming home to." He grabbed his bags, then stopped at the entrance, one hand under my chin. "I think you should come with me."

My stomach flipped, and I could feel the heat rise to my cheeks, my neck.

It was what I should've said nineteen years earlier, if I hadn't been so stubborn. If I had let myself believe I could deserve something so good in my life. If I had been kinder not only to him but to myself.

I held his gaze. "I want to," I said. "I really do. But I think I need to clear up some things at home first."

When he looked at me, I could see another life. I could see the possibility—not only back then but now. He smiled slightly and opened the door. "Tomorrow, then?"

I nodded. "Tomorrow," I said, but it caught in my throat.

After I locked the door, I turned to find my mother waiting at the entrance of the kitchen. I felt like a teenager caught with a boy who shouldn't have been there.

"I could use your help," she said, gesturing to the back of the house. "Moving the boxes back to the attic. Those are your father's things."

"Was he still selling his collection?" I asked.

"Yes, but he was doing things a little smarter. Fixing the pieces up. Waiting for the right price. Keeping them protected in the meantime." She ran her hand back through her hair. "I don't think he needs to do that anymore."

"No," I said.

"And I'd rather he didn't know that you found out."

I nodded. They managed to keep some secrets from each other after all.

When the call came in from an unknown contact with a local number, I answered it tentatively. It was very late already, but I'd gotten nervous with Delilah out of my sight.

"Beckett, this is Fred Mayhew," he said. "I know it's late, but I was hoping to set up a meeting for tomorrow morning."

I rubbed my forehead, closed my eyes. "What's this about?"

"Well, we finished going through the local footage from outside the shops downtown. We tracked you coming out of the woods and walking down the street behind the deli. We'd really like to get a complete statement on the record. Make sure we're clear on what you were doing there."

"I already told you. I was looking for Delilah. Why don't you ask other people why they were out there that night? I know I wasn't the only one." I'd seen Bryce Wharton walking right back through those woods that same morning. And Delilah had said she'd received a text marking Cryer's Quarry as home base. The area must've been teeming with people in the night.

"No, Beckett, that's where you're wrong. You and your daughter are the only two people, at night or in the morning, that we can track heading toward the quarry."

The room was suddenly buzzing again. It wasn't possible. It didn't make any sense. I worried he was lying to me, trying to trap me. He'd done it before. Twenty years earlier. Finding the gaps and pushing.

You were the one yelling for people to call 911—

You were screaming for Adalyn—

Someone saw you—

"I'll call you in the morning," I said.

I needed a lawyer. I needed a plan.

I added Fred Mayhew's cell number to my contacts and dropped my head on my father's desk, where I'd been trying to work through Delilah's defense.

I didn't understand. If the quarry had been home base, of course kids would be out there. They must've been running through the shortcut to downtown, to the path for the quarry.

Unless Delilah had been the only person to receive that text.

Everything was spiraling outside my control. I was growing desperate. There must've been other evidence that could support her story. If not from the cameras downtown, then maybe from the other side—by the access road. A car would have had to drive up that way to move a body.

Sierra had said the new owners were turning the quarry into a park. Maybe they'd put up cameras along with their private-property signs.

I couldn't remember the details from the signs, but I searched *Cryer's Quarry* and *new ownership* on my phone, and a single local article popped up.

Residents Divided over New Plan for Cryer's Quarry

I scanned the article and quickly found mention of the name I'd forgotten—JW Enterprises. *"The new park, complete with lifeguards and food vendors, will provide a safe family experience for all," says the new owner, a local resident himself—*

And then I froze, a wave of nausea rolling through me.

JW Enterprises was the name of the business owned by Joseph Wharton.

My vision was going blurry. I kept drifting off on the futon, planning on a quick nap. But when I woke this time, I saw a cup of tea on the desk blotter. Something my mother must've brought in before finding me asleep. When I picked it up, it was cool to the touch.

There was a message on my phone that must've come in sometime earlier in the evening. A reply from FordGroup. My hands shook, hovering over the message.

In response to my curt question—*Who is this?*—there was finally an equally curt reply:

The witness.

There had been so many witnesses the night of the fire. Students in the woods and kids from town, just out of sight. I couldn't even begin to guess who was contacting me now.

Like Fred Mayhew had threatened long ago. *Someone saw you . . .* I'd thought he was bluffing. There was no one else in the tunnels. What else could they have seen?

I knew what they were trying to prove. The same thing Delilah had said over dinner the night before: That I'd helped Adalyn. That I'd been in on her plan. It's what had marked me as a person of interest. But in Adalyn's absence, and without any evidence, such as the key—no one could prove it.

The witness.

Not part of a group but a singular person.

I stared at the sender's address, trying to make sense of it. I knew no one with that last name. The only Internet hits took me to finance groups and automotive clubs . . .

Then I realized. My heart pounded, shoulders tensed.

FordGroup. They'd been telling me exactly who they were from the start.

That night, Charlie and Micah had arrived in Charlie's truck. The same one that Adalyn had taken her key to, carving deep into the paint. His brand-new F-150.

Someone had dropped them off and backed away into the night. I'd been caught in the beam of their headlights, but I'd been wearing a mask.

Unfortunately, the driver was the one person who would know it had been me that night.

Cliff, who came to warn me. Who tried to stop them. Who told me he was supposed to be with them that night.

This whole time, he'd been playing me, and for what? Drawing me closer in order to take me down? He had eyes on the entire campus. Knew how to contact me. Had read Delilah's file. He knew I was a ghostwriter—he'd told me so himself when I drove him home.

Of course it was him.

I was fuming. So angry I called him immediately, but he didn't pick up.

The message hadn't been sent that long ago. Surely he was still awake, waiting for my reply. Waiting to see how he'd rattled me.

I grabbed my purse, stuffed my phone inside, and headed for the door.

I didn't care that it was almost midnight. I didn't care if I woke him by pounding on his front door. I didn't even care if his neighbors heard or came out to see what the commotion was all about.

Secrets were getting people killed here.

The street was quiet and dark except for the porch lights dotting the homes, marking the way. The construction vehicles sat idle in the empty plot, casting ominous shadows against the night sky.

Cliff's house appeared totally dark, but I was intent on waking him up. I walked up the steps and pounded on the door with the side of my fist—but the door cracked open under the impact.

I stepped back, frowning. It hadn't been latched.

I pushed it open farther, the noise creaking in the empty foyer.

"Cliff?" I called.

Something felt wrong. Either someone had been in here, or Cliff knew I was coming, drawing me in—like I'd once done to his friends. Like he was still playing the game.

"Cliff?" I called again, stepping deeper inside. "I swear to God, if you're messing with me . . ."

I flicked the foyer light, saw a shadow down the dark hall, slumped on the floor at the base of the steps. I ran to him: It looked like he'd fallen, hit his head. I was scared to move him. Scared to do anything at all.

"Oh shit, oh shit." I fumbled for my phone, called 911 while I held my other hand to the side of his neck, feeling for a pulse. "I'm at Cliff Simmons's house on College Lane," I shouted into the speakerphone. "I don't know the house number. The one right beside the empty plot. He's hurt. He's unconscious. It looks like he fell. I can feel his pulse."

A clatter came from the dark end of the hall. I froze, held my breath. Someone else was in here.

I heard the woman on the other end of the line. "Ma'am? Can you tell us what you see?"

"Someone's here," I said, then grabbed the phone, standing up.

A door at the back of the house creaked open, a shadow slipping into the night.

I raced toward the back exit. My hand shook as I called the one person I trusted the most in that moment.

"Beckett?" Trevor answered, sounding like I'd woken him.

"I need you to get to Delilah," I said frantically. His hotel was on the other side of campus, closer to the dorms. "Please, go fast."

Someone was running in the night, heading for the college.

Someone was running toward my daughter.

CHAPTER 33

Wednesday, October 8
12:00 a.m.

I followed the shadow across the street, desperately trying to call Delilah while I ran. It was so late; she wasn't picking up.

Stay inside, I thought. *Lock the doors. Call for help.*

I hoped Trevor was on his way.

I veered onto the footpath of the main gate behind them, heading to lower campus. The academic quad was deserted in the middle of the night. There were only the dim lights lining the path, and the emergency blue-light system, spaced out in steady intervals.

I tried to keep up as the shadow wove behind buildings, avoiding cameras. I worried that Bryce was heading back to upper campus—to the dorms.

I didn't wait, couldn't risk it. I stopped briefly at the nearest blue-light emergency phone and pressed the button. I remembered from orientation—the promise that help would be here soon. But then I kept going, scared of losing him.

The shadow slipped around the back of Beckett Hall, near the woods.

I trailed behind at a careful distance. Once behind the building, I couldn't see where he went next. The woods were dark except for a dim blue light between the trees, on the path to upper campus.

I started heading that way, then stopped at the sound of a door creaking on its hinges behind me.

I spun, but the night was empty. Behind me, the back entrance of Beckett Hall stood open.

There was no camera on this end. No card-swipe system. Only the key for a lock—a set of security keys that Bryce had in his possession—something that had given him access to Delilah's dorm room. Something that let him slip through every unseen part of campus.

He's a kid. He's just a kid, I kept repeating to myself. I knew this place better than he did. Every in and out. Every secret. *He's just a kid.* Nineteen and very angry. Acting out in desperation.

Cliff must've believed me when I'd told him it was Bryce who had the keys. He must've called Bryce in, confronted him. He must've assumed that Bryce had set the fire next door, where Cliff had started to move in. He had backed me up to the police twenty years earlier. He'd said he even had to leave town because of it. He must've been hated almost as much as I was. Bryce had the access, and he had a motive.

Maybe it had started as a taunt, a lit match, a glowing ember. But it wasn't anymore. The game always grew beyond the players' control.

I pushed the door open, calling Bryce's name. I listened to the word echo back, resounding through both ends of the building.

I stood under the red glow of an exit sign and took out my phone to use as a flashlight. I had to keep him here, in this building, until help arrived. I had to keep him from going to the dorms.

I dropped the phone to my side, finger over the side button, in case I needed to call emergency services.

And suddenly I understood why I'd received a call in the middle of the night from Delilah's phone.

I was her emergency contact. The number accessible without opening the phone. Adalyn must've been calling for help. My stomach sank: I'd heard the gasp of her last breath before the phone fell from her grip.

I sent a text back to the FordGroup number: *I'm right here.*

I heard a ping, and it sounded like it was right beside me. I shone my light around the space, but there was no one here.

The other atrium. That eerie echo, a feature of Beckett Hall.

He was in here, at the other end of the hall, so close.

I thought better of waiting and decided to place a call right now. I pressed the new contact for Fred Mayhew, then turned the phone to silent, stuffed it inside my purse. I'd called so they would hear the truth. I'd called to clear my daughter's name.

I knew it was late. I hoped, above all, that Fred picked up.

"Bryce!" I called again, walking deeper into the building. There was a light at the other end, the red glow of another exit sign, but I didn't see him anywhere. "Bryce, come and talk to me," I said. "I know who you are. I know you've been following Delilah. I know you sent her a text during the howling, luring her to the quarry."

I saw the door to the tunnels, open and waiting.

I walked toward the entrance, peering down. Cliff had told me the tunnels didn't connect across campus anymore. I didn't think Bryce had gone that way to escape. He was luring me down—the same way he'd tried to lure Delilah.

"I'm not coming down there," I called, just as I felt two hands collide with my back. And then I was falling—tripping down the short flight of steps, hands bracing for impact at the bottom.

I landed on my shoulder and felt something pop. My purse had been crushed between the cement and my body, and I could feel the phone inside digging into my rib cage. I had no idea if anyone was on the other end of the line, listening. I had no idea if anyone was on the way to help.

I scrambled back as a shadow appeared in the red glow of the exit lighting behind them. The person was shorter than I'd first thought.

"Well, this is fitting." A woman's voice.

She descended the steps, wearing all black, with a hat pulled over her shoulder-length blond hair.

"Violet?" I called, a throb working its way down my arm. "What are you doing? Why were you just in Cliff's house?"

She reached the base of the tunnels and stopped. "I went over there to have a simple chat. He called me today, said we needed to talk. Figured we could sit down like old friends, hash it out."

I saw it then: after I left his office, Cliff calling Violet instead of Bryce. *We have a little problem with your son—*

"Now, you tell me why *you're* looking for my son," she said, leaning over me.

I pushed myself to standing so I was facing her, one arm held awkwardly in front of me. "I know what happened at the quarry."

"No, you don't." She stepped closer, so I had to back up, spine pressing into the pipe running along the wall. "But I know what happened down here with you and Adalyn. I saw you."

"You're the witness," I said. Now I understood. The first text had arrived right after I'd shown up at orientation. Right after she'd seen me here. The emails started after she'd done a little bit of digging on me, figured out what I did for a living. "You drove the truck that night?"

She stepped back, looked over her shoulder, making sure we were truly alone. "I told them I saw you, but no one believed me. You were both in masks. They said any identification couldn't be trusted. That it was too far to see in the dark. But I saw *you* in the headlights." She raised her arm, like I had done back then, to block the glare.

"And you know what I saw?" she said, one finger on her wrist. "The mountains."

The ridge, like my own heartbeat. Proof that it was me.

"I wasn't the type of person people listened to back then. Except for Fred, who knew me. But everyone else, they believed *you* and Cliff. I had no proof. I knew it was you, though. I always knew it. I saw *both* of you that night from the truck. Don't you think I'd remember something like that? It was the last time I saw Charlie."

My stomach dropped. There were people who died that night and other people left behind. They remembered. Of course they remembered.

"I didn't know you were together," I said, trying to pivot away, closer to the exit.

"Why would you have known?" she said, turning with me. "You had nothing to do with the town anymore. But I heard about *you*. I heard about you and your friend down at the Low Bar. I was pregnant, so I wasn't really in the scene at that time, as you can imagine." She took a step to the side, blocking my view of the exit again. "I've done well for myself, don't you think?" she continued. "Charlie's family made sure the settlement went to me and Bryce. They're really good people. So was Charlie."

"You have," I said. "You've built a good life." I placed my hand on the side of the tunnel, trying to orient myself. Looking for a chance.

"I *have,*" she said, voice rising. "But I've had to carry this for the both of us for *years*. *Decades,* Beckett. I've learned to be patient. I've learned that justice sometimes takes time."

As if that's what we were doing down in the tunnels where two men had lost their lives. "This isn't *justice,*" I began. But what did I really know of that, either?

"Bryce was so excited to start here, and the school was happy to welcome him. His roots are strong. He never wants to leave this place."

She took another step closer, so that I had to keep moving away. We were backing slowly away from the exit, the red glow of the sign fading to dark.

"I couldn't believe you were back, Beckett. I really couldn't. The *nerve* of you after all this time."

"Bryce has been harassing Delilah, even though she had nothing to do with anything that happened then," I said, trying to get back on topic. To get her to tell the truth about what really happened in the woods. To prove Delilah's innocence. "He'd been stealing her things, following her. He broke into my parents' house and left her threatening messages. He was luring her to Cryer's Quarry that night, I have proof—"

"You have no such thing," she cut in. "So here's what *I* want to know. Tell me how you did it, Beckett. Tell me how you got away with killing them."

"I didn't," I said. "I swear I didn't know what she was doing."

"That's the lie I kept hearing. But I saw you both. You had a plan."

She was right. I was guilty by association. Haunted by the choices of someone else.

Maybe this was all it took to break everything free. Reach back to the past and bring it into the room with us.

Maybe we were all reaching for something here. Something we couldn't give up. Cliff and Violet and me, all saying in our own way, *Please, I can't go back.*

It made you the most dangerous type of person, with nothing left to lose.

"They were coming after us," I said softly. "Cliff warned me. We were just going to keep them here. To keep them away from us." I shook my head, felt the tears coming. For the second time in a day, I was confessing. "They were chasing her, and I closed the door behind them. I didn't know what she was doing—the fire—I swear."

"I don't believe you."

"I tried to get them out!" I said. "I really did."

She grabbed me by the arm, twisting my shoulder again, and I cried out in pain.

"Then don't you talk to me about my son," she said, voice dangerously close. "He didn't mean to do anything, either. But we aren't always believed, are we."

"He was waiting for Delilah at the quarry. But Adalyn showed up instead."

"Stop *saying* that. He didn't even know who she *was,* Beckett, when he called me in a panic."

I stayed silent, letting her speak. Counting the seconds. How much longer until security checked the cameras, saw us running through the night? How much longer until they found us here? Was my phone even working?

Violet went on, "He said it was supposed to be a prank. That he'd run into someone in the woods, scared them by accident. The quarry is so dangerous, you and I both know that. We're trying to fix that up. Bryce said that she fell. And he was confused because it was some older lady."

I didn't believe that. He was so angry. I believed he had wanted to hurt Delilah; maybe not kill her, but he'd definitely wanted to give her a good scare. He had taken her things, sneaked into our house. And then he'd lured Delilah—and only Delilah—out there in the night, wearing a mask. He'd lured her to the place his family now owned. It was a one-sided game that kept escalating. Something she hadn't even known she was a part of.

"You're the one who moved the body," I said. Violet couldn't leave it there. Not on their property. Not with evidence that could lead straight to her son.

Fred Mayhew had it right, he just had the wrong people. Instead of me covering for Delilah, it had been Violet helping Bryce cover up the crime.

"I made him wait in the car," she said. "I got into the water, checked her ID. Can you believe my shock at seeing Adalyn's name." Violet shook her head. "She was after my son, Beckett. Charlie's son. You can see that, right?"

"No," I said, finally understanding why Adalyn had stayed. She had been watching, and she'd seen what was happening: a girl who looked so similar to me; Bryce, going after her, sneaking into our house.

She had protected my daughter. Gone to confront Bryce in her place. And she'd died because of it.

"You were trying to frame Delilah," I said. "You took Adalyn's key to our house and planted Delilah's phone in there." I'd heard the cabinet open in the kitchen—it must've been the door to the dumbwaiter, up above.

It was Violet inside my house that day. Violet who saw the mask on the table—and took it.

"Delilah's phone was on the body," she said. "Bryce said she'd been staying at your folks' place. Do you think she knew Adalyn? Do you think they were acting together, like you and she did, so long ago?"

"No," I said. Delilah had never noticed that Adalyn was there. The shadow following her. Watching her from afar. Sierra had noticed her presence only in hindsight.

"What were you even doing here so early that morning?" she asked, but I could sense her backing away. *Soon,* I thought. No one was coming. I had to move soon. "I dropped Bryce by the edge of the woods so he could get back to the dorms while I figured out what the hell to do. Then I find out you were already *there*? And you want me to believe you didn't know what Adalyn was planning."

"She was calling for help from Delilah's phone when he *pushed* her," I said. "I thought the dropped call was from Delilah."

"I told you to stop saying that."

I was running out of time. Couldn't talk my way out. Couldn't push my way past her.

Violet stood between me and the exit. "Wouldn't it be fitting, to die in this place that shares your own name?" A place to begin and a place to end. "Do you think they put any fire sprinklers in here after the last time?" she asked, taking a matchbook from her pocket.

The skeleton key was in my bag. I had a way out, but I wouldn't make it past her to the door. Not with a fire. I had no idea if the pipes were flammable. I wouldn't make it. Not in time.

"I have the key," I yelled. "I have the key to the tunnels. The one I gave Adalyn. It's the proof. I'll give it to you."

She paused, considering. That was all she ever wanted—to be believed.

I fumbled in my purse, seizing the moment. My fingers brushed the loops of the skeleton key. But I grabbed the phone instead, held it up so she could see that someone was on the other end, listening: *Fred Mayhew.*

The clock keeping time of our call kept ticking forward. He'd been listening for a long while.

Her eyes widened, and in the glow of red, I saw her make a decision. The sirens were audible now, growing closer.

The clock had begun. She turned and ran.

I followed her out of the tunnels, saw her standing at the entrance of the double doors, frozen, hands raised.

It was too late. The police had arrived—and so had a crowd.

Violet exited the building to a sea of red and blue lights waiting for both of us.

BEFORE:
THE CRIME

After I exited the tunnels, I stepped out of Beckett Hall into the steady snow. And then I started to run. It was a long way on foot to the old president's house, but I knew these woods so well. I knew this whole place by heart.

I smelled the smoke far sooner than I thought I should—it drew my gaze up. And there, through the falling snow, I saw flames above the tree line in the distance, licking the sky.

I started running faster. Something was burning. I burst into the clearing to find that the entire barn was up in flames. Students stood around it like it was nothing but a raging bonfire.

I pulled the mask from my face. I couldn't breathe. And then I screamed: "Does anyone have a phone? Call 911! There might be people in there!"

Then I started screaming for Adalyn. Adalyn, with the key. Adalyn, with the only way to save them.

A girl turned around, eyes glassy. "It was her. She set the fire. I watched her do it," she said. "She's not here anymore."

I shook my head, backing away.

I started to run in a blind panic. Twigs hitting my face. Tripping over roots poking through the snow. I kept moving until I was back at Beckett Hall.

I'd left the whole series of tunnel doors open for when we released them. But the final door was shut and locked.

It wouldn't budge. I rammed it with my body, pulled against it with my foot braced against the stone wall. I tried to get my dorm key to work, my house key, my car key. But the smoke had already seeped into the space where I was standing, and I couldn't get a breath. I couldn't get them out.

I'd gone off looking for her after. I screamed her name into the cold dark until my voice was gone, lungs seized by the smoke and the fear. All through the night, I'd searched, as if finding her could somehow undo it all. As if it weren't already too late. An accident, *I wanted to believe, so desperately.* An accident, *and I couldn't find the key.*

I raced down to the quarry. Stumbled back through a dark alley behind the Low Bar, wild with panic. I couldn't stop moving, or searching, or calling her name. Couldn't stop the tears of rage and grief and shame, ice-cold in the bitter air.

Even then I feared the stillness.

Eventually I made it back to the dorm, thinking: One last place.

Thinking: Maybe she got them out instead.

But I knew it as soon as I saw that open window: She was gone.

She'd taken her things, and she'd left. Left me. Left nothing behind. Not even the key to the tunnels—the only thing that could've freed them.

In the stillness, I knew, there was nothing left to look for; nowhere left to go; no one left to save.

I curled up on my bed, where I waited for someone to come and find me.

To discover what I had done.

CHAPTER 34

Wednesday, October 8
1:00 a.m.

I stepped out into the night, watching as Violet was led away through the crowd.

Students had started to arrive from upper campus, drawn by the lights and the sirens. I wondered if Bryce was somewhere in there. If he knew what was coming for him.

I saw several men in uniform talking to one another, fanning out—with orders.

And at the end of the path, the man in charge: Fred Mayhew, staring at me.

He started walking slowly toward me. He'd heard it all. And I knew what was coming. I'd known it when I'd said it.

When I'd chosen it.

Adalyn was gone, and there was no one left to take the blame; there were only people left to take the fall. My mother, for helping her escape; and, years later, for paying her off to protect me. Delilah, for coming here, to this place I once loved so much.

No matter how many times I went back in my mind to that cold November night, I couldn't undo it. Couldn't justify it. Couldn't atone for it.

But I saw how to make sure Delilah went free.

It had been a game, but that was just an excuse. It was a crime wrapped up in the guise of tradition. One that we molded to fit the confines of the accepted parameters. It was planned and then it was executed, and I was guilty by the rules we had agreed upon.

I had always known this.

I noticed Trevor pushing through the crowd, wide-eyed. "Beckett," he said, coming closer, pressing me to his chest. My heart thundered; I couldn't breathe—I was running out of time.

"Sir," a voice came from behind him. "I'm going to need you to step aside."

Trevor kept a grip on my hand as he pivoted. "No, I think I'll be staying right where I am."

Fred Mayhew stood in front of me, looking like he had something he wanted to say. But there was only a downward twitch of his mouth. Like he'd found the thing he'd been searching for only to discover he wasn't sure he liked the result.

"Trevor," I said, releasing his grip. "It's okay."

"Ready?" Mayhew asked, not without sympathy. But how could I be? How could I ever be?

I felt the rough skin of Mayhew's hand raise my arm gently between us.

The click around my wrist sounded like the lock of a door. An echo in my heart. Something I had been hearing for the last twenty years. Something I had always been waiting for.

Time stopped.

"You're under arrest," he said.

Twenty years—a suspended sentence.

My mother had bought me that: nineteen years, ten months, twenty-one days—and I felt I had used it well. I was grateful I could use it to absolve her, too.

"Hold on," Trevor said, voice rising. "Beckett, what—"

I shook my head. "I'm sorry. Please . . ." But I couldn't find the words. *Please forgive me. Please take care of our daughter. Please wait for me.*

I felt the tears stinging my eyes. I wasn't ready.

"Mom?" I heard.

I saw Delilah pushing through the crowd. She was supposed to be safe, inside her dorm. She'd promised me. But of course she wasn't. She did what she wanted. She was just like me that way.

"Wait," I said as I saw her racing toward me. I wanted more time with her. With Trevor. A life, all together.

Someone yelled at her to stop, but she didn't listen.

Time cycled back, to her toddler run, and the scent of oatmeal and baby shampoo. A spotlight illuminating her on center stage. The call of my name in the dark.

She threw her arms around my back, hot tears on my neck.

I breathed her in, and I wished for eternity.

EPILOGUE

423 Days Served

Sometimes I count the hours and minutes instead of the days. Time does not leapfrog here. It shuffles along the floor, slides sideways. Each day feels like a circle, ending once more where it began. The first line and the last line, bookended together.

I count the days between visits. Measure the gaps between letters. Recalculate everything again after meetings with the lawyer.

I have a hard time orienting myself without counting. Without keeping track.

I've worked it forward and back, night after night, trying to find the moment I could've stopped it.

Was there another way? Another chance emerging in hindsight? Another option to save Delilah and me, together? Or was it only at the very start, when I could've just told the truth the first time I was interviewed?

Or further back still.

Sometimes, in my dreams, I don't close the door. I don't steal the key. I don't play that game of darts.

But those are dangerous thoughts. Because in those same threads, I don't move to London. I don't meet Trevor. I don't have Delilah.

My life has a different sort of calculus to it now.

I took a plea for my role in the crime, sparing us all a trial. Three years. Though my lawyer thought I'd be out in half that.

Involuntary manslaughter is treated as a felony in Virginia. I already knew this. Had known it for two decades. I'd looked it up from a different continent, separated by a body of water, where no one would look too hard at what I was doing online. I'd checked the statute of limitations: There wasn't one. And so I had decided—I would never go back. And then there was Delilah, another reason, a better reason—the only reason, at the end of the day.

If Adalyn returned, I feared what she would do. She would play it as a game, play her cards, show her hand. Trade a year, or two, or three, for me. Wouldn't we all do it? Trade in time?

I never wanted her to come back. But then she did, and Delilah was alive because Adalyn had died in her place. I had to reconcile these facts.

That in her return, Adalyn had saved my daughter.

I was no longer a threat to anyone, but I did owe time. Not just for Charlie Rivers and for Micah White. Not only for their families. But maybe for Adalyn, too.

Sometimes I can hear the wind, higher-pitched, a whistle against the concrete. I know it's the same wind that funnels through the valley—blowing from her on its way to me—and I start counting again. I can feel it getting closer. There's not much time left.

It's a countdown now, to all the things that are waiting for me out there.

Three, and I can feel my blood pulsing under the tattoo of the mountains, calling me back to the place where they are.

Two, and I see Delilah and Trevor in a car outside, waiting for me.

One, and I'm home.

ACKNOWLEDGMENTS

I'm so fortunate to work with a fantastic group of people who've helped see this project through from the spark of an idea to the final, finished book.

First, many thanks to my editor, Marysue Rucci, and agent, Jennifer Joel, for the sharp insight and continued guidance on every new project. I consider myself a very lucky author to work with such an incredible team!

I'm very grateful to the entire teams at Marysue Rucci Books and Simon Element, including Clare Maurer, Elizabeth Breeden, Emma Taussig, Richard Rhorer, Suzanne Donahue, Jessica Preeg, Nicole Bond, Sara Bowne, Laura Wise, and many others who have helped see this book into the world. Thank you also to the team at CAA, especially Sindhu Vegesena for the fresh eyes and early feedback.

Thank you to great friends Elle Cosimano and Ashley Elston for all the support along the way on each and every book. What a journey this last decade-plus has been together!

An extra special thanks to my family, who have always been a huge part of the publishing journey, but also contributed in very specific ways on this one: My daughter, who encouraged me to write this story after our college-visit road trip initially sparked the idea. My son, who talked through the plot with me when I was stuck during the first draft and provided a key insight that brought everything together. And my mother, who fittingly named my main character.

Lastly, as always, to all the readers—thank you.

ABOUT THE AUTHOR

Megan Miranda is the *New York Times* bestselling author of *All the Missing Girls*; *The Perfect Stranger*; *The Last House Guest*, which was a Reese Witherspoon Book Club pick; *The Girl from Widow Hills*; *Such a Quiet Place*; *The Last to Vanish*; *The Only Survivors*; and *Daughter of Mine*. She has also written several books for young adults. She grew up in New Jersey, graduated from MIT, and lives in North Carolina with her husband and two children.